MANIAC

NECESSARY EVILS
MANIAC

ONLEY JAMES

MANIAC

NECESSARY EVILS BOOK SEVEN

Copyright © 2023 Onley James

WWW.ONLEYJAMES.COM

Cover and Interior Design by We Got You Covered Book Design

WWW.WEGOTYOUCOVEREDBOOKDESIGN.COM

ISBN: 979-8-88722-437-4

TRIGGER WARNING

This book contains discussions of child abuse, sexual assault, intimate partner violence, suicide, and torture of bad people who totally deserve it.

PROLOGUE
DR. THOMAS MULVANEY

After years of single-handedly raising a small group of psychopathic children, Dr. Thomas Mulvaney was rarely surprised anymore. But sitting across from Marshall Kendrick in his large stately home in Annandale, he had to admit, he was taken aback by the man's audacious request.

"This is a blatant abuse of your power," Thomas said, doing his best to keep his voice even.

Kendrick sniffed, shoulders raising at Thomas's admonishment. "Maybe so, but I'm doing it anyway, and you have far more to lose than I do."

That wasn't exactly true. In the grand scheme of things, Project Watchtower was probably worth more to the government than the man sitting across from him, but beneath Kendrick's defensiveness, Thomas could sense his fear. So, he didn't call him out on the validity of his statement. Besides, he'd be lying if he said he wasn't intrigued.

Instead, he shook his head. "But he's your son."

Kendrick set his jaw, shaking his head before Thomas

even finished his short statement. "Whoever that is in there? That's not the boy I raised. That…thing… He's a monster."

Thomas stared at Kendrick, eyes boring into him, like if he just studied him long enough he might glean whatever it was inside that would make him say such a thing about his own child. "What happened?" When Kendrick hesitated, Thomas pushed. "I won't take him if you're not honest with me."

"He beat a kid to death with a fifty-pound weight," Kendrick said, voice raw, eyes welling with tears he quickly pushed back.

That was aggressive. A blitz attack most likely. Something born of fury, not a well-thought-out plan. "Why'd he do it?" Thomas asked.

"Does it matter?" Kendrick spit back, looking at Thomas like perhaps he was a monster, too.

That was a question many who knew the real him had likely volleyed about several times over, but the truth was, it didn't actually matter. Part of Thomas felt life would have been easier for him if he'd lacked guilt or empathy. Unfortunately for him, he had both in spades.

Thomas rephrased his question. "Did you ask him why he did it?"

"He won't speak to me," Kendrick said, digging his thumb and forefinger into his eyelids, like he was hoping he could just make the situation disappear if he rubbed hard enough.

Making a dead kid disappear was damn near impossible without the proper backing, but Kendrick had the government on his side. "What can you tell me about what happened?"

Kendrick dropped his hands to his desk, then found his glass, slugging back whatever clear liquid was within before saying, "He did it in my garage. We were all home. He didn't care. He walked into the house covered in blood. Scared the shit out of his mother. He just walked right past us and went to take a shower. Left the kid's corpse where he killed him."

"Kid? You keep saying kid. If he murdered a child, I'm not taking him, Watchtower be damned."

Kendrick's hand flailed. "Not an actual kid, but a kid to me. He was nineteen. Three years older than Aiden."

Aiden. The A name wasn't lost on Thomas. All his sons had A names. Was this fate? Kismet? Perhaps. Or maybe Kendrick's son was just a hot-tempered monster who'd beaten someone to death for no reason.

But none of this would matter if Kendrick hadn't taken the necessary steps to shield his son. Thomas shifted in his seat, propping an elbow on the arm of the chair. "What kind of damage control has been done?"

"Once I managed to calm my wife down and prevent her from calling the cops, I called in professionals. They disposed of the body, sanitized the garage, and got rid of Aiden's clothes. I did manage to get him to admit he and the kid weren't friends or even associated in any way people knew. Also, it's been over ten days and the family hasn't even filed a missing persons report. I'm not sure what to make of that but it bodes well for us."

There was no 'us.' Not to Thomas. He wasn't taking Aiden off Kendrick's hands until he knew exactly what had caused the boy to snap. It was easy making a child in the foster system disappear and reappear but Aiden was sixteen, almost seventeen. He had friends, high school transcripts. A social security number. This was going to take more than a few phone calls to make Aiden his.

But if this was an isolated incident, something that happened in a moment of anger, Aiden should be punished by the law, not taught to kill others. He didn't fit the code. But it was clear Kendrick would never allow Aiden to be punished properly. Not that it was Thomas's problem. If the boy had snapped, he wasn't right for Thomas's…program.

"I want to speak with him," Thomas said.

Kendrick nodded grimly. "I figured you would. He's in the dining room."

Thomas got to his feet, and Kendrick let out a deep breath before doing the same. Thomas followed the man, trying not to lose his patience at his cadence. His footsteps were glacial, like the cars in a funeral procession.

When they reached the formal dining room, Thomas found a boy slumped in his chair, the hood of his white Quiksilver sweatshirt pulled low over his eyes, hiding all but his lips from Thomas's view. Those full lips were parted, his chest rising and falling slowly.

He was sleeping. Interesting. To sleep that peacefully after taking someone's life took a special kind of person. Often a psychopath. But psychopaths rarely acted in haste. Perhaps he was a sociopath. So many questions.

He had kicked his feet up on the antique dining table, his long legs stretched out before him. He wore ripped, faded denim jeans and a pair of well-worn but expensive high-top sneakers. He was skinnier than Thomas had envisioned given Kendrick's large stocky frame.

It took a lot of strength to beat someone to death. Or a lot of rage.

Kendrick marched to where his son reclined and kicked the chair, causing the boy's feet to fall, startling him awake. Kendrick snatched the hood off the boy's head, glaring at him. "Wake up. This isn't a vacation."

The boy sneered at his father but then seemed to realize they weren't alone. He turned ocean blue eyes to Thomas, and a shock of awareness rocketed through him. A sullen expression replaced his look of confusion, then he folded his arms over his chest.

Thomas blinked, trying to force his brain to focus on anything other than the boy's looks. But it was hard. Aiden was…pretty, objectively speaking. That was the only word that came to mind. Model pretty with chiseled cheekbones, full lips, and a shock of wavy blonde hair that fell messily into his eyes.

Thomas swallowed as Aiden gave him a thorough once-over that made him feel a bit uneasy inside. When they locked eyes, Thomas couldn't look away. He wasn't even sure he blinked until Kendrick cleared his throat.

"Aiden, this is Dr. Thomas Mulvaney. He's going to talk to you about what happened. You will answer his questions. Understand?"

Aiden's gaze flicked to his father, releasing Thomas from the prison of his far too interested stare.

"Sure, Dad," he said, infusing the words with as much sarcasm as he could seem to muster.

Thomas sat to the boy's left, clenching his fists in his lap when Aiden returned his full attention to him. Thomas had been face to face with a number of killers in his day. Hundreds, in fact. Some very young, others with a body count that spanned decades, but looking at this boy had him shaken. Literally.

"Leave us," Thomas said to Kendrick, unwilling to break eye contact with Aiden.

Kendrick hesitated but finally relented. Still, Thomas waited another moment or two before finally opening his mouth to speak. Before he could, Aiden's tongue poked free of his mouth, licking over his teeth in a gesture that Thomas found both fascinating and disturbing.

"So, you're him, huh? The psychopath wrangler?" he said, every bit of sarcasm he'd given his father still dripping from his words.

"I am raising a group of children with a very specific psychopathy," Thomas agreed carefully.

"'A very specific psychopathy,'" Aiden mocked. "How careful you are, doctor. Are you really even a doctor? You barely look older than me."

"I assure you I'm far older than I look," Thomas lied.

"Well, I'm not a psychopath," Aiden said with an authority Thomas found confusing. "So, you probably wasted a trip."

"How do you know that?" Thomas asked.

Aiden shrugged, slouching farther in his seat. "I checked."

Thomas's lips twitched, amused. "Checked how?"

"I've read a lot of books on psychopathy, behavioral profiling. John Douglas, Robert Ressler. I don't…fit. I can experience guilt. Remorse. Empathy. I have feelings, Dr. Mulvaney."

"Are you sorry you killed that boy?" Thomas asked, propping his elbow on the arm of the chair, then placing his chin on his fist, studying him.

Aiden once more looked him dead in the eye. "I'm only sorry he didn't suffer more."

Thomas blinked at him. "What?"

"He died too quickly," Aiden said. "I'd hoped to hear him scream. To watch the life drain out of him."

Goosebumps rose along Thomas's arms. "Tell me why you did it."

Aiden shrugged. "Because he wasn't a good person and he deserved to die."

Thomas tilted his head. "Why do you believe he wasn't a good person?"

"Because I'm the one who had to carry the guy he raped and beat near to death to the hospital."

Thomas processed this information. "How do you know it was him?"

"I saw him. I scared him off. I would have killed him if I caught him, but I had to make a choice: help the guy bleeding to death or kill the guy who caused it. I chose the first one," Aiden said, jaw muscle twitching. "Not that it mattered in the end."

Thomas's brow raised. "Why's that?"

For the first time, Aiden broke eye contact, gaze floating somewhere over Thomas's shoulder. "He's been in a coma for months."

"Months?" Thomas repeated.

"With what he did to him, they said they're lucky there's any brain activity at all," he muttered. "Considering what the guy did to his body, I think I'd prefer to be brain dead."

"Why didn't you just tell the police?" Thomas asked.

Aiden looked at him as if he was stupid. "I did. They didn't care. They said it's a gay thing. High risk lifestyle. The kid was from a poor family. There was hardly any evidence since he used a…since he used an object to rape him. My description was vague at best. It was dark. We were on a street with broken lights. It's not like Brett can tell anybody what that piece of shit did to him. The cops tried to imply it was some kind of romance gone wrong. Not even Brett's parents wanted to pursue it. They were too humiliated."

"Brett?" Thomas questioned.

"The victim." Aiden shook his head. "What that guy did to him wasn't romance. It was rage. He… I've never seen someone do that to a person before. It was brutal."

Thomas felt something unknot in his chest. It was interesting that Aiden had named the victim but refused to call the man he'd murdered anything but 'that guy.'

Aiden definitely wasn't lacking in empathy. His face was pale, his eyes haunted. What he'd seen had scarred him for life. The human part of Thomas wanted to hug the boy, but the scientist in him wanted to pick his brain. How did Aiden differentiate the horrors that happened to Brett from what he'd wanted to do to his abuser?

Thomas sat up a bit straighter. "How did you find him?"

Aiden shrugged. "I took the police sketch and showed it around. Went to gay clubs. Places close to where he'd attacked Brett."

"Why gay clubs? You think Brett was targeted because he was gay?" Thomas asked.

Aiden's gaze darted upwards, and once more, that arc of electricity jolted through Thomas's whole body. "It seemed like the best place to start. Like I said, what he did to him… it was meant to hurt, to inflict as much pain as possible. He wanted him to suffer. That level of rage and evil usually comes from some kind of self-hatred. No?"

Thomas blinked in surprise. Clearly, he had been reading up on psychopathy as more than just a passing fancy. "Seems likely."

"Brett was small, frail. There were rumors he was gay, but who fucking knows. It's high school. It's not like the rumors have to be true for anybody to believe them or spread them. I asked his friends, but they said he didn't really have prospects from any gender. That he was kind of a weirdo."

"How did you know you had the right guy?" Thomas asked. "How can you be sure the kid you killed was the same one who hurt Brett?"

"Because I watched him stalking his next victim for weeks. Luckily, he never had the opportunity to act on whatever he wanted to do. But he was definitely ready. I was ready, too. If he'd tried to hurt someone, I would have done what I had to do."

Thomas didn't ask him to clarify. "How did he end up in your garage?"

"I followed him, started hanging at the same pool hall he did, played a few games with him, overheard him saying he was looking to buy a Playstation 2. I introduced myself and told him I had one for sale. I gave a ridiculously low price, and told him I was getting a Gamecube instead. Gave him my number. When he called, I invited him over."

"But your parents were home," Thomas said.

Aiden shrugged again. "Yeah, that was unfortunate."

Unfortunate. "Did you plan to kill him?"

"Yeah. Eventually. I was hoping to have more time with him. But he knew something was up. I don't know what I did that gave it away. I've been thinking about it since it happened, but I can't figure out where I went wrong."

"Why?"

Aiden frowned in confusion as if the answer was obvious. "So I don't make the same mistake twice."

"You do know that you'd be in jail right now if not for your father, right?" Thomas asked.

Aiden scoffed. "Please, if you believe my father's ego would ever allow him to have a murderer for a son, you're not as smart as he thinks you are."

"Do you know what I do, Aiden?" Thomas asked.

"You train psychopaths to kill bad people," Aiden said.

"Did you know that before you killed that boy?" Thomas asked.

Aiden's smile was cold. "Sure. But don't tell my father. He thinks a locked door keeps his secrets safe from the rest of us."

A chill shot through Thomas. Had Aiden...had he planned this? All of it? Right down to this moment? No. That wasn't possible. That would mean he was playing a master level chess game, guessing his father's movements from the very first moment Aiden's world had collided with that boy, Brett's. Thomas found himself momentarily speechless at the notion.

"Do you want to be part of my program, Aiden?" Thomas finally asked.

"If the alternative is prison, sure," he said, like he didn't care either way.

"My other sons have been with me for quite some time. I've raised them from an early age to follow my orders without exception. Can you follow my rules, Aiden?"

"Yeah," he said, tone bored.

Thomas sat forward, closing the distance between them until they were almost nose to nose. "Listen carefully. I've had years to instill the fear of God into my other children, but since you're almost an adult, I will be blunt. You do as I say when I say it. You go where I tell you when I tell you. You never go off-book. You never waver from the plan. You never take matters into your own hands. Ever. There's no pass or fail in my program. You follow my rules or you disappear just like that boy did and I never waste another moment thinking of you. Understand?"

Aiden opened his mouth and closed it again before he

gave a couple of jerky nods. "Yeah. Yeah, I get it."

"Good," Thomas said, leaning back.

Once there was some distance between them, Aiden's sullen expression returned. "I'm not calling you Dad."

"I—" Thomas had no idea what to do with that statement. "Yeah, that's fair."

ONE

THOMAS

Thomas sat in his office, a half empty bottle of whiskey beside him, the only light coming from his laptop screen and the image frozen on the display before him. A sea of unfamiliar faces. Five white coffins. And Thomas—a much younger Thomas—standing over them all. How long had it been since Thomas had seen that photo? Decades.

Hubris. That was what had led him to this moment. He scrubbed his hands over his face, trying to collect his thoughts as they swirled around his alcohol-soaked brain. It had only been a matter of time before his sins came to light. In truth, he'd managed to keep them hidden longer than he'd ever imagined. So long, in fact, that he'd let his guard down.

He took another large swallow of the whiskey in his glass, letting it burn its way down. He was fucking Icarus and he'd finally flown too close to the sun. His harsh laugh cut through the silence of his study. Christ, he was losing it. Had he ever really had it? Tears pricked at the backs of his eyes, and he dug the heels of his palms in until he regained his composure.

Thomas understood he was wallowing, his thoughts scattered, his timeline no longer linear. Memories he'd buried painfully deep erupted from the darkest recesses of his brain, tearing apart his carefully crafted lies in their wake. Bleached hair. Green eyes. That wicked smile. Those perfect teeth. That chain he wore that would brush against Thomas's skin whenever he leaned over him.

"We're the same. Nobody gets you like I do."

It had been years since he'd heard that voice. Years. But it was still as clear as day. Low. Raspy. The pain in his heart was knife sharp, twisting until Thomas felt the tightness in his chest had to be from the bleeding. Yeah, he was fucking drunk. But what the fuck else was he supposed to do?

It had finally happened. He'd thought if he suffered enough, was miserable enough, was sorry enough, he could right his wrongs without ever having to admit what he'd done. Without having to admit who he was on the inside. But years of killing monsters couldn't eliminate the monster within him. Years of suffering hadn't alleviated the agonizing way his family had died.

Maybe this was karma? Though he was loath to admit it, these days he was happier more than he wasn't. His children were healthy, happy, and thriving. He had two gorgeous granddaughters who looked at him like he was their hero. Maybe he'd gotten too comfortable? He'd let his guard down and the universe had taken swift action to rectify his mistake.

He'd thought if he denied himself the one thing he wanted more than anything, maybe the universe would just let him have the rest. He could compartmentalize. He could focus on Addy and Arabella, could focus on the work, could focus on his family as long as he didn't have the one thing—the one person—he wanted above all other things.

Aiden.

Thomas picked up his half-full glass and flung it against the fireplace, the flames jumping as the alcohol made contact.

Fuck.

He scrubbed at his face once more, pacing. He should go to sleep. He could think more clearly in the morning once he was sober. But he wouldn't do that. He couldn't. His thoughts were too powerful. If he laid down, he'd feed those thoughts until they became sentient demons who perched on his chest, depriving him of sleep, reminding him he'd brought all of this on himself.

Once more, he pictured the palest green eyes he'd ever seen and the two of them on the floor of the ballroom gazing up at the hammered tin panels on the ceiling.

"I hate them."

"You don't mean that."

"I do, though. I hate them. All of them."

He glanced back at the laptop screen now facing away from him. Maybe he should just pay them?

Even as he thought it, he rejected the notion. Blackmailers never went away. Besides, that video was someone's way of warning Thomas they intended to destroy him. They wanted him humiliated, defeated, brought to his knees. Only then would they pull the trigger and take it all from him. They wanted to see him suffer. He just didn't know why.

Maybe it was time. Maybe this was always how it was meant to go. But Thomas wasn't worried about himself. He was worried about the rest of them. His family. His sons. His grandbabies. Thomas had built a skyscraper on quicksand and now it was about to collapse and swallow them all.

He roared, the sound doing nothing to quell the turmoil churning within him. It wasn't about the money. He didn't give a fuck about the money. What they were asking for wouldn't even put a dent in the Mulvaney fortune. But that wasn't the point. This was personal. That video was personal. But it didn't make any sense. They were all dead. Everybody who knew the truth was dead…weren't they?

Thomas collapsed back into his office chair. He usually had all the answers. He almost always knew exactly what to do but, this time, he was lost. Usually, he could call in favors, get the boys involved, but he couldn't do that with this. He couldn't tell his sons what he'd done. He'd spent years drilling into their heads that there was only one unforgivable curse. One thing he could never forgive. How could he tell them he was the one who was unforgivable?

He picked up his cell phone, pressing the send button before he could even acknowledge what he was doing.

"It's three in the fucking morning, Thomas," a voice rasped.

Thomas. That was all he called him anymore.

Thomas got his agitation. He did. This wasn't his first

drunken call to the man he'd tried to call his son. Hell, he couldn't count on two hands the amount of times he'd called Aiden when he'd had too much to drink. He'd made his suffering Aiden's problem one too many times, but he didn't know what to do. He was scared. Thomas was scared to death, and when the world got to be too much, there was only one person who quelled his fears.

"Aiden." Thomas said his name like a plea, like a prayer.

"What's wrong?" Aiden barked, far more alert than seconds before. "Is someone hurt?"

Me. I'm hurt. I'm bleeding.

He wanted to tell him everything but all that came out was, "I need you."

Silence stretched before Aiden finally said, "I can't fucking do this with you anymore. You can't keep doing this to me. I won't let you."

That was fair. More than fair. Thomas had dragged Aiden down into his own shit again and again. It was only fair Aiden was done. But he had nobody else.

"I need you—your help," he corrected. "I need your help. Please. It's important."

"Tom—"

"Please…please, Aiden." Thomas would be humiliated by this when he sobered up, but he couldn't stop. "I'm begging. Please, help me. Please."

Thomas would've liked to say he took the time before

Aiden got there to sober up, but that would've been a lie. He finished off the bottle of whiskey, then fell asleep in his chair, only waking when Aiden slapped him hard enough to penetrate the fog of unconsciousness.

He opened bleary eyes to find Aiden on his knees before him, his cock taking notice of the position before his alcohol-soaked brain could catch up. Thomas reached for him, touching his bearded face before his hand fell, remembering Aiden wasn't his to touch. Not anymore. Not ever, really.

Aiden seemed to forget that as well, reaching up and cupping Thomas's face. "What have you done to yourself?" he asked, his voice that same low rasp that did things to Thomas's insides.

Thomas did his best to focus on the question and not the way Aiden's thumbs were gently brushing his cheekbones, like he was something Aiden cared about. Like he was someone Aiden still loved. "I fucked up," he blurted.

Aiden studied his face like he was trying to figure out what the hell was going on. He probably was. It wasn't like Thomas was making any goddamn sense.

"What are you talking about?" he asked, sounding almost hopeful at Thomas's confession.

Thomas scanned Aiden's handsome face in anticipation of his next words. "I-I did something bad. Really bad. A long time ago. I…lied. And someone knows it. And they're going to expose me."

Thomas watched in real time as the window on Aiden's hopeful expression slammed shut, leaving behind his usual hostility. A well earned hostility. Thomas knew he was a bastard for doing this to Aiden…again, for constantly leaning on him while giving him nothing in return, but he didn't have anybody else.

Aiden sighed, getting to his feet and hauling Thomas up by his arm, pushing him towards the office door. He allowed Aiden to manhandle him up the stairs and into the east wing to his bedroom. He didn't even protest when Aiden shoved him into the bathroom and turned on the shower. He would have let him undress him, too, if he'd tried. He'd let Aiden do almost anything…but that was almost what put miles between them.

Aiden didn't try to undress him, though. He just shoved a towel into his chest. "Sober up. I'll be downstairs when you're done."

Thomas didn't argue, just waited for the door to close before stripping down and stepping beneath the near frigid spray, letting the cold penetrate the haze of alcohol as goosebumps erupted along his skin. He leaned his forearms against the wall, the spray from multiple jets beating against him at once like tiny little daggers, driving away all his thoughts until his mind was blissfully quiet. Only when he started to shiver did he quickly scrub and rinse himself before turning off the water.

When he emerged from the shower, he spotted a pile of clothing folded on the counter. Gray sweatpants and a black Chanel hoodie. He couldn't remember ever wearing the sweatshirt. It had been part of a swag bag he'd received after a movie premiere. He'd tried to give it to Adam, but he'd refused it, saying he already had something similar.

Thomas had no idea why he remembered that in that moment, but he let the thought come and go as he toweled off and dressed quickly, combing his fingers through his hair before heading back downstairs.

He found Aiden in his office chair, light from the laptop screen illuminating the lines on his face as he frowned at the video as it played. Thomas didn't want to move closer, didn't want to have to explain what Aiden was looking at, what was happening. But he'd have to. He couldn't ask for Aiden's help but not explain what happened to his family. At least, in part. But how much? How much could he reveal and still live with himself?

"What is this?" Aiden asked as Thomas came to stand beside his chair.

"Someone is blackmailing me, threatening to expose our family's secrets. This is their way of letting me know," Thomas said.

Aiden handed him an insulated cup. "Which family secret? The one where we kill people? The global conspiracy where we teach the government to do the same?"

Thomas took a sip, the bitterness biting at the back of his tongue before the coffee burned its way down. "No, those secrets are well protected. It's something else. Something that happened a long time ago."

"What is it? What do they have on you?" Aiden asked. "What does it have to do with these dead bodies? Those coffins are your family, right?"

Aiden knew about Thomas's family? Of course, he did.

He was a private investigator. The boys had probably all done a deep dive into the Mulvaneys at least once in their lives, curious to know their family legacy. But Thomas had never worried about them stumbling onto the truth.

Several people had worked in tandem after the tragedy to assure that what really happened that night would never see the light of day. Of course, those people never suspected Thomas was the real villain that night. But then again, that had been the whole point.

"Yes. My parents. My siblings. My...cousin, Shane," Thomas said, the last part sticking in his throat just a little.

The shrill laugh pierced Thomas's already throbbing skull as Aiden restarted the video, causing him to wince. Whoever had created the video knew the truth and they had a real flair for the dramatic. Superimposed over graphic images of his family's dead bodies were words like *guilty*, *sinner*, *liar* along with their demands. It was all very over the top. If Thomas didn't know the pictures in that video had supposedly been destroyed years ago, he might have just written it all off as a hoax.

But there they were, in full color.

In all these years, Thomas had never seen the crime photos. Pictures of his siblings' bloated bodies. Pictures of Shane. What was left of him, anyway. They'd only been seven. Too fucking young for the horrors they'd endured that night. His uncle had assured him it was better that way.

He had only been fifteen after all, even if he was taking college level classes. Even if he had suddenly just had a fortune dumped in his lap. Even if he was suddenly expected to act as the head of a global empire. He had only been a kid.

"Why are they doing this?" Aiden asked.

Thomas shook his head. "I truly don't know." Aiden gave him a baleful look. Thomas sighed. "They want to hurt the family. They want to hurt me."

"But why?" Aiden asked. "Who's doing this?"

The fullness in Thomas's chest expanded to the point of pain as he tried and failed to search for the right words, the right phrase, something that would explain this all away without having to say the truth. Finally, he just blurted, "If I knew who was doing this, would I have called you?"

Aiden flinched, then scoffed, his face contorting in disgust, though whether it was with Thomas or himself, he didn't know. "No. I guess you wouldn't."

Something withered inside Thomas. "Aiden, I—"

Aiden turned the office chair back towards the laptop, hands flying over the keys as he opened Thomas's email. "I'm sending myself an encrypted copy of the video. Did they send anything else?"

Thomas clenched and unclenched his jaw. He just couldn't stop saying and doing the wrong thing when it came to Aiden. It was always *just Aiden*. He'd been Thomas's undoing since the moment he laid eyes on him, and some small part of him wanted to vomit the truth about who he was and what he'd done so Aiden would finally cut him off, once and for all. It was nothing less than he deserved.

But doing that would endanger more than just him. "There's a link to an offshore bank account embedded within the file. I'm assuming so I can transfer the money they're demanding."

Aiden turned the chair to face him, their knees brushing, sending a jolt through Thomas. How long had it been since they'd touched? Not since that last night. Right there in the study. Right where Aiden sat now. Only that night, it had been Thomas sitting right there when Aiden crawled into his lap. *"Why can't I stay away from you?"*

But he'd stayed away after that. Far away. All the way across the country, only returning home for the occasional job, always careful to avoid Thomas. Had it really been almost four years since that night?

Thomas forced his attention back to Aiden as he said, "What do they have on you? Why are you even entertaining this bullshit? Call Kendrick? Call one of the fifty senators you have on speed dial."

"I can't do that," Thomas said.

"Why not? You call in favors all the time. 'For the good of the program,'" he air-quoted.

"It's not that simple this time. These people—this person—isn't making idle threats. They know something. They wouldn't have those photos if they didn't. If they know everything, it will ruin our whole family. It will ruin everything I've worked for. It will wreck your brothers—the others—" he corrected. "Their whole lives."

"What? How?" Aiden asked, clearly bewildered.

"What we do…who we are…it's all a house of cards. This family. Project Watchtower…it all exists due to mutually assured destruction. If the truth about my family comes out, the rest of our secrets will fall like dominoes. We cannot let that happen."

For the first time, Thomas realized that was why he'd really called Aiden. That was what he needed from him most. Not comfort. Not a wake-up call. He needed a plan. He needed someone like Aiden. Someone who didn't lack the capacity to feel, but someone who used those feelings to promote the suffering of those who deserved it. Aiden would find out who was behind this. Aiden would destroy that person. And when Aiden knew who Thomas really was, what he'd done, he'd destroy Thomas, too.

Thomas's destruction at Aiden's hands felt right. It felt just. And Aiden would make it hurt, make him suffer. But he'd do it quietly. He'd save the family the burden of bearing the weight of his sins. But not yet. Thomas wasn't ready yet. He needed to see this through. He'd come clean to Aiden when it was necessary. But only then.

"What are you hiding?" Aiden pressed. "What did you do?"

This time, it was Thomas who went to his knees, shock rocketing through him as he took Aiden's rough hands in his own much softer ones. He forced himself to look him in the eye. "Don't ask me to tell you that. Not yet. Please. If you ever fucking loved me, just let me keep my sins to myself a little bit longer. Please, Aiden."

Aiden thrust his jaw forward, clenching until the muscle there jumped, as he studied Thomas's face with an anger and frustration he fully deserved.

"Please," he said again.

"I hate you sometimes," Aiden told him, voice raw. "So much I feel like I'm choking on it."

Thomas nodded, trying to pretend Aiden's words hadn't just ripped through him like a bullet. "I know. I deserve that…but I'm asking just the same. Don't make them suffer for my sins. I promise I'll tell you before this is all over. And when you know the truth, I'll accept the consequences. Just let me keep my secrets. I can't deal with you hating me more than you already do. Not with this hanging over our heads."

Aiden yanked his hands away from Thomas and jerked to his feet, grabbing Thomas's laptop. "Pack a bag. We're getting out of here."

"What? Why?" Thomas asked, standing once more.

"Because whoever is doing this to you is clearly unstable. You want to keep the family out of it? Well, keep them out of it. All the way out. If they see me here, they'll have questions, and once they smell blood in the water, they won't let it go. If you want to keep your secrets, then you'll come with me. That's the deal. Take it or leave it."

Thomas's head was spinning. Being alone with Aiden would be nothing short of torture. Just the two brief touches they'd shared had Thomas in pieces. He kept distance between them because when they were in the same room, they were magnets, drawn together by something impossible to fight. Except now, Aiden hated him. Thomas was many things, but he'd hardly force himself on someone who didn't want him.

What the fuck was he even saying? Why was he thinking about touching Aiden when someone was threatening everything he loved? He knew the answer. He suspected Aiden did, too. Because he loved Aiden most. He loved Aiden above all others. And he didn't even feel guilty about it. He couldn't. Because he'd never loved Aiden as a son. Aiden had never been his child and was barely a child when they met. The love he felt for him was nothing like the love he had for his sons.

Because he didn't just love Aiden. He was *in* love with him. Had been for longer than he'd ever admit to another soul, even himself.

"Thomas," Aiden said sharply, pulling him from his spiraling thoughts. Why did the use of his own name feel like a punishment?

"Yeah. Yeah, okay. We'll do it your way."

For now.

TWO
AIDEN

Thomas slept the whole way out of town, slumped in the passenger seat of Aiden's '95 Jeep Wrangler—a gift that had sat forgotten in the back of Thomas's garage since their fight on the night of his college graduation. A night Aiden had analyzed a million times, in a million different ways, for almost two decades.

But, now, he had a new question to analyze. Why had Thomas kept the Jeep in working order and why had none of the others told him? Surely, they'd fucking noticed?

Stop overacting, Aiden. It's not like Thomas takes care of the cars himself.

Hell, he had so many cars he likely forgot it was even in there. It was probably just the mechanic performing routine maintenance on all the vehicles in the garage. His gut twisted at the thought and that self-loathing he usually drank away at night started rearing its ugly head.

He hated how much the answer still mattered to him. He could torture a man for hours without so much as a drop of remorse, yet when it came to Thomas, he was so fucking weak. Even now, he was just sitting there, wallowing. Nobody else did this to him. Just Thomas. Always fucking Thomas.

He disappointed Aiden at every turn, but when he'd said, 'I need you', Aiden's hopes had soared…until reality set in. He banged his hand on the steering wheel, feeling a modicum of satisfaction when Thomas stirred in his sleep. Why should he get to rest?

Aiden shook his head, forcing himself to focus on the task at hand: saving Thomas's ass. He needed to call Lola. He had several open cases he needed covered. He scrubbed a hand over his eyes, then blinked as the world became blurry, making everything the headlights touched look warped like something out of a Dali painting.

Calling Lola would just open a whole other can of worms. She'd never let him just ask for help and go. She'd start prying. It was what she did. And he couldn't afford to alienate her. She was a great detective, a better bounty hunter, and the only friend Aiden had.

He spared another glance at Thomas, noting the worry etched on the older man's face even in sleep. Aiden pictured opening the door and letting Thomas roll on out, and he could even hear the satisfying clunk he'd make as he hit the ground. It was no less than he deserved. Aiden had punished people for lesser crimes—had tortured them until they were past the point of begging for the hurt they caused.

Yet, somehow, he could never punish Thomas. No matter how much he hated him. And he did. He fucking hated Thomas Mulvaney almost as much as he loved him. It was that hot and cold in near equal measure that combined inside him and created this tornado of emotion that made him want to destroy him, to tear at him until he was just as shredded as Aiden felt.

But what good would that fucking do?

He envied his brothers. Their relationship with Thomas had always been so clearly defined. They were brought in so young they'd only ever known Thomas as their father. But Aiden had a father. A shitty father but a father nonetheless. He'd never seen Thomas as anything paternal.

If anything, he was the only one to truly see the cracks in Thomas's supposedly stable foundation. A foundation that was crumbling. Finally. Aiden had spent countless nights wondering what sins Thomas had committed that left him rejecting any amount of love in his life.

Aiden would know now. He'd finally get to know the source of their combined misery. He'd allow Thomas to think he'd won, to think he was in control. If he needed Aiden's help, he'd give it, but he'd also keep digging until he knew it all, every deep, dark, dirty fucking secret Thomas was fighting to keep buried.

And then what? Aiden shook his head. Fuck if he knew. Could he punish Thomas for his crimes? That was why the code existed, after all. To ensure they never strayed from the path. Had Thomas strayed? Whoever was blackmailing him seemed to think so. Thomas seemed to think so, too. But what could Aiden do to Thomas that was worse than what he did to himself?

If after all this time, Thomas was the real villain, where

did that lead Aiden? Thomas had never been Aiden's father, but he had been the only person who'd ever given a shit about him, had confided in him. So, Aiden had done the same. He'd told him all his secrets.

In retrospect, maybe that was why Thomas had confided in him in the beginning? Maybe it was simply a way to get Aiden to trust him in return? But then Aiden had ruined everything by falling in love. He winced, picturing the face Thomas had made the night Aiden confessed his feelings.

He'd been so young. So fucking stupid. Thomas had been horrified. He'd blamed himself for giving Aiden the wrong idea and had sent him away with his friends for the summer just to get away from him, all while blaming himself for Aiden's 'crush.'

Thomas the martyr. So put upon. So broken. Aiden tried to force the past back down into the deep, dark recesses of his mind, but it was impossible with Thomas sitting right there beside him. So many fucking years had passed between them.

At seventeen, a fourteen year age-gap was insurmountable. It couldn't be ignored. Aiden had known that when he confessed. It had never occurred to him that Thomas wouldn't feel the same. That he'd misinterpreted his niceness for love. But even then, he'd thought Thomas would eventually come around and would stop seeing him as a child. And he had. Eventually. Years later, after Aiden's heart had been run over again and again.

Aiden blinked behind his glasses, his eyes feeling like sandpaper. He couldn't believe he was rehashing this shit in his head again. Every time he made peace with slamming the door shut on his feelings, Thomas found a way to drag him back in.

Every fucking time.

It was near pathological at this point. Aiden wished he'd been born a psychopath. The peace he could have had if he'd lacked the capacity to love. It would have been easier that way. Or maybe that was just what Aiden told himself to justify spending twenty fucking years loving someone who refused to love him back.

Who refused to act on it anyway.

Maybe that was the real salt in Aiden's wound. Thomas loved him. Not then, but later, when Aiden had come home from college graduation, when he'd finally put a voice to his feelings and reminded Thomas he was a fully grown adult…that was when he'd known there was something between them. Or there could have been if Thomas would have just stopped being such a goddamn martyr.

But no matter how Aiden had tried, there had been this fucking wall he'd run up against again and again until he was battered and bloody. Thomas telling him that he did love him, he did care for him, but it didn't matter—it could never fucking matter—because they could never be together.

But it was Aiden who Thomas called when he was drunk and lonely and desperate for some crumb of affection he couldn't get from his sons. It was Aiden he called when he was in trouble. It was fucking Aiden he called in the middle of the night just to hear his voice. And Aiden answered. Every. Fucking. Time.

Aiden reached over and turned the knob on the radio, music blaring through the speakers and rocketing Thomas upright in his seat. Aiden tried not to gloat as he watched him look around in confusion before seemingly remembering where they were and why this was happening.

"Where are we going?" Thomas asked, voice raspy with sleep.

"Safe house," Aiden said, offering no further explanation.

Just looking at Thomas made him ache, made him mad, so mad he fought the urge not to punch him in the face. He stole another glance at him, watching as he scrubbed his hands over his face for probably the hundredth time since he'd arrived.

Even then, sleep deprived and hungover, Thomas could have easily passed for ten years younger than his true age. Maybe it was genetics or the miracle of modern pharmaceuticals, but he was aging like fine wine. His hair wasn't gray but an almost pristine silver that made his pale blue eyes look silver, too. His usually clean shaven jaw was now hidden by scruff, but it just added a ruggedness to a man most viewed as elegant.

Nothing detracted from his looks in Aiden's eyes. That was part of the problem. Thomas never aged. And clearly, the same could be said for Aiden. Because even though Aiden was forty, Thomas still acted like he was a child. Like he was *his* child. Like being together was taboo.

Thomas turned down the radio, turning in his seat to look at him. "Aiden, I—"

"Don't. Seriously. Just…just fucking don't," Aiden said,

the rage he'd been choking on for hours bubbling to the surface. "You asked me to come and I'm here, and I'm going to fucking help you, but I cannot listen to you fucking apologize again."

Thomas opened his mouth and closed it, and Aiden felt some small sense of satisfaction knowing he'd kneecapped Thomas. If he couldn't constantly apologize to Aiden, he had nothing to say. Sober Thomas was always painfully polite. Reserved, classy, put together in every way.

Aiden preferred drunken Thomas. Alcohol had always been the key to unlocking Thomas's real thoughts and feelings. With enough whiskey on board, it was hard to shut him up. Drunken Thomas loved Aiden more than his pride, more than his suffering. But only from a distance.

Except for that one time.

"I should call Calliope, make up an excuse…" Thomas mumbled, staring out the window.

"I already did. I told her you're helping me with a case, but it was clear she didn't believe it. We only have a limited amount of time before the others realize something is happening. You should just tell them. They deserve to know."

Thomas gave a stilted nod. "I'll tell them. I will. I just don't know what to tell them."

"You could start with the truth," Aiden said. "But that would be too easy."

"Aiden…"

Aiden rolled his eyes at Thomas's tone. The way he said his name like he was begging for understanding. But Aiden *had* been understanding. He'd been so understanding he'd choked on it. He was done being understanding. He was just fucking mad. "Don't fucking 'Aiden' me. Just get some sleep until we get to the safe house."

Aiden could feel Thomas's gaze on him, but he ignored it, ignored him, until he rested his head against the glass once more. Thomas didn't sleep, but he stayed silent, his sorrows and regret filling the car like radiation until they infected Aiden, making him feel almost sorry for him.

Aiden wished he was a different man. A better man. Someone who learned his lesson and walked away from a relationship that, at its very core, was far more toxic than anything his emotionally stunted brothers had managed to create with their spouses. But even as he sat there, he wanted to take Thomas's hand, wanted to drag him to him, bury his face in his scent, wanted to hold him until they both felt whole again.

Just like that one night.

He shook his head, disgusted. With himself, with the situation, with Thomas. He was so fucking tired. Of everything. He reached over and cranked the music back up. He just needed to stay awake for a little while longer.

"I need you to take over my cases for a bit."

There was a long pause on the other end of the line. "What's a bit?" Lola asked.

That was a fair question, but one Aiden couldn't answer with any accuracy. He collapsed into the overstuffed leather chair taking up the corner of the sprawling safe house living room.

Thomas had called it a cabin, but it seemed more like a lodge to Aiden. There were two floors, four bedrooms and several windows. It would have been a security nightmare. But there was also strong wi-fi, a thirty-thousand dollar alarm system, and a ten-foot privacy fence.

This was Thomas's idea of roughing it.

Aiden sighed. "A week, maybe two. It's a...it's an emergency."

The moment the words left his mouth, he regretted them. Aiden didn't have emergencies. Emergencies meant obligations, and short of his cases, Aiden had been very good at avoiding obligations. At least, as far as his friends knew. Well, friend. His one friend. If he could even call her that. She was more of an associate.

Aiden could hear Lola judging him from a thousand miles away. "This is about him, isn't it?"

Aiden didn't ask who she meant. It was obvious—even to her—this was about Thomas. He had half a mind to lie about it. But if he did, she would just keep pressing him until he said something he couldn't take back. "Yeah, fine. It's about him. But it's not what you're thinking."

"I'm thinking that he called you—probably drunk—and begged you to help him with some random problem that, somehow, only you can solve," she said, voice tight.

So, maybe it was what she was thinking.

Lola Nixon was a lot of things, but she wasn't a fool. Aiden was the fool. Aiden was doing exactly what he said he wouldn't do and making lame-ass excuses in the process. But even knowing all that, he wasn't going to leave Thomas alone. Not now. His brothers meant too much to him.

Thomas means too much to you.

Aiden clenched his teeth until the thought went away, then glanced at the staircase leading to the bedrooms upstairs. He'd exiled Thomas upstairs the moment they'd arrived, mostly just to get him away from him before he did something stupid like smother the man with a five-hundred-dollar throw pillow.

He was too mad. He could barely stand to look at him. But, even now, sitting there talking to Lola, all Aiden wanted to do was go upstairs and put himself in Thomas's way so he could look at him…fight with him. It was so frustrating that it felt like someone tightening a noose around his heart.

"Hello?" Lola said, irritation obvious.

Right.

"Okay, yeah, but this time he really does need my help," Aiden said lamely.

Lola snorted. "You sound like every client we've ever had, making excuses for their shitty relationship. Except, you don't even have a relationship. This man uses you, twists you up, rings you out, and then spooks himself…every time. I don't get how he makes you so dumb."

"It's not like that," Aiden said. Except, it was. "He… there's a lot you don't know." Aiden didn't really know either. But he knew—deep down—that there was a reason Thomas kept doing this to him.

"That man is a hundred red flags made out of silk sheets and you're too busy worrying about the thread count."

Aiden didn't even know what that meant but he wasn't going to be lectured again. It wouldn't change anything. "The last guy you dated was literally on *America's Most Wanted*," Aiden recalled. "So, sticks and stones…"

Lola scoffed. "I didn't date him. I fucked him. Then I took him to the Marshall's and collected a big, fat bounty on him. We are not the same."

Arguing with Lola was pointless. She was as stubborn as she was cunning. They weren't business partners exactly, but they shared a caseload when things got to be too much to handle. She tended to deal with the more domestic side of things. Cheaters. Domestic abusers. Cases that didn't get in the way of her bounty hunting gigs.

Aiden covered a lot of fraud cases, sometimes missing persons. It kept him in the industry but gave him enough plausible deniability when it came to the extracurricular activities the Mulvaneys still required of him.

"I also need a favor—"

"*Another* favor," Lola corrected.

Aiden frowned. "What?"

"*Another* favor. Taking over your cases is the first favor," she pointed out. "But go on."

Aiden sighed. "I need you to—discreetly—do some digging into something?"

"Discretion is my middle name," she said mockingly.

Aiden rolled his eyes. Discretion was barely in her vocabulary. There was nothing about her that was discreet, from her wild, kinky curls that fanned around her like a crown to the knee-high boots she wore that made her look like a heroine in some movie. Lola liked to be seen. "I thought your middle name was Mabel?"

"I told you not to bring that up?" Lola muttered. "*Anyway*...what do you need me to do?"

Aiden didn't know how to phrase his question without making her suspicious. The last thing he needed was her getting a bug up her ass about his family. But he also couldn't ask Calliope. Not yet. "I need you to look into the explosion that took out the Mulvaney family."

Once more, that hesitation, then, "You want me to look into your family?"

It was on the tip of his tongue to say, "They're not my family," but he just couldn't bring himself to say it. His brothers were his brothers. Thomas just wasn't his father. But that got complicated and Aiden was so fucking done with complicated.

"I don't need you to investigate how they died. It's hardly a mystery." Except, it actually was. "I need a list of everybody who worked on the case. And I mean everybody. From the coroner to the dude who strung the crime scene tape. Everybody."

The crime scene photos were ground zero. Whoever made that video had access to them. That couldn't have been a huge pool. Not with the cover-up that clearly took place. But why the cover-up? What had Thomas done? Aiden refused to believe he'd killed his family as the video implied. Thomas was a lot of things, but he wasn't a family annihilator. They were a very specific breed of killer.

"Yeah, yeah, I got it. Everybody," she said, like she was quickly tiring of his shit. "Is that it?"

Was it? Yeah. Did he want to hang up with her? No. Talking to her was better than dealing with the man currently unpacking upstairs. Aiden was too pissed.

The minute he hung up the phone with her, he would go upstairs and find Thomas and push his buttons until they both snapped. That was what happened last time. But it wasn't the only thing that happened last time. And Aiden wasn't sure he could taste Thomas and then pretend like nothing happened.

Not again.

He leaned his head back against the chair and closed his eyes, seeking patience he'd never had. "Yeah. Let me know what you find."

THREE
THOMAS

They were ghosts haunting the same house, floating past each other in otherwise empty halls, but never communicating— never acknowledging the other existed. Thomas stood in the living room, gazing out the huge window, doing his best to avoid Aiden, who was moving around the kitchen out of sight.

Outside, snow blanketed the ground, but despite the artificial heat pumping through the vents, it felt far colder inside. Aiden couldn't look at him, and when he did, there was a barely contained…*something* that caused a grimace to appear on his face, like Thomas's mere existence pained him.

He hadn't uttered a single word since he'd ordered Thomas upstairs the day before and it was untenable. The worst kind of torture. Like when his parents would give him the silent treatment when his grades slipped, or how they'd take his siblings on trips and exclude him as punishment. Aiden had unwittingly found the perfect way to torment Thomas. A dark empath indeed.

It was ironic, really. Thomas rarely felt lonely despite living alone in a house far too big for him, but with Aiden within arm's reach, he'd never felt more isolated. The compulsion to touch him, to hold him, to bury his face in his throat and just inhale him was a physical constant ache inside him. But they were like magnets with the same polarity, repelling each other at every turn.

"Breakfast."

Thomas snapped his head around, startled by Aiden's gruff announcement. By the time he went to say thanks, Aiden was already gone. He should've followed him. Maybe this was an olive branch of some kind. A way for them to work together amicably…at least, until Aiden learned the truth.

Surely, he must have softened a bit. He'd gone to the trouble of making breakfast. Now was Thomas's chance. But try as he might, he found himself rooted in place. The back door opened, then shut, then Aiden appeared on the other side of the large glass window of the main room.

Thomas watched, riveted, as Aiden crossed the yard, and he imagined hearing the snow crunching beneath his booted feet as his gaze snagged on the wide strides he made as he walked. Somewhere along the way, Aiden had passed Thomas in both height and muscle mass, turning him into an imposing figure, not only in stature but in appearance. His hair was too long and his jaw remained covered in a permanent five o'clock shadow.

Aiden pulled something from his pocket and then scraped his hair off his face into a knot before pulling off his flannel and tying it around his waist, leaving just an eggshell-colored thermal that hugged his well-muscled arms and torso. Thomas couldn't help but take notice.

Aiden snatched an ancient-looking ax from a tree that was likely just as old, then grabbed a log, setting it on a wooden stump, before bringing the ax down in a perfect arc, splitting the wood in half and tossing it onto the ground.

Thomas watched, eyes glued to Aiden, as he broke down log after log. He was just letting off steam. There was already more than enough firewood inside. Thomas always made sure the safe houses stayed stocked.

Aiden was working up a sweat, his breath visible with every grunt. Thomas should have put real clothes on instead of staying in the flannel pajamas and long-sleeved shirt he currently wore. There was no way of hiding his very obvious arousal. Not after witnessing that level of exertion on Aiden up close and personal. He'd felt those straining muscles beneath his fingertips, knew the way Aiden's teeth felt scraping over his skin a moment before he sucked on his neck, his jaw, his collarbones.

He closed his eyes, his fingers flexing, as memories overtook him. The taste of his lips, the rough whisper in his ear as he'd begged him not to say no. Just once. *"Just one night."* And Thomas had given in, had been unable to refuse. Just one time. He'd told himself it might help. Just scratch the itch and get it out of their system. No matter how good Thomas was at lying to others, it never beat the lies he told himself.

Christ.

He forced himself away from the window and into the

kitchen. On the counter, sat an omelet and a cup of what was likely now lukewarm coffee. Thomas spared another glance out the window, relieved he didn't have a view of Aiden from there. He sat on a stool, taking a couple of sips of the mediocre coffee and forcing down half of the omelet with its rapidly congealing cheese.

When he finished what he could, he didn't move, just sat, staring at nothing, quietly contemplating his options. Maybe he should call the whole thing off. Maybe he should go home, accept his fate. Surely, the blowback couldn't be worse than this. Whatever punishment they doled out was bound to be quicker than this torture. When they found he'd broken the code, his children would kill him quickly and efficiently, executioner style.

Or maybe they wouldn't. Maybe they'd make him suffer. But nothing could be worse than this. Less than twenty-four hours with Aiden was agony. It was a Civil War doctor sawing at a soldier's leg without anesthesia. But the masochistic part of Thomas liked it. Aiden was his most exquisite pain, and if they were together too long, Thomas would be infected once again until his need consumed him and he was feening like some kind of addict.

The sound of the screen door slamming shut dragged him from his thoughts. Aiden stormed past with an armful of logs, carrying them into the living room to the already full container. Thomas sat paralyzed, listening to the sound of wood hitting stone until Aiden returned.

He poured himself a cup of coffee from the near full pot then leaned against the counter, glowering at Thomas until he had no choice but to look away or be consumed by the flames of Aiden's fury.

"Are you ready to start talking?" Aiden asked, like Thomas was some common criminal in an interrogation room.

He supposed he was. He forced his gaze upward until their eyes met. "About what?"

Aiden's jaw clenched until Thomas swore he could hear his teeth grinding. "I'm not playing these games with you. I already have someone looking into your family's deaths—"

That brought Thomas up short, a sudden terror shocking his nervous system and flooding him with adrenaline until he couldn't help but say, "You what?"

Aiden's eyes gleamed with satisfaction. He liked that he'd thrown Thomas, that much was clear. He shrugged, taking another casual sip of his coffee. "I have a detective friend. She's getting me a list of people involved in the original investigation."

Thomas felt dizzy. The doctor in him knew it was just his fight or flight instinct kicking in, but it didn't make it any less uncomfortable. "What? Why? Why would you do that? Why would you involve strangers in family business?"

Aiden gave him an astonished look, like he couldn't believe Thomas's nerve. "Because you won't fucking talk to me. Seems pretty obvious."

Thomas shook his head. Why couldn't Aiden understand? "I just asked for a little bit of time to…gather my thoughts. I didn't say I wouldn't tell you. You know how dangerous it is to get others involved in this. We can't trust outside—"

"She's not an outsider," Aiden snapped. "Not to me."

What the fuck did that mean? Was she... Did Aiden have a...girlfriend? Jealousy tore at him like the blades of a lawnmower until he was certain the tightness in his chest was blood pooling where his heart had been. He fought the urge to grab his chest, even though it felt a little bit like he was having a heart attack.

"Oh... I didn't realize you were seeing someone," Thomas managed, voice tight.

Aiden's mouth fell open, then his face contorted into a look of disgust.

"You're so fucking unbelievable," he snapped, knocking his coffee cup into the sink with enough force to cause the handle to crack. "Are you seriously fucking jealous right now? *Now*? With everything that's happening?"

Thomas shook his head before Aiden even finished, but he couldn't stop the strained expression staring back at him in the distorted reflection of the toaster. "It's not that. I—"

Aiden cut him off. "Right. Of course, it's not that."

Thomas's head was spinning. Why was he trying to fight him over this? There was no winning. "I—"

Aiden thrust a finger in his direction. "I have the right to date whoever I want. That's what you said. Remember? In the library that night? Before the sweat had even dried? You couldn't wait to explain it away. To shove me out the door."

"That's not what I was doing."

Aiden ignored him. "You said you had no right to keep holding me hostage. That I was...free to be with whoever I wanted. That's what you said you wanted, too. For me to be happy. For me to find someone who matters."

"It wasn't what I wanted. It was what needed to be done!" Thomas shouted, lurching to his feet, but he made no move to close the distance between them. He rubbed his hand over his face. "Fuck. You know that. You have to fucking know that. None of this is what I ever wanted for you. Not me, not us, not this fucked-up situation."

Aiden's lip curled at Thomas's words. Fuck. That was not what he meant. God, he just kept getting it wrong with him. Every fucking time. Every conversation was a goddamn landmine.

"Oh, I know you never wanted us," Aiden growled. "You've made that abundantly clear over and over again. Except when you can't fucking take it anymore. Right? Except for when you're drunk and lonely and tired and there's nobody around to fill that giant fucking hole inside you. Nobody but me."

Thomas swallowed the lump of sand in his throat, not sure whether he should tell him that it wasn't true, that he was wrong, even though he was a hundred percent right. He had no defense. None. And they both knew it. This was the same conversation they always had. Over and over again. Caught in an endless loop like a residual haunting. Two souls destined to just keep reenacting the same tragedy again and again. And the worst part was…it didn't even matter.

None of it mattered.

Aiden's anger was a vacuum, sucking the air from Thomas's lungs and swallowing the words desperate to come out. It took every ounce of willpower he contained to not fight back. This was why he tried to keep some distance between them.

But today, there was no escape. They were trapped together on this mountain. At least, for now. "Aiden…" he managed, trailing off when he realized he had nothing more to say.

Aiden was across the room and in his space before Thomas could even register the movement, looming over him. "What? *What*? You just keep saying my name… Aiden…Aiden…what? Aiden *what*? Fucking say it, you fucking coward. What do you want to say? You're sorry? You wish things could be different? What? For fuck's sake just fucking say it and put me out of my misery."

Aiden was close enough that each coffee-laced breath puffed against Thomas's cheek. He opened his mouth and closed it again. He couldn't breathe, couldn't think. His hands shook with the effort it took not to reach for him, to pull him in, to give in to the longing that was killing him.

He was right there. Right fucking there. Everything he'd ever wanted and the one thing he could never have and it was so goddamn sad. No, it was infuriating. Maddening. Thomas had spent a lifetime learning how to deny himself— to give himself just enough, but never everything. It was about self-control. Willpower. Mind over matter.

"Don't do this," he whispered, half-praying he would, that he'd have the courage Thomas never did.

Aiden moved until their bodies were pressed against each other, his lips so close that all Thomas had to do was turn his head just the tiniest bit and they'd be touching his.

"Do what?" Aiden said, his voice raw. "Tell the truth?

47

Yeah, that would be fucking tragic, wouldn't it?"

Thomas took a deep breath, and Aiden's scent flooded his nostrils, imploding that tiny last remnant of self-control he had left. He couldn't stop himself. He couldn't. It was just the barest movement, hardly noticeable if it didn't bring their lips together in a kiss that did nothing to quell the fucking desperation raging through him.

Thomas regretted the decision the moment they connected, tried to course correct, but it was too late. Aiden's arms were around him, dragging him tightly against him, smashing their mouths together in a brutal kiss designed to punish.

Thomas should have resisted, should have pulled away, but when Aiden's tongue prodded against his lips, he yielded. God fucking help him, he yielded. Aiden grunted his approval, walking Thomas backwards until he met the counter, his hands clenching Thomas's ass as he plundered his mouth mercilessly.

Thomas's head was swimming with nothing but Aiden. His taste, his scent, the feel of his roaming hands and his wide-legged stance that put them eye to eye all made it so easy to just keep letting their mouths slide against each other again and again.

Thomas lifted his hands to push him away, but instead, he gripped his shirt, stepping in-between Aiden's thighs until their hips were flush together and Thomas could feel his hard length pressing against the zipper of his jeans. Fuck.

Thomas groaned, unable to stop himself from grinding against Aiden, letting him feel he wasn't the only one turned on.

Aiden made a sound that was close to a snarl, then shoved away from Thomas so fast he felt dizzy. "Un-fucking-believable."

Thomas stood blinking, his brain and body fighting to catch up with each other. "I'm sor—"

Aiden cocked his head, livid. "Fucking say I'm sorry. I dare you. I will punch you in the face. I swear to God. Try me."

Thomas snapped his mouth shut, giving a stilted nod before finally saying, "Yeah. Okay."

Aiden paced the kitchen, pulling the elastic from his hair only to pull the upper half back up and secure it in a knot on the top of his head once more, like some kind of nervous tic. "You need to tell me what happened with your family before I fucking learn it from someone else. I'm tired of the secrets and the lies."

Thomas shook his head, his pulse jack-hammering against his throat once more. "You said you would give me time."

Aiden stopped to glare at him. "Yeah, well, I guess that makes us both liars," he said before beginning to pace once more.

"Aiden…"

"I'm starting to hate the sound of my own fucking name, *Thomas*," he said, spitting his full name at him like a curse.

Thomas was trapped. For the first time in as long as he could remember, he didn't know how to fix this. He didn't have a plan. He was just winging it. He didn't wing things. That wasn't who he was. He was a general. He was strategic.

Precise. Calculating. Formulate a strategy. Send his soldiers to execute the plan. Victory. Every time.

But he was out of his element with Aiden. Especially *this* Aiden. So different from the boy he'd met all those years ago. He was the monster Thomas created. He supposed they all were, but it was doubly true for Aiden. Thomas had used him as a crutch for far too long—had leaned on him until he had warped him into the man before him now.

"I am not trying to piss you off," Thomas started, trying to figure out how this had gone so far off the rails so quickly. "I want to tell you."

"Liar."

Thomas shook his head helplessly. "Okay, fine. I *want* to want to tell you."

Aiden's laugh was bitter, his face twisted into a look of disbelief. "Save your insane double-speak for your children. That shit doesn't work on me."

Thomas fought the urge to scream or punch something. He couldn't remember a time in his life he'd felt this impotent. At least, not as an adult. Not since he'd freed himself from the prison of his family. He shook the thought away.

"Can you just put yourself in my shoes for five minutes?" Thomas pleaded.

Aiden was in his face once more. "Which shoes? Be specific, Tommy. We're standing in a really big fucking closet. Thomas Mulvaney, altruistic billionaire? Thomas Mulvaney, vigilante wrangler? Thomas Mulvaney, self-centered narcissist? Thomas Mulvaney…possible murderer?"

Thomas Mulvaney, the man who loves you.

Tommy. Nobody in the world had ever gotten away with calling him that. It started as a joke, something that was just for Aiden. But it had blossomed into something more. Until it wasn't. Jesus. Maybe he was a fucking narcissist. Because even with their relationship in tatters, he heart still soared hearing *Tommy* fall from Aiden's lips. Because no matter how unfair it was to ask Aiden to wait for him to open up about his past, he still didn't know how to tell him the truth. He'd guarded this secret for decades. He'd shoved it down and fed it a steady diet of lies and self-loathing, and now, it was so big inside him he was choking on it.

But Aiden deserved to know. They all did. They deserved to know what kind of man he really was. But he just couldn't do it. Aiden was right. He was a coward. The irony was that his sons would all take it with a grain of salt. They'd explain it away, negate his guilt, but the others… Noah, especially…they wouldn't be so easily swayed. And his relationship with Noah was already fragile. Almost as fragile as his relationship with Aiden.

No, not fragile. This thing between him and Aiden…it was brittle. Years of hot and cold had left what was between them rigid and unbending, straining under the weight of a lifetime of regret.

Aiden wouldn't offer up platitudes when he learned the truth. If anything, he'd use it as further proof that Thomas was exactly the person Aiden made him out to be, and then, he'd put an end to Thomas, once and for all.

Thomas closed his eyes and took a deep breath. "Okay.

Fine. I'll tell you. But for you to understand the whole thing, you have to know how it started…who I was…who my family was…"

"You're just stalling," Aiden snapped.

"Yes. I am. But that doesn't make what I'm saying any less true. Telling you the whole thing in one sitting would take days. What happened to my family didn't happen in a vacuum. There were circumstances, outside influences. Mistakes were made. By me and lots of others."

Thomas forced himself to maintain eye contact with Aiden as he studied him. He knew it was a big ask. But it was no bigger than the things he'd been asking of Aiden since they'd first become trapped in this constant push and pull.

"Fine. But you're not dragging this out for weeks. You've got the next seventy-two hours to get it all out," he said. Thomas grimaced, but before he could agree, Aiden added, "And you can't impede the investigation. If something comes up, then you need to fucking answer honestly. And I'm not calling off Lola. She's going to keep digging. Discreetly," he ground out. "Someone is threatening your family."

"Our family," Thomas said without thought.

"Do you agree or not?" Aiden asked, ignoring Thomas's words.

Thomas's eyes burned and he felt tired in his bones. It was a weariness that came from somewhere deep within. He sagged against the counter, crossing his arms over his chest and taking a deep breath. "Yeah. I agree."

Aiden stalked back to the coffee pot, turning over two

new mugs and filling them to the brim before carrying them to the table. He set the mugs down then sat. The chair diagonal to him shot out as he kicked it with his booted foot. "Good. Let's get started."

Thomas stared at the chair, his mind racing. "Can I shower first?"

"No."

Thomas closed his eyes for a long moment, then nodded. "Fine. Let's do this."

FOUR
AIDEN

Aiden's lips still buzzed from their kiss and his thoughts tumbled around his skull with no cohesion, his entire body as turned on as he was furious and frustrated. Less than a day together and they'd fallen right back into each other. Aiden had given in so easily. Or maybe Thomas had.

Aiden didn't know who'd moved first, but the second their lips met, all rational thought had abandoned him, leaving behind only thoughts like *yes*, *fuck*, and *mine*. And he would have kept going…*could* have kept going until he'd buried himself inside Thomas.

Finally.

Or let Thomas bury himself inside him. It hadn't really mattered then, and it didn't now. When they touched, when their lips met, it triggered something deep within, and all sense of reason and logic just ceased to exist.

Aiden couldn't explain the effect Thomas had on him, like he was a match and Aiden was gasoline. The moment they kissed, it was like they consumed each other, burning bright and hot until they ate up all the oxygen in the room and the flames died again. Then Thomas would pull away once more and make excuses until Aiden wanted to scream.

Christ.

He wrapped one hand around his coffee mug to quell the shaking, hiding the other in his lap. Thomas needed to talk, he had to. Aiden needed to find out who was responsible for this so he could kill them and retreat back to his cabin in the woods, back to peaceful isolation where nothing could hurt him. Where the world couldn't disappoint him again.

Thomas sat diagonal to Aiden, this air of desolation swirling around him. He was lost in his thoughts or maybe dreading what was to come. He didn't look good. He was pale and haggard and more broken than Aiden had ever seen him. Even now, it tugged at something deep within his chest. He wanted to be heartless about this, about *them*. But he didn't know how. How could he stop caring when Thomas had owned his heart his entire adult life?

Even mad—even furious—Aiden still hated seeing him suffer. That was what was so frustrating. How could he be so pissed and still feel so bad for Thomas at the same time? How could he care so much about the suffering of someone who didn't seem to care that he suffered, too? Aiden killed people, tortured them, delighted in finding out exactly what made them tick so that he could disassemble them in the most horrifying way possible.

But he could never do that to Thomas. Never Thomas. Somewhere along the way, he'd just…grafted himself to Aiden's heart, and removing him now would cause a wound so deep he'd bleed out in seconds.

Death was probably the far more peaceful option, but Aiden had never had the sense to take the easy way out. Still, he wasn't letting Thomas worm his way out of this conversation. Not this time. Not ever again. He was going to force Thomas to do the one thing he'd demanded of them their whole lives. He was going to hold him accountable. He had to. The stakes were now far too high.

"Well?" Aiden finally said when it seemed Thomas would never begin on his own.

Thomas closed his eyes briefly, then gave a weary sigh. "I don't know where to start."

"Start at the beginning."

Thomas shook his head. "The beginning of what? Their deaths? Before that? After? I don't even know when the first domino was knocked over."

Aiden clenched his jaw until it felt like his teeth might crack, praying for patience. "Guess."

Thomas picked up his mug and took a sip then winced, like the liquid was too hot. One final stall tactic. How bad could this story be? Why was he so leery of talking about his family? As long as Aiden had known Thomas, his family was the only thing he'd ever truly cared about. "I guess it started with Shane."

"Your…cousin?" Aiden asked, recalling Thomas had mentioned the name the night he'd called. Body number five. The one with no face. Had that conversation only been yesterday?

Thomas started to give a stilted nod that became a shrug.

"My…cousin, yes. But before I tell you about him, I need to say some things about my family. Things maybe you already know, but it matters…for context."

"Alright," Aiden said, suddenly feeling wary himself.

Thomas nodded. "The Mulvaneys aren't special. We made our money the way most disgustingly wealthy people did."

The Mulvaneys' road to billions was well-documented. As someone who had once bore the name Mulvaney, it was only right that Aiden had learned their history. Thomas's great-grandfather Gerald Mulvaney had made his money in the 1800s by having his fingers in many lucrative pies. Oil. Railroads. Hotels. But that wasn't what Thomas said.

"We made our money by stealing it." He flicked his gaze to Aiden. "Legally, of course. We weren't bank robbers or mafia. We were far worse than that. We stole land, exploited people, lied, cheated, took from those less fortunate until we amassed a fortune we couldn't spend in a hundred lifetimes."

Aiden frowned. He could feel Thomas's disgust like an actual living, breathing thing between them. But why now? Thomas had never been averse to the finer things in life. His wardrobe alone was probably equal in value to the salary of several congressmen. He had private jets and even a yacht. Thomas was the liberal elite. And Aiden had never seen him appear even slightly apologetic about it.

"By the fifties, my family had transformed their image from greedy robber barons to benevolent oligarchs. We gave generously to numerous charitable causes, had several foundations set up to help those who fell on hard times, and were shoveling money into things like pharmaceutical and cancer research as well as advanced technologies. To my father, the Mulvaney name was everything. And it was to be protected at all costs."

What did that even mean? Protected from what? From who? Thomas was equally protective about the Mulvaney name, but that was out of necessity. The only scandals Thomas allowed were those that promoted exactly the image he needed to continue his work. Did that make him like his father?

"To say I grew up with immense privilege is a vast understatement," he continued. "My father was golfing buddies with sultans and dictators. He played polo with royalty. I truly had no concept of money. My parents kept me deliberately shielded from those who struggled. I knew not everybody had money like us, but I didn't realize there were people without food or shelter. That seemed impossible to me."

Thomas stared into his coffee cup now like he was scrying his memories from the dark liquid. He shook his head, expression pained. "Maybe if my father had allowed me to see the suffering of others, I might have had some perspective. Maybe I wouldn't have found my own suffering so…all-consuming."

Aiden hated this. He hated how much he wanted to call this off after only a few sentences because Thomas looked so distraught. He'd said next to nothing but it was like every word seemed to physically pain him, like he had to drag his tongue along broken glass just to spill them.

"I was gifted. Like August. IQ off the charts. Homeschooled with private tutors then entered school already light years ahead of my peers even in my ivy league-like prep school."

Aiden's head swam at the sudden shift in perspective. He knew all of this. The whole world knew Thomas Mulvaney had Doogie Howser'd his way into a degree before he was even old enough to drink. Was Thomas processing or stalling? "That had to be hard."

Thomas's lips twitched in an aborted smile. "It sucked, but nobody was going to be mean to a Mulvaney. I was a slightly bigger fish in a pond filled with big fish. People pretended to like me. I let them. It was my home life that truly sucked. Shocking, I'm sure."

It was. Thomas had never spoken of his family with any malice. Of course, Thomas had never spoken of his family at all unless forced. Perhaps that was a red flag they should have examined closer over the years, but given Thomas's current reluctance, Aiden imagined it wouldn't have been a productive conversation.

"My earliest memories of my parents were them trotting me out during parties to perform for their friends. Reciting every country from memory, speaking foreign languages, recalling obscure information I'd read from a book far too advanced for me. People would always fawn over me and say 'you must be so proud' and my parents would smile and nod." Thomas was scowling now, the words dripping with bitterness.

"It was all an illusion, though. I wasn't their beloved child,

I was a parlor trick, meant to lure people into believing we deserved everything we had. A distraction meant to dazzle people while my father swallowed up more wealth than any one person should ever have a right to. When the party ended, I was handed off to the nanny, forgotten again until they needed me once more. It became apparent at a very young age that any crumb of affection I hoped to get from my parents would only be won with effort."

Aiden's stomach churned. "How young?"

"Diapers. I was raised by whatever nanny was on the payroll at the time, and there were several because my mom was a monster and would get drunk and verbally abuse them until they quit. If she had just let the nannies raise me, I might have been okay. If she had just stayed distant, I could have coped maybe."

What did that mean? Aiden didn't have the patience for this.

"But she couldn't stay away. Especially not when she'd been drinking. She used her love like a reward. A merit badge I had to earn by excelling, by getting things right. Whether it was potty training or learning to read, my mother dangled hugs and affection in front of my face like carrots, and if I wanted a smile, a hug, or even acknowledgment, I better do what she wanted right the first time.

"I wish I could blame the alcohol. But that wasn't it. She liked being cruel. She was calculating about it. Methodical." Thomas was suddenly looking him dead in the eye. "You know what that does to a child, right? We've seen it again and again. That attachment disorder. It warps children somehow. I was no exception."

Aiden's heartbeat tripped. He didn't know if the sudden heat flooding his system was over Thomas's mother's cruelty or because Thomas seemed to be implying he was warped somehow. Had Thomas actually killed his parents? Had he actually committed the crime this random stranger accused him of? Aiden couldn't blame him for snapping at his parents, but his siblings? It couldn't be. Thomas would never kill children, even if he was a child himself. He just couldn't. Was that why this was so hard for him? Had Aiden spent the last two decades in love with a true psychopath?

He shook the thought away. "What about your father? Why didn't he step in?"

Thomas shrugged in a way that was so unlike him that it spooked Aiden, ignoring his question to say, almost to himself, "Maybe because it worked? I did whatever they wanted, made as few mistakes as possible, became their perfect child. I just hated myself. I hated them, too. I wish they would have just hit me. That was quick. Efficient even."

Thomas jerked to his feet then and, for a split second, Aiden thought he was going to leave, but he just started pacing the kitchen island as Aiden had earlier.

"It got worse as I got older. When I didn't need hugs or affection, my parents had to get more creative with their punishments."

"What the hell does that mean?" Aiden ground out before he could stop himself.

"It means they had to deprive me of my own right to exist. I didn't think there was anything worse than my own parents looking through me, but I was wrong. Do you know what it's like to have a household staff of thirty treat you like a ghost? To not even be able to acknowledge your existence? To ignore you completely, even if you're crying? Even if you're bleeding? It's maddening. It makes you feel crazy. And my parents knew it."

Thomas stopped pacing, once more looking at Aiden. "I'm not telling you all of this for sympathy. I am not trying to get you to excuse their deaths. I know other people had it worse. I need you to know that."

Aiden blinked in surprise. How often had someone said that to Thomas? That others had it worse? Aiden knew what it was like to be ignored, forgotten in his own home, but to have the entire world treat you as if you didn't exist? To ignore you when you're standing right in front of them? That would be a special kind of hell...especially for a child.

Thomas leaned against the counter, crossing his legs at the ankles and his arms over his chest, like he was trying to close himself off, to distance himself from his past. "If they had treated us all the same, maybe it would have been bearable. We could have been—I don't know—allies? But when the twins came along...they doted on them. Loved them. Cared for them. Denied them nothing." Thomas shook his head. "It just didn't make any logical sense to me."

Aiden's heart squeezed as he imagined Thomas as a child, trying to rationalize his own abuse while his siblings got everything. There was no rational explanation for something like that, but children didn't know that. But Thomas's parents had known it. They'd exploited it. It was sick and twisted and punishable by death based on Thomas's code alone.

"I thought my acceptance to the international boarding school would be my escape, but it was just a brand new form of torment. There were kids of all ages, but those who were my age were in eighth grade. I was already taking advanced college-level classes. My peers were much older. And unlike my old school, everybody was the child of someone with money, power, and status, so I'd lost my only advantage.

"Like August, I was thirteen taking classes with eighteen to nineteen-year-olds who resented the fuck out of me. But unlike August, I very much cared about the opinions of others. The school work was easy. The social aspect was a nightmare. I wasn't bullied, but I was, once again, ignored." Thomas resumed his pacing. "Except for Shane."

"Your cousin."

"For all intents and purposes, yes. But not by blood. His mother married my uncle on my mother's side when Shane was fourteen. We never even spoke until I started school there. He was already attending. His mom was an heiress in her own right. He was fifteen when I got there but already a star. Junior varsity team captain. Straight A student. Bleached his hair blond and wore it just long enough to annoy the teachers." Thomas gave a grimace that might have been his attempt at a smile. "I thought he was so cool."

A hornet's nest kicked up in Aiden's stomach at the way Thomas spoke of this boy. This dead boy. Shane. His cousin. But they weren't cousins. They weren't blood-related and something about the look on Thomas's face made Aiden want to punch something.

"So, you and Shane were…friends?" he asked, voice strained.

Thomas gave a rough laugh. "I thought so. But looking back, it was more…hero worship on my part. At least, at first. Shane McAvoy, soccer star, wanted to be friends with the school freak. Should have been my first clue something was wrong."

"Wrong?"

"Mm," Thomas said. "What fifteen-year-old wants to forsake his cool friends to hang out with a nerdy thirteen-year-old who has no friends? At least without having hidden ulterior motives."

Aiden sat forward. "And what were Shane's ulterior motives?"

Thomas didn't answer, just stared out the window like he was caught up in a memory.

"Tommy, what were Shane's ulterior motives?" Aiden asked, the name slipping out for the second time that morning.

Thomas blinked at him. "Can we be done for today?" He gave him a tight smile. "There's a reason therapy sessions only last an hour. I'm…I'm going to go shower."

He didn't give Aiden a chance to confirm or refuse, just turned and left the room. Aiden listened as he took the stairs at a run, then as his heavy footsteps moved about the upstairs. He wasn't sure how long he stood there, rehashing everything Thomas said to him before his curiosity got the better of him and he headed to the study.

Once he sat at the desk, he opened his laptop and rewatched the video Thomas had received, freezing it on Shane's corpse. There was no face. But by process of elimination, it had to be him. All the others had remained intact, but it was clear Shane's skull had been obliterated, likely with a bullet. That made him the anomaly.

All the others had died of strangulation. Up close and personal. But not Shane. Shane, who'd possibly had ulterior motives. At first glance, a bullet seemed impersonal, efficient. But this wasn't just a bullet. This was a shotgun blast. There was nothing left. Whoever had done this to the kid had wanted to make them disappear in every conceivable way. Just him.

Why? Did Thomas know? Had Thomas done it? Had he pressed a shotgun barrel to his forehead and pulled the trigger?

Aiden closed out the video and opened his browser window, suddenly desperate to know what Shane had looked like before someone had tried to erase him from existence. It took a moment to find Shane's mother, but once he did, he found his date of birth easily enough.

Shane wasn't the boy's first name. It was his middle. Quincey Shane McAvoy. Heir to a soup empire turned chemical company turned international conglomerate that owned a good sixty percent of the items purchased in any grocery store. Aiden's hands shook as he clicked the images tab, dreading what he would find.

The first images of Shane made Aiden's blood run cold. Not because of his calculating stare or his charming smile completely devoid of any true feeling, but because, at a quick glance, Shane looked like Aiden at that age. They were both tall and lanky. Both had dyed their hair shock-white. They weren't twins by any means, but the similarities were there. They were close enough to make him question everything, even his own sanity.

Was that why Thomas had agreed to take him in all those years ago? Because he reminded him of the person he lost? Did that make sense if Thomas pulled the trigger? Maybe it had nothing at all to do with Thomas and he was just projecting.

So then, did Thomas just have conflicted feelings about his friend and a heavy helping of survivor's guilt? But Thomas himself said Shane was the catalyst to everything, the one who set it all in motion. How did Shane go from Thomas's friend to a crime scene photo in the middle of Thomas's dead family? What had been his ulterior motive?

Aiden brought his fist down on the desk and slammed the laptop shut before rocketing back in the chair hard enough to temporarily throw it off-balance. What the fuck was going on here?

FIVE
THOMAS

Thomas stayed in the shower longer than he'd intended. He stayed under the spray until his fingers were pruned and goosebumps had erupted along his skin from the chill of the water. His head was a mess, his heart felt bruised, his psyche flayed open. And that had only been one part of the story. The easiest part. The most innocent part.

He'd hidden from his past for so long, but now, it was bubbling up from the cracks of his mind and he couldn't push it away. He and Shane lying on the floor of the solarium, the shrill sounds of their parents' laughter echoing from the ballroom down the hall as they regaled their rich friends with their business triumphs, usually at the expense of those less fortunate. Some things were still so clear. The pungent scent of night blooming jasmine. The smell of potting soil and fertilizer. The musty scent of the mist that would jet from the sprinklers at just the right intervals to keep the thousands of plants alive under the huge glass dome. The feel of Shane's foot as it tapped rhythmically against Thomas's while they talked.

"I hate them. I wish…"

"Wish what?"

"Nothing…"

"You can tell me. You can tell me anything."

How was his voice still so clear in Thomas's head all these years later but nothing else? The mind really was a strange creature. Memories were just neurons firing in various patterns, triggering a sequence of events that could make or break someone's day based simply on what it pulled from archived files. Somewhere, Shane was an archived file. One Thomas had done his best to bury deep down. One he'd convinced himself was now only fragments of memories— nothing left that could hurt him.

And over the years, his hazy, broken thoughts of his past had convinced him he was right. That the truly horrible stuff was all gone, erased by time. But he'd been wrong. They were still there, still buried. Once too far away to see, but now almost crystal clear because he was right beside them down in that hole. And that hole was looking a lot like his own fucking grave.

But even down in it, even close enough to touch, it felt so far from him, so removed, like it had happened to someone else while he watched. But it wasn't someone else. It was him. What would happen when Aiden knew the truth? The thought of it made Thomas want to vomit. If it was this hard to tell Aiden—who only thought the worst of him, who saw him when he was weak and petty and jealous— what would it be like telling his children? The ones who respected him? Who loved him? His family, as fucked up and dysfunctional as they were, they were his. His pride and joy. A shining example of his own fucking brilliance.

He snorted. His own fucking narcissism. It was all bullshit. Smoke and mirrors.

He swallowed back the helpless sound trying to break free. What was wrong with him? He needed to get it together, needed to try to put the armor back on. He needed to be the Thomas Mulvaney the world knew. Somehow. He'd never make it through this if he didn't go back to faking it.

He took a deep breath and let it out, then wrenched the handle, abruptly cutting off the water before stepping out of the shower. He grabbed the heated towel, letting it return some of the warmth to his body as he dried himself briskly, before wrapping it around his waist and brushing his teeth.

He thought about shaving but quickly dismissed the idea. His hands were shaking so badly he'd likely need stitches before he finished. Instead, he scrubbed his hands over his face, then combed his fingers through his damp hair, his gaze falling to the large tattoo on his side.

His only tattoo.

Medusa holding the scales of justice, her hair made of seven snakes. One for each of them. His children. His weapons. His eyes burned as he blinked back tears. He'd been so fucking righteous. So convicted in his beliefs. No better than any religious zealot, killing in the name of their god. But Thomas had been his own god. Playing judge, jury, and executioner.

He was a hypocrite of the worst kind. How had he

thought passing judgment on others would ever do anything to assuage him of his own guilt? He was no better than those he sentenced to death.

Jericho popped into his head then. Of all his sons-in-law, Jericho was the one who spoke his mind plainly. He'd told Thomas to his face that he'd made a mistake with Atticus. That he was no psychopath. That Thomas had taken someone soft and turned him into a monster to suit his own twisted need for vengeance. And Thomas had argued with him.

But maybe it was true. Atticus was content to spend his days in his lab and let Jericho—who was decidedly *not* a psychopath—do his killing for him. Jericho's boys weren't on the psychopathy spectrum either, but they did what needed to be done and they didn't wrestle with their conscience about it. So, maybe he'd been all wrong. Maybe Thomas had gone so very wrong.

But…they were happy. His children were happy. Thomas had taken them from broken homes and taught them to kill, but he'd given them every advantage, had put them in circumstances where they'd met the people they loved. August and Lucas had children. Adam…his most broken child…had a boy he loved more than anything and two dogs he doted on. So, he wasn't wrong. Right?

Project Watchtower was in its final phase. If everything Thomas believed was wrong, what did that mean for the thousands of children in various stages of the project? He closed his eyes, weary in his fucking bones. Had he saved his sons? Or had he turned them into monsters? Would he now be responsible for corrupting thousands of others who might have gone on to be normal upstanding citizens?

He flipped the light off, exiting the bathroom into his bedroom, these thoughts swirling round and round in his head. What if he was wrong? What if he was right? His brain was just an endless feedback loop of what if.

He was so in his thoughts, he didn't notice Aiden sitting on the corner of his bed until he was almost on him. It brought him up short, his hand tangled in the second towel he'd looped around his neck.

Aiden leaned back on his hands, expression bleak. "He looks like me."

Thomas blinked. "What?"

"He looks like me. Shane," he clarified. "Looked, I guess."

Thomas took a step back at Shane's name, feeling like Aiden had invoked some kind of curse. Did Aiden look like Shane? *Had* he looked like him? He closed his eyes, trying and failing to picture Shane's face with any level of detail but time had stolen that, too.

He remembered some things. Shane and Aiden had once had the same artificial hair color. The same cocky demeanor. But Aiden had been so broken and angry when Thomas first met him. Nothing like Shane. Shane had been…hollow. Void.

Thomas opened his eyes, almost shocked to see this Aiden sitting before him, not a single trace left of the boy he'd been all those years ago. Aiden was a man, tall and broad, with creases at the corners of his eyes. Older, but still so broken and angry.

Because of Thomas.

"I…" Thomas started but then trailed off, uncertain as to what he wanted to do. Deny it? Reassure Aiden? To what end? What did it matter?

"Is that why you took me in?" Aiden asked, not angry, but…defeated. "I reminded you of him? Is that why you can't look at me?"

Couldn't look at him? There were days when Thomas couldn't see anything but Aiden, when he was the only thing on his mind for hours at a time. But telling him that would do nothing. "What does it matter?"

"So, now the past doesn't matter?" Aiden spit. "It's been your excuse forever, but now it doesn't matter?"

Fuck. As usual, Thomas was getting it all wrong. When it came to Aiden, he just always got it wrong. "I didn't say that. I don't know why I took you in all those years ago. But I did. I chose you." Aiden continued to look at him with that same vacant look. Thomas shrugged helplessly. "Shane's been dead for thirty years, Aiden."

"Then why does it suddenly feel like he's been standing between the two of us this whole time?" Aiden asked, voice raw. "Fuck. I don't even know what he did, but I'm fucking jealous. Do you know how fucked up that is? I'm jealous of the person you said is the catalyst for the worst thing that ever happened to you. That's so fucked up, you know? You've fucked me up so fucking much."

Thomas felt like his heart was being shredded at Aiden's words. He was right. Thomas had fucked Aiden up so much. "He's not what matters. This isn't about him. It's about what I did. It's about who I am."

"That's bullshit. I might be dumb about a lot of shit, Tommy, but not you. That kid meant something to you then, and I know it has something to do with us. You say it's not about him, but he's somehow more important than me. This ghost from your past is important enough for you to keep me at arm's length for decades."

Thomas's eyes went wide at his words. Was that what he thought? That he'd been…so in love with Shane or something that he was still hung up on him all these years later? Did he think Thomas had killed him and regretted it? He supposed it wasn't that far off from the truth, and he couldn't blame him for drawing conclusions from the crumbs Thomas had fed him, but he was wrong about Shane…and about Thomas's feelings. About how he felt about him.

"What? No." Thomas shook his head. "Christ, Aiden. Do you think I'm harboring some—what?—crush on him? Whatever mixed up feelings I have about what happened between him and I when I was a kid have nothing to do with my feelings for you," Thomas assured him. "The three fucked up years with him are nothing compared to the twenty-three years I've had with you in my life."

Aiden's lip curled like he didn't believe him. Not that Thomas blamed him. He'd spent every moment of their lives together assuring Aiden that his feelings weren't valid, that what they felt for each other wasn't real, wasn't right, wasn't okay. Why should Aiden believe him now that Thomas had finally given him a villain to fight, someone to be mad at other than Thomas?

He shook his head, helpless. "Don't you get it? The only person who haunts my thoughts is you, Aiden. You're in my head. Every day. A million times a day," he admitted, taking a step closer. "At any given moment, at any time of day, you're the ghost standing just out of view."

Aiden looked…shell-shocked. When Thomas stepped between his open knees, he didn't protest. When he pulled him to his feet, he went willingly. Thomas wrapped his arms around him, buried his face in his throat, inhaling his scent like a drug, letting his warmth bleed into his bare skin.

"What are you doing?" Aiden managed, body stiff.

Thomas kissed the spot on his throat, feeling his pulse pound beneath his lips. "I have no idea."

He wasn't lying. He had no fucking idea what he was doing, but he couldn't let him go. He couldn't stop touching him, kissing him. He wanted to hold him like this more than he wanted to keep drawing air into his lungs. The pull was gravitational. It was selfish and borderline evil to give Aiden what had to be false hope, but Thomas couldn't will himself to let him go.

This was why they stayed away from each other. Being together was death by paper cut and it would hurt so much worse when it was over, but he couldn't stop. He wouldn't.

He needed him to stop looking at him like he'd destroyed him, like he thought someone in Thomas's life meant more to him than Aiden. Nobody meant more to him than Aiden. They didn't. They couldn't. His world started and stopped with him. He just needed him to know that… somehow. And this was all he had.

"Thomas." Aiden said his name like a warning, or maybe a threat.

"Are you going to stop me?" Thomas asked, heart slamming against his ribs as he pressed the words into Aiden's skin, relishing the feel of him. "Please don't stop me. You're the only one on my mind. You're always the only one on my mind. Let me prove it to you."

This time, when their mouths collided, it was Thomas who deepened the kiss, his tongue sliding home with no resistance. Like always, something in him gave way, forgetting everything but the taste of Aiden's mouth and the heat of his body. How was it possible to feel so instantly consumed by another person, to forget every ounce of sanity?

Aiden's hands were squeezing his back, then sliding lower, gripping his ass through the towel. Thomas was already painfully hard, his cock trapped between the softness of the fabric and the hardness of Aiden's hip. Fuck. He felt so fucking good. He smelled so good. There was nothing better in the world than being so wrapped up in Aiden that nothing else mattered.

Thomas's fingers went for the hem of Aiden's shirt, and he mourned the loss of Aiden's hands when he stopped groping him long enough for him to lift his arms. Thomas tossed the shirt aside, already going for the button on Aiden's jeans.

Thomas's heart dropped when Aiden slapped his hands away, but then he was shoving Thomas down onto the bed, unknotting the towel before going to his knees on the floor between Thomas's open thighs. Christ. This was so much more than last time. That was just drunken fumbling, fueled by years of longing and rage.

This...this was something else entirely. He hissed as Aiden's mouth landed on his inner thigh, sucking a mark there before dragging his teeth over it. The pleasure/pain of it felt right, felt like them. He gave the other thigh the same rough treatment before pushing his legs wider, dragging him down until his hips were off the bed and Aiden had him completely exposed.

"Aiden..."

"Shut up," Aiden said, spreading him open and burying his face in the heart of him, his tongue spearing against his hole in a way that had Thomas's muscles contracting and his hands grabbing for Aiden's hair just for something to hold onto.

Fuck. Was this really happening? It felt like some kind of fever dream. But if it was, he didn't want to wake up because Aiden's talented tongue had him hard and leaking and he was afraid he might come just from that.

"Fuck. Aiden."

Aiden only deepened his efforts, licking and sucking at him until Thomas couldn't stop the moans falling from his lips. This hadn't been his intention. Or maybe it had. Fuck. He'd always been so selfish when it came to Aiden. Never letting him go but never letting him stay.

Thomas cried out as Aiden's mouth closed over his cock, sucking him from root to tip. His hips rolled upward against his will, forcing himself deeper. He groaned when Aiden gagged, but he recovered quickly, so quickly Thomas had to fight the sudden jealousy bubbling within him. How many others had sampled Aiden's mouth? His body?

He had no right to be jealous. To be irrationally angry. It was nobody's fault but Thomas's. It was always his fault. But that didn't stop the irrational surge of possessiveness. Of ownership.

Aiden was his. He belonged to him, whether it was right or wrong. He locked his hands in his hair, holding him in place as he worked himself in and out of the wet heat and suction of Aiden's mouth, some part of him wanting to punish him. "Fuck. Fuck."

Aiden let him, groaning around him. His fingers dug into Thomas's hip bones as tears streamed down his face as he used him. God, how could he have refused him all these years? Even as the thought entered his head, he knew it wouldn't be the last time he did.

He shook the thought away, focusing on the heat building at the base of his spine and the toe curling pleasure Aiden's mouth was giving him. "I'm gonna come."

He didn't tell him so he could pull off, he just wanted him to know it was happening. He wanted to flood his mouth, wanted to watch him swallow it all, needed it, really—needed it to chase away all the thoughts of other men Thomas had no right to hate but did anyway.

He shouted as his orgasm hit, his body curling as Aiden kept sucking, kept swallowing around him until it felt like a punishment.

When he could think again, he released Aiden, who stood like he might be the one to run this time. Thomas grabbed him by the waistband, hauling him back and yanking his pants open, pushing them and his underwear out of the way until his cock sprang free.

Thomas refused to look up. He didn't want to know what Aiden was thinking. He just wanted to taste him. To give him some of the same pleasure he'd just received. He ran his tongue along the underside of his cock before sucking on the head, precum sharp on his tongue. Thomas had never known anything could feel so wrong and so right at the same fucking time, but it did. *This* did.

"Tommy…"

If Thomas could have gotten hard again, just the way Aiden said his name would have done it. Not a curse this time but a fucking prayer. He closed his mouth around him, relishing the heavy weight of him on his tongue, the way his hands flexed on his shoulders, the sound of every sharp exhalation as he sucked him.

Thomas gripped his ass, taking him deeper, swallowing around him, hoping it bruised, hoping it left behind some tangible evidence that this happened, that for just a brief fucking moment, Thomas had let him have something he truly wanted before everything was ripped away from him forever.

But it was over too quickly, Aiden's blunt nails digging into his skin as he came, the bitter taste of him there and gone as he drank him down. When Aiden pulled free, Thomas wrapped his arms around his hips, resting his cheek on his hip, desperately trying to remember everything about that moment.

But all too soon, Aiden was stepping back and righting his clothes. Then he turned and walked out of the room. He didn't look back. Just left Thomas sitting there in his bed. Just like Thomas had done that night in the library. He'd just left Aiden there. What the fuck was wrong with him? He'd wasted his whole life denying the one person who wanted him, flaws and all.

Because he didn't deserve him. Aiden deserved better. But Thomas had never let him go and find better. He'd just trapped him there in his misery. Because misery loved company and Aiden was just damaged enough, just needy enough to take Thomas's scraps.

Whatever this fucking blackmailer wanted, Thomas would give it to him. Then he'd let his family put him out of his misery once and for all. Maybe then Aiden could finally be free of Thomas's narcissism, this fucked-up version of love or penance or whatever it was Thomas had spent the last twenty years doing to both of them.

Death was more grace than Thomas deserved, but it would be best for all of them. Excise the cancer he was on the family and let them all be whoever they wanted to be. Give them the choice he'd never offered.

He fell back on the bed, letting his eyes close. He just needed to sleep. It didn't matter that it was barely noon. It didn't matter that the sun was blazing through the window or that he'd only been awake a few hours. He would sleep. And when he woke, he'd tell Aiden the next part of his story and let the chips fall where they may. There was nothing else he could do. Not anymore.

SIX
AIDEN

Aiden left Thomas before he'd even fixed his towel back into place, escaping to his own room and dropping down onto the bed. He covered his eyes with his pillow, almost instantly assaulted with flashes of what had just happened between them. Just those brief glimpses had his skin burning.

What the fuck was wrong with him? Every time. Every fucking time Thomas so much as crooked his finger in Aiden's direction, he folded like a cheap lawn chair.

Every. Time.

But how could he not? It was in his nature to crave instant gratification. He had zero impulse control on his best day and when something he wanted, craved, feened over, was right there, willing…begging even, he lacked the ability to say no.

Even when he knew it was going to hurt like this as soon as it was over. But he couldn't even muster up the energy to be mad about it. Talking about his family had mentally broken Thomas. It was written all over his face.

The story Aiden dragged out of him—whatever it was—had its claws in him all the way out. His suffering quelled Aiden's fury, leaving a deep ache that was a hundred times harder to ignore.

His phone began to vibrate along the side table, snagging his attention. He frowned at it for a moment, then answered it without looking, expecting Lola's sarcasm-laced voice.

"Hello," he grunted.

"What the fuck, Aiden? Have you lost your fucking mind?"

Nope. Not Lola.

Aiden sat up, heart dropping. "Noah?"

The anger in the younger man's voice was immediately replaced with confusion and a bit of indignancy. "Yeah, didn't you look before you answered?"

No. He hadn't. He'd forgotten that not only Thomas had this number. Noah was Thomas's second-in-command so it was only logical that he would have Aiden's emergency contact. He ignored Noah's comment, assuming it was rhetorical. "What's up?"

"What's up?" Noah snapped, instantly angry once more. Aiden winced as his voice rose an octave. "*What's up*? Are you fucking serious right now, Aiden? You kidnapped Dad. What do you mean, what's up?"

Aiden rolled his eyes, his misery temporarily paused by Noah's sulky tone. "I didn't kidnap your father, you drama queen."

Noah made an indignant sound. "Did you or did you not abscond with our father in the dead of night?"

Adam's garbled voice could be heard in the background, like he was talking around a bite of food. "A thousand dollars says they ran away and eloped…finally."

Noah must have him on speakerphone. "Tell Adam to fuck off. And who says abscond anymore?" Aiden asked, doing his best to deflect, hoping they would just let this go as something innocent and easily fixed. "We left pre-dawn at best."

"Don't be an asshole, Aiden," Noah muttered.

Aiden smiled in spite of himself. "It's kind of my default setting, Noah."

Noah fell silent, forcing Aiden to listen to the sounds of their domesticity as Adam could be heard roughhousing with their dogs. Aiden wasn't sure if he was supposed to say something more, but just as he was about to say Noah's name, the boy spoke, this time sounding ten years younger and more than a little afraid.

"What's going on, Aiden? Seriously. Who's blackmailing him and why? What do they think he did? Are they implying he killed his family? Because you know that's fucking insane. Why did we not know about this? Why did he call you and not us? Why didn't you tell Calliope the whole story? What are we doing about this? How do we—"

Aiden pulled the phone away from his ear as Noah became progressively more upset, finally interrupting to say, "Jesus, kid. Breathe. Just…just breathe, man."

Aiden wasn't sure if he was talking to Noah or himself. He'd obviously expected them to know Thomas was gone, that was why he'd told Calliope. But how had they known about the video? Or had something else happened? Had the blackmailer contacted the family? Sent more copies of the message?

"What are you talking about?" he asked, just in case Noah was fishing somehow.

Noah scoffed. "I'm talking about the blackmail video sent to Dad. Why didn't you tell us about it? Why did you just kidnap Dad and tell Calliope not to worry about it?"

Aiden frowned. How did they know about the video? He shook his head. Fucking Calliope. She must have been monitoring Thomas's emails. Did she read all his correspondence? His heart galloped as he thought of some of the heated emails he and Thomas had exchanged over the last twenty years. Fuck. She was so nosey.

"I took Thomas with me to get him away from the family. If someone is after him, you're all safer with us gone. I'm… figuring it out."

"Figuring it out?" Noah echoed, his exasperation obvious. "Without us? Without his family? *Our* family? Without Calliope? How?"

"That's no way to talk to your future stepfather," Adam called from across the room. Aiden huffed out a sigh. The next time he saw Adam, he was going to punch him in the face. That was a promise.

"Adam," Noah snapped. "You need to fucking take this more seriously."

"Why? Dad didn't kill anybody. I don't care what some rando perp says. We'll find this guy and rip out his insides and everything will go back to normal. You need to just relax. You're going to give yourself an aneurysm before the wedding," Adam said.

"Did you finally set a date?" Aiden asked.

"I meant yours and Dad's," Adam said, then cackled like a super-villain.

"I'm going to kill your fiancé before you ever make it to the altar," Aiden promised Noah.

Noah gave a long-suffering sigh, then asked, "How serious is this? You know you can't do this without us, right? You need the family. You need Calliope."

Aiden huffed a breath out through his nose. How did Thomas tolerate these kids every goddamn day? "I have connections, too, you know. I do this for a living, remember?"

Adam's voice was suddenly blaring in his ear like he was now lying on top of the phone...or his fiancé. "You bust cheating husbands, bro. You're not the FBI. Even Calliope hasn't been able to find anything in that video and she's searching frame by frame."

Well, that was disconcerting. He didn't tell them that he wasn't working on tracking down the blackmailer yet and hadn't even started going over the video.

"What's the game plan here?" Noah asked.

When had Noah grown up so much? He sounded just like Thomas. The corner of his mouth lifted in a half-smile. Somehow, in Noah, Thomas had managed to get the devoted acolyte and son he'd so desperately wanted. Noah believed in Thomas's vision. He truly saw the benefit in turning villains into anti-heroes.

"We can't even begin to break this down until I know

what Thomas knows. I have someone looking into the deaths of Thomas's family. I'm hoping we can see who was on the case and work our way forward. If Calliope has her hands on the video, then I'll leave that analysis to her."

There was the sound of something brushing over the speaker and then Noah said, "Did…did Dad say anything? About…what the video implied? Do you really think he did it? Do you think he killed his own family, Aiden?"

"He didn't do it, babe. He's not like us," Adam said before Aiden could answer.

Aiden wondered how much of Adam's confidence in Thomas was faked for Noah's comfort. But maybe Adam really didn't think his father was capable of committing murder. Of course, Adam would see that as a weakness. But it was clear Noah's confidence was wavering. The last thing Thomas needed was Noah and the rest of the feelings faction losing faith in him.

"Of course, not," Aiden reassured him. "Look, I'm not going to sugarcoat this. Whatever happened to his family is bad. And he clearly feels guilty about it. But your dad would never hurt an innocent person."

"Parents are rarely innocent," Noah said bitterly.

"But his siblings were killed, too," Aiden reminded him. "They were children. Tommy would never hurt a child. You know that."

The sound of Adam choking on something alerted him that he'd said something shocking.

"Did you just call him Tommy?" Noah asked, sounding stunned.

Aiden felt his face flush. He had. He really fucking had. "Noah," he warned.

He didn't need his nickname for Thomas hitting the feelings faction group chat. The one that didn't include Aiden.

"What? You're the one who said it," Noah said, his voice filled with mock innocence.

"Don't you dare tell the others," Aiden muttered.

Noah snickered. "You think Adam isn't texting your brothers as we speak?"

"We're not his brothers. He's our new stepdad," Adam called.

"Adam, stop being a dick," Noah snapped.

"It's kind of my default setting, Noah," Adam said, mimicking Aiden's earlier statement in a crude mockery of his own voice.

"Adam," Noah said, tone terse enough to cause Adam to make a whining noise like a dog.

"Are you sure you didn't kidnap Dad for another reason?" Noah asked.

"Noah," Aiden snapped.

Adam's voice was in the speaker again. "This is your problem, Aiden. You never take the opportunities presented to you. You've been in love with him for forever. You two are finally alone together after all this time. Maybe you should, like, you know, use this time to your benefit?"

"You've been in love with him forever." Was he that obvious? Were *they* that obvious? Was it when he'd reversed the adoption? Before that? The night in the library. Right

after Adam met Noah. That was when things had changed. Before he'd made it legal. He wasn't sure if he was pissed or embarrassed. Maybe a little bit of both.

"What are you talking about?" he mumbled.

Noah was back. "You guys aren't subtle, dude. Everybody knows. We all know. We all support you. We all want you two to figure your shit out so you can come home once and for all and stop living in the woods like some kind of antisocial survivalist nut-bag."

"I don't know what you mean?" Aiden lied.

"Oh, my God. Do you really think we don't see it?" Noah asked. "You guys have secret meetings we aren't supposed to know about. He bought a house near you, has cars near you, keeps a jet at the airport closest to you."

"It's for work," Aiden managed.

Noah continued as if he hadn't spoken. "Gives you more jobs just as an excuse to talk to you. Pouts when you go out of your way to avoid him. Do you know you're the only one he insists on handling personally? Just you. Oh, and even though you're never home, Dad finds a million reasons to bring you up a hundred times a day."

"You're reading into things," Aiden said.

"You cut your hair every time you FaceTime him." He did not. Did he? "You never bring Dad up in conversation. You go out of your way not to bring him up, go so far as to pretend he doesn't exist, but, on FaceTime—in front of God and everyone—you stare at him like he's the only person there and so does he. It's…awkward."

Aiden opened his mouth and closed it again, unsure what

to say to that.

"Yeah, you two are so fucking weird, we had to call a meeting to discuss it," Adam said.

Noah snorted. "*You* had to call a meeting to discuss it."

"You were the one who pointed it out in the first place," Adam countered.

Aiden ground his teeth, tired of their bickering. "You what?"

"Called a meeting. Keep up, dude," Adam said. "Everybody just wants Thomas to be happy. You make him happy. Well, when you aren't making him a short-tempered, day-drinking lunatic. But I think you and him being together forever would fix that."

This conversation was killing Aiden. Of course, he wanted that. He'd wanted nothing but that since he'd known him. But it had been dangled and snatched away so many times over the last two decades, he definitely didn't have the strength or courage to reach for it again. Just being alone with Thomas was masochistic enough.

"Whatever he did…whatever happened to his family… it convinced him that he doesn't deserve happiness. He's going to spend the rest of his life torturing himself, and by extension me, if I don't break this off. We're not leaving this cabin until I get to the bottom of what happened to his family and why he's let it shape his entire fucking life. Once we find this blackmailer and punish them, I'm going back to my life…alone. Once and for all. Thomas can do whatever he wants after that."

"Aiden—"

Aiden cut Noah off. "Have Calliope call me if she gets a break on the video. Otherwise, leave us alone. We'll be back when we get back."

He disconnected before Noah could keep the conversation going. He stood, trudging down the stairs to the bar tucked into the corner of the living room. He poured himself two fingers of whiskey and sprawled into the large chair in front of the fireplace, staring into the flames.

How long had he and Thomas been public knowledge? A while, it seemed. Aiden didn't know how to feel about that. On the one hand, at least Thomas could no longer hide behind the family as an excuse not to be together. But on the other, the amount of ribbing they were going to take over this was going to be beyond painful.

If they made it past this. Adam seemed to think there was nothing to worry about. That this was some garden variety bad guy, but it didn't make any sense. Who knew any of this? Thomas had said those photos of the crime scene shouldn't even exist. Yet, they did. They did and someone had sat on them this entire time…for what? To what end? Who were they trying to avenge?

There were no Mulvaneys left outside of Thomas's children. No aunts or uncles. No nieces and nephews. They'd all died. That left cops. Maybe a prosecutor. But why would any of them wait this long to blackmail Thomas? Were any of them still alive? The case had happened almost forty years ago.

Nothing made any goddamn sense. He was tempted to harass Lola for more information but she would have called if she had something. She was also picking up his other cases. He couldn't nag her about this also.

He heard Thomas before he saw him, but when he rounded the corner, it still sent Aiden's heart racing. He wore gray sweatpants and a pale blue hoodie that made his eyes look the same light shade.

"I didn't expect to see you down here again before dinner," Aiden said.

"I tried to sleep but couldn't." He took one look at the drink in Aiden's hand and frowned. "Is this about…" He pointed upwards. "Upstairs?"

Aiden shook his head and took another large swallow. "No. Calliope has the video. She's analyzing it as we speak."

Thomas's brow furrowed. "I thought we weren't involving them."

Aiden snorted. "So did I. Do you know she goes through your emails?"

"What?" Thomas said. "Who? Oh," he said as he seemed to catch up with the conversation.

Aiden didn't know why he was taking this out on Thomas. It wasn't his fault his kids were nosey. Or maybe it was. It wasn't like they'd had much supervision once they'd come of age. Thomas had been super strict with all of them growing up, but he'd softened by the time each of them were eighteen.

All of them except Aiden.

But, to be fair, Aiden was practically eighteen when he'd arrived. Neither of them had ever truly known what to do with each other. While Aiden had developed the world's biggest crush, Thomas had been trying to treat him like a little brother, like he might someday be his future protégé, as Noah was now. It had all gotten so messy so quickly.

"Yeah, and do you know your kids are hoping we eloped because they think we're in love with each other?" Aiden asked.

"What?" Thomas said again, looking more bewildered and distressed with every new statement. "Stop calling them '*my* kids,'" he air-quoted.

Again, Aiden ignored him. "They have clandestine meetings about the two of us. They think we should be together so we're not…what was it they called us? Oh, right, an antisocial survivalist nut-bag and a short-tempered, day-drinking lunatic."

Thomas opened and closed his mouth a few more times before settling on saying, "Oh."

Aiden snorted. "Yeah, oh."

"Aiden—"

Aiden pointed a finger at him. "Apologize to me at your own peril, Mulvaney. I swear to God, I can't take it. It's fine. We're fine. Everything's fine. Have a drink. Do whatever you have to do to get yourself together because we're not done talking about your past yet."

Thomas seemed to take Aiden's advice, walking to pour himself a drink before taking the seat across from him. "Can't it wait until tomorrow?"

Aiden watched him from over the rim of his glass. "You tell me. Someone wants to expose you to the world as a murderer. You're doing your best to act guilty as hell. You are drowning in your own misery. Your kids are already on the case and we're not leaving this cabin until I know the whole story. So, you decide how you want this to play out."

Thomas gulped down his whole glass in one swallow, then set it on the small table between them. "I'll tell you what I can."

"You'll tell me everything," Aiden corrected.

Thomas made a noise of frustration. "You have no idea what this is like."

"What would you say if the tables were turned? Would you let me get away with hiding?"

Thomas clenched his teeth until the muscle in his jaw twitched, shaking his head. He knew Aiden was right. Thomas would have forced the secret out of him one way or another. Aiden would do the same. They needed to know the truth in order to get to the bottom of things.

"I need another drink first," Thomas said, rising to fill his glass.

"Have two. It helps," Aiden promised.

Liquor always loosened Thomas's tongue, usually to both their detriment. Today, Aiden would use that to his advantage.

When he was sitting across from him once more, Aiden met his gaze. "Tell me about Shane. Tell me everything."

SEVEN
THOMAS

"Where did I leave off?" Thomas asked.

"Shane's ulterior motives," Aiden said gently.

Something died inside Thomas at Aiden's patient tone. He could handle him being hostile, furious, argumentative... but not this. Not the softness. Fuck. He didn't want to do this. He didn't want to tell this story. How could he squeeze the most confusing three years of his life into one cohesive narrative?

Had he really thought he'd be able to go his whole life without admitting his part in his family's murders? He clutched his glass in his fist, trying to quell some of the shaking, at least long enough to get the words out. Maybe he needed to detach? Tell the story clinically, like it happened to a patient? Would that make it easier? Did he even deserve easy?

No. He didn't.

Thomas took a deep breath and let it out. "Looking back, I think I was...flattered. Shane was all I had. My only friend. Choosing him wasn't a hard decision. It wasn't a decision at all. He was my only choice. But Shane had a million friends and he chose me. He ignored them all for me. They didn't get it. I didn't either if I'm being honest. But I was grateful. After thirteen years as a ghost, someone finally saw me. Chose me. I was…" Thomas closed his eyes. "An easy target."

Shane's attention had been like the sun on his face after living in darkness, but Thomas didn't say that. Shane didn't deserve that praise. It had all been so fucking contrived. And thinking about how stupid and naive he'd been just made his stomach churn.

"He convinced me that the others didn't get what it was like to be us. That they didn't know what it was like to have parents who demanded everything but gave us nothing. He protected me, listened when I talked, validated my feelings, hid with me at our parents' parties. He convinced me nobody would ever get me like he did."

Thomas's heart skipped as memories flooded back. Shane's smile. Thomas had once thought it was the best thing in the world, but now, it seemed evil—as evil and deceitful as Shane himself.

"Thomas…"

When he realized he'd fallen silent, he shook his head. "I didn't know what he was doing."

Thomas didn't realize he'd spoken the words out loud until Aiden said, "What do you mean?"

"Looking back, it was textbook, really. Isolation. He didn't need any help with that. I was already lonely. Then it was liquor. Not enough to get me drunk, but just enough to make me more receptive. After that was porn. It was totally normal for boys to…help each other out."

"Are you saying—"

"I see it now, obviously," Thomas said, cutting him off. "The…grooming. But at the time, I just wanted to make him happy. Wanted him to keep liking me. He was cute. I was gay. It wasn't like I didn't already have a massive crush on him, but I wasn't ready for what he wanted. I was barely thirteen and he was almost sixteen. I see what a massive age gap that is now. But it didn't feel that way then. I was in way too deep."

"You and he…" Aiden trailed off.

Thomas shook his head and took another sip of his drink, letting the alcohol burn its way down. He was grateful Aiden didn't finish the sentence.

"It somehow happened slowly but also overnight. We would do things…sexually, but then we would just go back to being friends. Then, suddenly, he said I was his boyfriend but that we had to keep it a secret. He said people wouldn't understand. He never even asked, he just declared it so. And, as usual, I never questioned it."

"You were thirteen."

Thomas turned to look at Aiden then back at the fire. "I had a genius level IQ. I was studying psychology. I should have seen the warning signs."

"You wouldn't say that if this happened to someone else," Aiden assured him.

That was true. But it hadn't happened to anybody else. It

had happened to Thomas. He should have known better. Should have seen the warnings. They were everywhere. Red flags. Alarm bells. Sirens. Thomas had ignored them all.

"At first, it was nice. Like a secret just between us. But almost immediately, he started getting weird. Jealous. Possessive. I was so…confused. One minute, he was my best friend, the next he would be mad at me for some perceived slight. I'd talked to a girl, looked at another boy too long, smiled at a teacher. I found myself constantly apologizing. I was getting whiplash."

"You like making me jealous. You just can't stand not having constant attention."

"What did I do?"

"You should just go back to your dorm room tonight. It's not like we were going to do anything anyway."

"I didn't get that the situation was toxic. It didn't seem abusive. It seemed…dramatic, I guess. But my parents were plenty dramatic. The constant push and pull felt normal. The cycle of feeling bad, apologizing, then getting his attention back was…what I knew. I spent years with parents who pretended I didn't exist, so to have Shane be so possessive felt good."

He didn't really want to talk about this next part. Especially to Aiden. He'd already seen the worst of Thomas, but this was just one more layer scraped away. He was already one big open wound. He wasn't sure how much more he could take.

"He wanted more than we were already doing… physically. He wanted everything, but I was scared. We fought about it constantly with him trying to push me into more almost every night until I was afraid to go to sleep because I knew I'd wake up with him touching me."

"Did you share a dorm?"

"No. But a locked door never stopped Shane in his life. He wanted something, he got it. Except that. With me." Thomas took a healthy swallow of his drink. "I was fourteen by then and he was almost seventeen. He tried every tired line to get me to see that he 'needed' sex. That it wasn't a big deal. But I just had this thing in my head...I wasn't ready. Finally, he just stopped."

"Stopped?"

"Yeah, he stopped being affectionate, stopped wanting to do anything...intimate. He told me he was fine with me not being ready for a relationship, even though that wasn't what I'd said. And then he brought home Holly."

"Holly?" Aiden echoed.

Pain arched through Thomas as he remembered the hurt of seeing the girl's face. She'd been everything Thomas wasn't. Beautiful. Smart. Funny. Age appropriate.

"Mm. He brought her to my parents' Christmas party. Introduced her to everybody as his girlfriend. Made sure I heard him. Made sure I got to see him dote on her all night. When I got upset, he dragged me upstairs to tell me that he had needs and that he loved me, but Holly was old enough for a real relationship. He told me if I stopped being a baby about adult things and just accepted that Holly was his girlfriend, then we could go back to the way things were."

"What did that mean?" Aiden asked.

Thomas closed his eyes, leaning his head back against the chair. "It meant, when we were alone together, we'd kiss, make out, fool around. He'd keep pushing for me to do more, but when Holly was there, I was just his friend. At least, at first."

When Thomas didn't continue, Aiden stood, taking his glass and refilling it before sitting once more. Thomas took another healthy swallow. He wished he could be more concise. He knew he was rambling, but there was just so much that happened back then. Too much to ever share in one sitting. He had no way of explaining the pain, the torment, the constant push and pull of never quite knowing where he stood with the only person in his life who'd ever shown him any affection.

"He was pushing us around like pieces on a chess board. But neither of us noticed at first. He wanted to see how much he could get away with. How far he could push us before we refused to do as he asked. It was a game to him. She was jealous of me. Of course, I was jealous of her, too. I hated her. She was pretty and sweet and socially acceptable. Exactly who Shane McAvoy should be dating. Which was what he wanted."

"He was pitting you against each other."

Thomas nodded. "And it worked. We both worked extra hard to give Shane what he wanted. I even...stopped fighting him off when it came to sex. I let him...take what he wanted. I thought if I just did it, he'd get rid of Holly. But that didn't happen. He wanted us both. Together."

"Together?"

Thomas nodded. "He set it up so she would find us together. It was like he wanted to gauge her reaction. I think he hoped, on some level, she'd want to join in. But she was horrified. Heartbroken. She lost her mind, screaming and crying until Shane had to shove her against the door and cover her mouth before we all got caught in his dorm room."

Her words still echoed in Thomas's head, crystal clear. *"You always pick him. Always. I knew there was something weird going on between the two of you. You're fucking disgusting. He's a little kid and he's your family. I'm going to tell everybody what you're doing."*

"She threatened to tell the whole school. She threatened to tell our parents. I was terrified. I begged him to fix this. If our parents found out, I'd never see the light of day again. They'd ship me somewhere overseas, for sure. Shane was so calm. He told me not to worry. That nobody would believe her."

"Did she tell?"

Thomas watched the flames dance in the fireplace, giving a stilted shake of his head. "No. She never really got the chance. Shane trashed her credibility before she could ever even think to start spreading rumors. He said he'd dumped her for another girl and she was just trying to get even. That she'd threatened to ruin his reputation. He did a good job of making sure nobody believed the truth. Which was why nobody believed her when she said he assaulted her. Not even me."

"Assaulted…"

Thomas downed the rest of his glass. "Yes. She claimed he

raped her in her dorm room."

"Did he?"

"Probably," Thomas said. "I-I didn't believe her at the time. He'd never forced himself on me. Not really, anyway. Guilted, coerced, manipulated, yes. But straight up forced…no. I convinced myself she was just mad that he'd broken up with her, that she was mad he chose me. That made it easier for me to stay in my denial. After that, it was just the two of us again. Sex seemed a small price to pay for his undivided attention."

Thomas snuck a glance at Aiden, who was quietly seething, his mouth a hard line, his jaw tensed.

"It was a long time ago, Aiden."

"He took advantage of you. You were a little kid."

Thomas shook his head. "We were both kids. Honestly, if it had just ended there, it might not have been so bad. Just a future therapy bill. If my parents had just left well enough alone, things probably would have turned out much differently."

Aiden's gaze jerked to his. "Your parents found out?"

"No." Thomas shrugged. "Well, maybe. We don't know what happened, but our parents stopped speaking. No more joint parties, shared vacations, family holidays. Nothing. My father said I was no longer to speak to Shane in school. That for all intents and purposes, that part of the family was dead to us."

"No explanation given?"

Thomas shook his head. "Our families didn't really feel the need to explain themselves. They just expected to be obeyed. But I was in way too deep with Shane. He was the only thing I had in the world. The only person who loved me. At least, that was what he said anyway. That he loved me. I didn't believe him, but I wanted the words just the same. I was desperate for them."

"With a family like yours, you were a perfect target for someone like him."

Thomas tried to smile but failed. "My father had spies everywhere. It only took a couple of weeks before he realized that Shane and I were still…friends. He dragged me back home, locked me in my room for my entire spring break, and said if he found us together again, he'd send me to boarding school in Switzerland. In my head, it was all very *Romeo and Juliet*."

"Did you…stop seeing Shane?" Aiden asked carefully.

Thomas shook his head. "No…" he managed. "I—"

"You what?"

He set in motion the events that would change the course of his life forever. He planted seeds that would eventually grow the most poisonous fruit. He inadvertently made the worst decision he'd ever made in his entire fucking life. He…

"I killed them," he managed, voice raw.

It was a gross oversimplification of a nightmare. But it was true nonetheless. For better or worse, Thomas had killed his family. And it all started with what came next.

He could feel Aiden's gaze boring into him. "What does that mean, Tommy?"

Thomas could feel his panic trying to climb its way up his throat, making his words stick until he felt like he'd choke on them. "I was mad. Furious. I didn't mean it."

"Mean what?"

Thomas ignored him, just trying to get it all out. "I'd just come off two weeks of what was essentially solitary confinement. I hadn't heard or seen another person in days and days. No television. No radio. Not even books. I was going out of my mind. Completely cut off from the world."

"What happened?" Aiden prodded.

Thomas shook his head. "I hated them. I need you to know that. I hated my parents more than anything in the world. But I loved my siblings. We weren't close. My parents wouldn't allow it, but I loved them. I didn't blame them. But I also never excluded them from my wrath either."

"What wrath?"

Thomas wiped the tear that rolled down his cheek. His insides churned as he tugged on these long-buried memories. "When I got back to school, Shane was waiting for me. He was sweet and attentive and everything I'd been lacking for the last two weeks, so when we were lying there in his bed, I told him exactly how I felt."

"Which was…"

"I told him I hoped they died. My parents. His parents. I said I hoped they'd get in a car crash or their plane would fall out of the sky. I just wanted them gone. I couldn't handle it anymore. He made a joke about it and I laughed, and after that, it just became a game. A way to blow off steam. We would joke about how we'd kill our parents and run off together."

Thomas swallowed the lump in his throat. "I need you

to know I wasn't serious. I know it sounds sick and twisted, but I didn't want them dead. Or maybe I did but I didn't want Teddy or Thea to die. They were babies. I didn't mean it. I didn't mean it."

"What happened?" Aiden asked yet again.

Thomas shook his head. "I made him mad."

"You made him mad?"

Thomas nodded slowly. "Another girl came forward alleging he'd assaulted her. Shane said it was another lie. Another girl trying to get even with him. But I didn't believe him this time. I could see the pattern emerging. Whenever he would get amped up, hostile, frustrated with me, he would disappear. It happened the night Holly claimed he assaulted her and then again the night this new girl made the allegation. I said maybe we just needed a break while he got things sorted."

"And that made him mad?"

Thomas glanced over at him. "That made him furious. It was my first real glimpse at who Shane was. At what he was."

"What he was?" Aiden echoed.

"Yeah."

Aiden shifted in his seat. "Which was what?"

"Isn't it obvious?" Thomas asked. "Shane was a psychopath."

A textbook psychopath, even. Cunning. Manipulative. Lacking guilt, remorse, or empathy. A psychopath who'd been left unchecked for years. No matter how many times Thomas ran the events over in his head, he couldn't pinpoint exactly when the turning point was. Was there ever a period of time where he could have prevented his family's deaths?

Thomas wanted to go back. He wanted to create a time machine and undo all the shit he'd said and done that led to him handing over his family to a fucking monster, but it was too late.

Aiden was silent for a long time, but Thomas couldn't bring himself to continue. Finally, he said, "Tommy… Did Shane kill your family?"

A quiet sob escaped before he could hold it back. He took a minute to collect himself. "I ignored him. I thought if I just left him alone, eventually he would get it and leave me be, like he'd done with Holly. But that wasn't the case. The more I ignored him, the more desperate he got."

"He killed them for revenge."

It was a statement, not a question, but Thomas shook his head. "If that was the case, maybe I could have found a way to live with it. A sick violent boy taking his revenge. But that wasn't why he did it."

"Then why?"

Thomas dug his fingers into his eyes, but no amount of pressure could stop the tears falling. "He said it was his love letter to me."

"What?"

"He killed them for me. To make me happy. To win me back. He did it because, in his sick fucking head, they were all that stood between us. And he had found the perfect solution."

"Tommy…"

Thomas shook his head. "He killed them because I told him, again and again, that they were the only thing that stood between us, and he took me at my word. They're dead because of me."

EIGHT
AIDEN

Aiden wasn't sure what he was supposed to feel. Disgust? Sorrow? Empathy? He didn't feel any of those things. What he felt was rage. This red, throbbing rage that blotted out logic and reason. Rage against the ghost of a seventeen-year-old monster who'd somehow managed to ruin multiple lives with his unhinged final act.

Shane was the reason Thomas had tormented himself—and Aiden—for years. He might as well have killed Thomas, too. It probably would have been less cruel. He wanted to hit something, tear it apart with his bare hands. He wished he had someone to kill in Shane's place, but there was nobody.

Yet.

Whoever was blackmailing Thomas would make a fine outlet for Aiden's fury and frustration. He just had to find them. And to find them, Aiden needed the rest of the story, even if Thomas wasn't ready to tell it. They were finishing this today. Then they'd find the motherfucker who'd had the audacity to go after the Mulvaneys.

Thomas was crying, but he didn't appear to notice, clearly too busy swimming in his own guilt, or maybe drowning in his memories. Aiden itched to comfort him, but it wasn't possible. There was no walking him back from the ledge, not until it was all out in the open. Every dirty fucking detail. No matter what that meant for either of them.

Aiden studied him for a few moments before finally forcing himself to ask, "How did he die?"

"Hm?" Thomas asked absently, staring into the flames.

Was he checking out mentally? Shutting down? Aiden wouldn't blame him. It was self-preservation. He was still hiding something. Something he deemed worse than what he'd admitted. But what? What did Thomas consider worse than the slaughter of his family? "Did you kill him? Did you kill Shane?"

Thomas turned to him, eyes red-rimmed, expression grim. "I should have. I could have, even. Easily. He handed me the shotgun. My father's shotgun. The one he kept in the closet."

"He wanted you to kill him?" Aiden asked.

Thomas shook his head, his mouth twisting into a brief smile that looked more like a snarl. "No. He wanted me to kill his parents—my aunt and uncle. I think he thought it would be…romantic? Killing each other's families. He called it 'removing obstacles.' That was what they'd been to him. Just things standing between the two of us."

"Your aunt and uncle were there?" Aiden asked, trying to follow Thomas's scattered thoughts.

"He'd called them. They were pulling into the drive when he handed me the gun. He said he chose the gun because he knew I wouldn't be able to handle something up close and personal like strangulation. He said I wasn't like him, that I was too soft, but that it was okay because I had him to protect me. To care for me. That I just had to point and shoot, like a camera. Like the hundreds of skeet we'd shot in my parents' backyard."

Aiden shook his head. "Why did he think you'd agree to this?"

Thomas scoffed. "It was my idea, wasn't it?"

But it hadn't been Thomas's idea. Not really. Aiden had said a million times as a teen that he hated his parents. He'd wished bad things on his father more times than he could even remember. Kids were shitheads with poorly regulated emotions due to a barely functioning prefrontal cortex. Thomas knew this. He was a doctor. But, somehow, all his training seemed to go out the window when it came to this one thing.

"You had no way of knowing that he would take you seriously."

Thomas laughed bitterly. "Didn't I? I knew he was violent. There were signs. Things I excused again and again. Things I romanticized, even. His jealousy. His aggression. Hell, I was flattered to be the only boy he took an interest in. But I wasn't a boy to him. I was a victim. Weak. Naive. Easily controlled."

"You were special to him. He chose you for a reason. And not because you were weak or naive. If that was the case, he would have just played with you and discarded you like the others. You were special to him in some way. Maybe he saw you as a partner in crime? Someone who would let him role play whatever deviant fantasies he had? Killing his parents may have been his final test."

It was all speculation on Aiden's part. He wasn't a psychopath. But he'd watched Thomas raise six of them. Each of them had latched onto their significant others with extreme prejudice. How had Noah put it? Like the werewolves in *Twilight*. Like a baby duck imprinted on its mother. Something in their psychopathy had seen their perfect match in their mate and chosen them almost on sight. Like Aiden had with Thomas. Maybe it wasn't a psychopath thing, after all. Or maybe Aiden was a little bit of a psycho, too. But Shane had recognized and imprinted on something in Thomas, and he'd fully expected Thomas would play his game. But, clearly, he'd been wrong.

"What did you do when he gave you the gun?"

"I told him I wouldn't do it. That I wasn't going to kill anybody. That I hadn't wanted any of this. I couldn't wrap my mind around any of it. My family was right there in front of me, but they weren't. They were gone. Just these vacant bloated bodies with sightless eyes. I didn't understand."

"What did you do with the gun?" Aiden asked, hoping he could guide Thomas out of whatever memory he seemed to be reliving.

Thomas wasn't listening. He was on auto-pilot, shaking his head like he was back there in that moment. "I told him he was sick and deranged and disgusting. I said I hated him. That he should just kill me, and if not, I'd kill him. He yanked the gun away from me and pointed it right at my head."

Aiden's heart raced at just the thought of a gun aimed at Thomas's head.

"I wanted so badly for him to pull the trigger. I wanted to be with Teddy and Thea. I wanted to stop looking at their bodies. I wanted to be gone, and death seemed a blessing. But I didn't have the balls to do it myself. I stared right into his eyes, hoping he knew how much I fucking hated him, hoping it would be enough for him to take one more life."

Once more, Thomas fell silent. Aiden gave him a moment before saying, "What happened next?"

"He obviously didn't do it. Maybe he thought it was crueler to let me live. He was right about that. He lowered the gun and told me to run. I don't know why I did. Maybe my sense of self-preservation kicked in. I was at the front door, staring at his startled parents, when we heard the gunshot."

Aiden blinked. It was the only logical conclusion, he supposed, but it was still out of character. "He killed himself."

Thomas nodded and scrubbed his hands over his face, then dug the heels of his palms into his eyes. "Do you know what a double barrel shotgun does to someone's face when you tuck it right up under the chin?"

Given the hundreds of dead bodies they'd both seen over their lifetimes, Aiden assumed it was a rhetorical question. Besides, they'd both looked at those crime scene photos half a dozen times at least. "His parents…"

Thomas swallowed hard. "His stepfather—my mother's brother—was rightfully horrified. His sister, his niece and nephew, his brother-in-law, all dead. Now, his stepson, too. He threw up. Sobbed. Wrang his hands and paced. But Shane's mother was emotionless. Not a single tear."

That was interesting. Not shocking, exactly, but interesting. Perhaps the apple didn't fall far from the tree. Was she in shock? A narcissist? Did she simply have the ability to compartmentalize in a crisis?

So many questions. "Who called the police?"

"Nobody at first. She went straight into cover-up mode. She forced me to sit on the love seat in full view of my dead family and very curtly demanded I tell her exactly what happened. I did my best to explain in-between my own bouts of nausea and shock. And when she was satisfied, she started making phone calls. Attorneys. The mayor. The DA. A senator. Hell, I wouldn't have been shocked if she had called the president. There wasn't anybody she didn't know."

"So, they all agreed to cover it up?"

Thomas took a drink, nodding again. "Myself included. Not that I had much choice. Nobody would believe a traumatized fifteen-year-old over the police. Over a senator. They moved bodies. Staged them. Took photos. Tossed around a dozen or so plausible suspects before someone simply suggested they make it look like an accident."

"Why would any of these high-powered figures agree to this? There had to have been hundreds of people who were agreeing to keep a very big, very dark secret."

"We were in the middle of nowhere. The police force was small. The sheriff and his two officers were easily bought. The others…well, it turned out they were all culpable in their own way."

"Meaning what?"

"Shane had shown signs of psychopathy from a young age. By the time he was ten, he'd already hit the markers for the McDonald triad. Arson. Bedwetting. Animal cruelty. She took him to therapist after therapist. But as his crimes worsened, she chose protecting her family name in lieu of institutionalizing him. She called in favor after favor. But she'd never expected things to go that far."

"She told you that?"

"She told my uncle. He demanded answers, and since I was there, I heard everything. She even said when he'd met me, she thought they'd gotten past the worst of it. That he'd just needed a friend. Someone grounded. Quiet. Someone who understood him. But then, he'd met Holly…"

Aiden's eyes went wide. "She knew about Holly?"

Thomas tipped the glass to his lips, looking down in disappointment when he realized his glass was empty once more. "Apparently. I listened, but I wasn't really absorbing things. My family was dead. I was responsible. My boyfriend was dead. He killed my family. His parents—his mom and his real dad—knew he was a ticking time bomb, but they'd set him loose on society anyway, gave him chances to harm others over and over again. It seemed impossible. Like a bad horror movie. I just sat and listened. Once they were sure I wouldn't tell, they took me home and my uncle did his best to coach me on what would be expected of me going forward as the only living Mulvaney."

"And that was it. You just became the new king."

"What else could I do?"

Aiden snagged Thomas's glass and took it back to the bar for a refill, but, this time, he kneeled in front of him, holding the glass out for him to grab. Thomas's gaze went hazy as he studied him.

"Drink," Aiden encouraged. Once Thomas took a sip, Aiden asked, "Why did you adopt them? If you knew Shane was a psychopath, why would you want to raise children like him?"

Thomas's hand inched closer but stopped short of touching him. "I had my chance to kill him and I failed. I had my chance to put down a killer and I couldn't do it because, even after what he did, I still had empathy. My feelings clouded my ability to do the right thing. When I began to really dissect the psychopath's brain, I realized there was nobody better to kill psychopaths than other psychopaths."

"But how did you know it would work?" Aiden asked.

"I didn't," Thomas said. "I could only hope. Because someone had to do the dirty work. Someone had to protect people, and I'd proven that I lacked the courage of my convictions. I had the gun in my hand, but I couldn't pull the trigger."

Was that why Thomas had been so hesitant to finish the story? Not just the guilt he felt over his family's death, but not being able to kill the man himself? He'd been barely fifteen. Why did he insist on dragging his guilt around when he'd never expect any other person in the same situation to bear that burden?

"Back then, I didn't realize that he needed to suffer for his crimes. That came later. After years of reading about the monsters living among us. Not just psychopaths, but rapists, pedophiles…falling through the cracks again and again. Bad laws. Bad investigations. Bad sentences that let the most vile creatures out so they could re-offend again and again."

"That wasn't your burden to take on."

"If not mine, then whose? Who else had the money, the connections, the knowledge? Do you think Shane's mother was the outlier? Just some rogue rich woman with connections? No. The rich get away with things the poor could never dream of. And I'm nothing if not filthy rich. So, I learned everything I could, talked to every expert imaginable. And then, when I felt I was ready, I began my experiment."

"Atticus."

"Mm," Thomas said. "He was perfect. The right age, the right temperament. A perfect mirror. He was fascinating. You all were."

Thomas's hand found Aiden's where it now rested on his thigh, and Aiden closed his eyes, letting the warmth of Thomas's skin bleed into his. For better or worse, Thomas was right. His experiment, though grossly flawed, was a success. His children, all psychopaths, were the perfect killing machines, yet they never crossed the line. Not one of them. But that didn't explain one final thing.

Aiden looked up, catching Thomas's gaze. "Why did you adopt me?"

Thomas sighed, pulling his hand off of Aiden's. He mourned the loss. But then his palm was cupping Aiden's cheek. "Because nobody knows better than me what it's like to live in a house where you're not wanted."

Something twisted inside Aiden. "Yet, you ended up not wanting me anyway."

Thomas shook his head emphatically. "That's not true. I never didn't want you. I just didn't want you the way you wanted me. You were a kid with a crush." Aiden opened his mouth to protest but Thomas covered it with his palm. "And by the time I did want you the way you wanted me, I knew I didn't deserve you."

Aiden slapped his hand away. "How was that your choice to make?"

Thomas gave another sharp laugh, looking miserable. "Whose choice would it have been? Yours? I couldn't tell you the truth. I couldn't tell anybody. How could I let you love me when you had no idea who I truly was? How was that fair to you?"

"You could have just told me. You tell me everything else, even when I don't want to hear it," Aiden said, thinking of all those nights Thomas had called him, drunkenly confessing feelings he had no intention of acting on.

"What should I have done? Married my adopted son? Caused a scandal that would have had the world looking at us under a microscope?"

"So you did it to protect the experiment?" Aiden spit, not surprised but still bitter.

"No. Not just that. What would we have been? I'm not husband material any more than I was father material. I drink too much, I never stop working. I don't just have two secret identities but three, sometimes more."

"But you were a father. You raised six kids. You didn't give them a choice in the matter. You just did it. Why couldn't you have just tried? For me?"

Aiden didn't know why he was bringing all this up now. It wasn't the time or the place. They had so many bigger things to worry about, but he'd been putting his feelings to the side for decades and he was so fucking tired of it. If he was getting answers today, he was getting all of them.

Thomas set his glass down. "Do you know what they would have done to you in the press? To me? To your brothers?"

"So what?" Aiden shouted.

Thomas looked at him like he was crazy. "So what?"

"Yeah. So fucking what? What crazy rich family doesn't have wild scandals? Hell, even the royals. Why couldn't you have just been willing to bear the weight of a little bit more scrutiny? For me? Do you think a man marrying his adopted son would be a bigger scandal than half the shit Archer has done? His marriage alone was a bigger risk to your experiment than anything you and I could have brought down on this family, and yet, you weathered that just fine. You've taken it all just fine. Even Avi's and Felix's hotel bloodbath scandal. Why were they more important than me?"

"They're not!" Thomas shouted back. "Don't you get it? I did this for you. I'm no good for you. You deserve better. You deserve so much better."

Aiden thought about hitting him, thought about how nice it would feel to have the cartilage give way beneath his fist. "I didn't want better. I wanted *you*. I still want you. Who knows you better than me? I know all your flaws. I know all your secrets."

Thomas shook his head. "You didn't. You didn't know the truth about who I was or what I'd done. And I couldn't tell you. It wasn't fair to let you love a lie."

Aiden wanted to scream. How was this man so goddamn stubborn? "What else are you hiding from me?"

Thomas closed his eyes for a long moment. "Nothing. That's all of it."

"Everything?"

Thomas opened his eyes and met his gaze. "Yeah, that's everything."

Aiden rose up on his knees until he was nose to nose with Thomas, close enough to smell the alcohol on his breath. "So, now I know. Now I know everything. What's your excuse going to be this time?"

NINE
THOMAS

Thomas felt like he'd aged fifty years in the last two days. He was tired in his bones—in his core. He was tired of hating himself, tired of lying, tired of denying himself the only person he'd ever truly wanted. He ached to touch Aiden, to give in to his instinct—to the near gravitational pull of him. But Aiden knowing the truth didn't change it. Just because he accepted what Thomas had done didn't make Thomas's involvement acceptable.

"Just because you can look past it doesn't mean the others can. You alone can't play judge, jury, and executioner," he said as he leaned in, pressing his forehead to Aiden's, wanting to cling to him. Always wanting to cling to him.

Aiden's voice was so warm. "Why? You've been doing it for years. You've condemned yourself to this fucked-up mental prison and you've taken me with you. When is it my turn?"

"When is it my turn?"

Was that what Thomas had been doing to Aiden all these

years? He'd thought letting him go would free him. But then, when had Thomas truly let Aiden go? He hadn't. He'd clung to him, used him, and kept dragging him back over and over again. When would it be Aiden's turn? Could he be happy without Thomas? Could he be happy with him?

Would there ever be a time when Thomas allowed himself to be happy? When he allowed Aiden to be happy? Did it matter? His sons still didn't know the truth, and when they found out, they'd never look at him the same way again. Maybe that was for the best. Maybe they would simply banish him. Would Aiden choose him then? Would he *allow* Aiden to choose him?

"Aiden…" Thomas breathed, closing his eyes, his hands reaching out and gripping his upper arms just to feel him, just to squeeze his muscles and reassure himself Aiden was there, flesh and blood. For better or worse, Thomas was addicted to Aiden—no, that wasn't right. It wasn't an addiction. It was like they were…fused to each other, so intertwined that no matter how far apart you pulled them, the connection never broke. It just tugged and pulled until they came back together.

Aiden's mouth was on his, like he could read Thomas's mind, a barely-there brush of lips that robbed Thomas of his sanity. It took him too long to realize Aiden was speaking, his palms cupping Thomas's cheeks as he pressed the words against his mouth. "This isn't going to go the way you think it is. Your sons aren't going to see you as a villain. They're going to see you as a victim and they're going to respond accordingly. They're going to turn their rage on whoever it is that's trying to fuck with our family."

"*Our* family?" Thomas echoed, his heart skipping and cock hardening. How long had he longed to hear Aiden claim the Mulvaney name as his own? It was so fucked up. He was so fucked up. They both were. Fuck.

"That's not the point," Aiden murmured softly, his tongue slipping past Thomas's lips to tease before retreating.

Thomas felt like he couldn't catch his breath, like every touch, every kiss, every word was robbing him of his reason—of his tenuous grip on his sanity. He needed Aiden like he needed the blood in his veins, like he needed his heart to keep beating. He couldn't explain it. He could *never* explain it. It wasn't fair to Aiden. But he couldn't force himself to pull away from him and from whatever this was.

"Then what is? I'm exhausted and more than a little drunk. What's the point, Aiden? What's the point of any of this? I'm losing the plot."

Aiden's rough cheek rubbed against Thomas's, then he kissed his closed eyelids. "The point is, your sons—all of them—love you in the only way they know how. They will never lay the blame at your feet, even if you do. This martyr complex you've been carrying around with you is useless."

"You can't know—"

Aiden cut him off with another hard kiss to his lips. "You've wasted so much of your life on a fairy tale where you've told yourself you're the fucking monster. Shane was the monster."

"But I created that monster. It's like Frankenstein. Who was the real monster? The doctor."

"You weren't the architect of Shane's disease. His mother was. His family was. You were a little kid from a fucked-up family, and you were coerced and brainwashed into a relationship you were in no way ready for. You know that. Deep down, underneath all those layers of guilt, the pragmatist I love fucking knows that."

The pragmatist he loved. Aiden *loved* him. Aiden loved him more than Thomas had ever deserved. This was when he usually pulled away. When he would find a way to ruin everything. Instead, he pulled him closer until Aiden was in his lap, his thighs on either side of his, their mouths crashing together in a kiss that never seemed to end.

He didn't know how long they stayed like that, mouths meeting and parting until Thomas didn't know if it was the alcohol or desire clouding his judgment. It was enough, having Aiden in his arms was enough. He didn't need more than this. But Aiden clearly did. He broke their kiss to pull Thomas's sweatshirt over his head, tossing it aside, before his mouth found his collarbone, then his ear. "I'm taking you upstairs. Don't say no."

For once in Thomas's life, it hadn't even occurred to him to say no to Aiden. He was too far gone to say much of anything at all.

He let him lead him upstairs, he let him undress him without so much as a word, and when they were both naked, he kissed him again and Thomas let him. He just let Aiden take control.

This was how it should be. Thomas was in no condition to make decisions. He'd been making the wrong decisions for so long that maybe the best thing he could do for the both of them was just surrender—to let Aiden do the heavy lifting when it came to the two of them. Thomas was so tired of fighting it, fighting Aiden. Just once, he wanted to know what it was like to have everything he wanted.

Aiden pushed him back on the bed and laid on top of him, settling between his open legs. There was fire everywhere they touched and they touched everywhere. Thomas didn't even know what to do, what to think. So, he didn't. He concentrated instead on the burn of Aiden's beard as he dragged his lips across his chest to capture his nipple in his mouth, and the way he licked and bit and sucked at it until Thomas was bucking beneath him, his brain a fog of want and pleasure.

"Aiden…"

"Don't move," Aiden demanded, switching his focus to his other nipple. "Don't talk unless it's to say *please* or *yes* or *more*. Understand? We're doing it my way now. You've said no to me for too long. We both want this. We both fucking need this. Don't we?"

Aiden's last question was more of a plea.

Thomas nodded. "Yes," he said, voice raw.

Aiden made a sound that was something like a growl or a rumble against his skin. "Then just let me do this. Let me have you. Please. Everything else can wait."

Thomas swallowed the lump in his throat. "Okay," he managed.

"Close your eyes. Don't think. Just feel. Just let me touch you. I've wanted to do this for so long."

This time, Thomas couldn't bring himself to form the words, he could only nod, letting his lids fall closed. Without his sight, his other senses were on high alert. The raw scrape of Aiden's face on his skin made him throb, the way his fingers squeezed at his hips, the feel of his hard cock pressed against his hip. Thomas was leaking already.

When Aiden's lips traced the large tattoo on his side, he shivered, and when Aiden slid lower, Thomas shook.

The moment Aiden's mouth closed over him, he groaned, his hands threading in Aiden's hair and pulling him off. "Don't. I won't last two seconds like that."

He thought Aiden might get mad, but he gave what sounded like a low laugh, then the weight of him disappeared entirely. Still, Thomas didn't open his eyes, he just laid there, naked and vulnerable. He didn't want to know what Aiden was doing or even if he was coming back. But when the bed sank again, something unknotted inside him. Aiden wasn't abandoning him—wasn't abandoning this, whatever it was.

Thomas was grateful for the alcohol in his blood. It made it easier to relax. When Aiden's mouth found his, he just opened for him, letting his tongue explore. Not just his tongue. His hands were moving, too, sliding between his legs, his now slick fingers probing his entrance. He hissed when Aiden breached him, invading his body in a way he'd imagined for longer than he'd ever admit to anybody.

"Can I?"

It took far too long for Aiden's simple request to penetrate his alcohol-soaked brain. *"Can I?"* Could he what? Fuck him? Love him? Have him? Thomas buried his face in Aiden's throat. He was tired of saying no. Tired of refusing himself the one thing he wanted more than anything in the world.

"Yes."

"Thank God," Aiden said in a rough whisper.

Then he was settling on top of him, forcing his legs apart with his body, putting Thomas where he wanted him. When the head of his cock pressed against his hole, Thomas had to force himself not to resist instinctively. It had been fucking years since he'd let anybody inside him. Shane had ruined that for him. Somehow, it seemed right that it was Aiden who changed it now.

Still, he couldn't stop the pained grunt that escaped as Aiden entered him, so much bigger than Thomas had anticipated. But when he stopped halfway inside, Thomas found himself wrapping his legs around his hips, his heels trying to spur him forward despite his discomfort.

"Are you…trying to make me move faster?" Aiden asked against his ear, amused.

Thomas felt himself blushing. "Maybe?"

"I don't think you have any idea how hard this is… I have waited for this forever. I would like to last longer than thirty seconds."

"I'm not sure I can handle you lasting longer than thirty seconds," Thomas admitted.

Aiden laughed softly. A real genuine laugh that shot through Thomas like lightning. When was the last time he'd heard Aiden laugh? Fucking years. So many fucking years.

"I do love you."

Aiden froze above him, and for a terrifying moment, Thomas thought he'd ruined everything. But then Aiden's mouth was on his in a kiss that melted Thomas's fears. It melted everything.

He just clung to him as he started to move, slowly at first and then in a tempo that scrambled Thomas's higher brain function and left him rolling his hips upward to meet every thrust until he couldn't stop himself from chasing the pleasure building in his spine, blocking out everything but the feel of Aiden on top of him, inside him in every fucking way.

There was no way Thomas could ever describe the feeling except to say it was the closest to God he ever felt. There was nothing but the scent of Aiden, the feel of him, the taste of him. He was consumed by him, absorbed by him. When Aiden shifted, lifting enough to take Thomas in hand, jerking him with purpose, he was so far gone it only took two or three strokes before he cried out, spilling his release on his stomach.

Aiden made a sound like a growl when Thomas came, fucking him hard enough to drive him up the mattress a few more times before he came with a hoarse shout, falling onto Thomas and burying his face against his neck.

They didn't speak. When Aiden made no move to get up, to pull out, Thomas let his eyes fall shut, and within seconds, he was sinking into blackness.

Thomas woke to find Aiden sitting in bed beside him, naked, the sheet wrapped around his hips and legs as he worked on something on his laptop. He thought about pretending to still sleep, but that seemed childish given the circumstances. He rolled over and propped himself up on his arm.

"What are you doing?" he asked.

"I talked to Calliope earlier. She asked if I'd take a look at the video frame by frame to see if maybe I could spot something she didn't."

"And?"

Thomas's heart sank as Aiden made a frustrated sound. "She's right. There's nothing. Literally nothing."

"What about your friend, Lola? Has she found anything?" Thomas asked, scrubbing a hand over his face, trying to rub some of the bleariness from his eyes.

Aiden shook his head, distracted. "She's still working on gathering the names." He looked at Thomas, meeting his gaze. "You know we need to go home to solve this. Right?"

"You were the one who said I was safer away from the family."

Aiden shrugged. "I was just being selfish. I wanted to be alone with you. Wanted to find a way to get you to open up to me."

"And now that you have, we should go home?" Thomas asked, feeling cranky somehow, like he'd fallen into Aiden's trap.

Aiden gave him a look like he could read Thomas's mind. "No. I talked to Atticus and he reminded me that you're safer surrounded by family."

"But they're not," Thomas reminded.

Aiden arched his brow. "You think they can't take care of themselves? They're all trained killers, Tommy. The real reason you don't want to go home is because you're avoiding the inevitable. Telling them the truth. All of it."

"I'm not ready," he admitted. "They're going to be so…" Disgusted. Disappointed. Angry.

"Sad," Aiden supplied. "What happened to you is sad. That's it. The feelings faction is going to cry buckets when they hear your story."

His insides shriveled as he thought of Noah, Felix, Zane, and Lucas. They were the ones he truly worried about. Mac and Jericho were killers in their own right. They had a strict moral code, but they were realists. They'd pity him, but they wouldn't condemn him. But the boys…Noah, especially. He was going to be so disappointed in Thomas. He didn't want to lose the way they looked at him. Like he was the father they chose.

"You just don't understand," Thomas said, shaking his head.

Aiden closed his laptop and turned his attention to Thomas. "No, *you* don't understand. The problem isn't me or the kids. The problem is you think you fell in love with the wrong guy and he murdered your family because of it."

"That's what happened," Thomas said.

"No. What happened is a young child was groomed, assaulted, and verbally abused by a narcissistic psychopath after years of emotional neglect from their parents. What really happened was a mentally broken boy convinced himself you were soulmates because he was too disturbed to understand the difference between shared trauma and romantic love. Until you see it for what it is and forgive yourself, it won't ever matter what me or your sons think."

Thomas felt like he'd been slapped. "It's not that simple."

Hearing Aiden say that felt like a betrayal somehow, like he was…minimizing what had truly happened between him and Shane. The drama. The feelings. The violence. It felt so real. So like a relationship. It felt like a cop-out to call three years of an emotional rollercoaster nothing but abuse.

They'd had so many deep talks. They'd understood each other in a way nobody ever had before. Shane had picked him. Over and over. Shane had picked him over Holly, over his family…again and again. Shane had chosen him— him!—and calling him a narcissistic psychopathic abuser made Thomas feel…like he was betraying his memory.

God, how fucked up was that? How fucked up that, even now, years later, the bodies of his family between them, Thomas still felt some weird fucked-up sense of loyalty to the boy who'd slaughtered his family? What was wrong with him?

He jumped when Aiden touched his shoulder. "I know that this is going to take a long time for you to unpack. I know that you will probably need therapy, but you've created a work of fiction in your head, Tommy. He wasn't your boyfriend. He wasn't your soulmate. He was your abuser. He was sick. And you have to make peace with that."

"I don't know how," he admitted.

Aiden sighed. "If you can't do it for me or for your sons, then think about the girls. Before the pattern repeats itself."

A pain, knife sharp, pierced Thomas's heart. "What does that mean? I would never hurt those girls. I would never withhold affection or allow them to fall into the hands of a monster."

Aiden squeezed Thomas's shoulder. "That's not what I'm saying. But if you can't forgive yourself for falling prey to an abuser, what does that tell the girls if it ever happens to them? Do you think they would trust you?"

"What?"

Aiden shook his head. "Let me put it to you this way. Imagine if Ara or Adi were in your position someday? If they were courted and groomed by someone like Shane. If they were abused and manipulated and something bad happened, should they subject themselves to a life of torture? Live their lives as martyrs to some cause that forces them to put their own wants and needs last forever?"

Thomas's chest tightened, his heart feeling like it was being squeezed by some invisible fist. This wasn't fair. "It's not the same thing. I should have known better. I wasn't like normal kids."

Aiden rolled his eyes. "August wasn't like other kids. Would he not be worthy of forgiveness? If the girls have August's IQ, does that somehow make them more emotionally mature? Are you saying smart children are more culpable in their own abuse?"

"What? Of course not. I would never say such a thing."

"That's exactly what you're saying every time you

romanticize your abuse and force yourself into the role of villain. Do you get it now? Do you? Do you understand now? Can we please move past this? Finally? Can you please fucking forgive yourself?"

Before Thomas could say anything, Aiden's phone gave a shrill jingle from the side table. "Who is it?"

Aiden picked it up and frowned at the name on the screen. "Lucas."

Fear sent a shockwave through Thomas. Something was wrong. Some superstitious part of him felt like they'd willed something bad into existence by invoking his grandchildren's names. "Answer it."

Aiden put it on speakerphone. "Hello."

"Tell Thomas to check his goddamn email," Lucas raged.

"Lucas," Thomas said. "What's wrong?"

Aiden snagged the laptop, opening it and logging into Thomas's email without asking for his password. They were long past privacy in such a short period of time.

"How did you know it was there?" Thomas asked, peering over at the screen. The email was from the anonymous user, not Lucas.

"Calliope has been monitoring your email. August and I got it, too," Lucas said, his impatience palpable.

There was a file attached. A movie clip. The thumbnail was just a blurry red brick building. Aiden hit play, and they watched as whoever held the camera away from them approached a group of toddlers playing on a grassy lot.

Thomas was going to vomit.

That was the campus where August and Lucas worked.

Somewhere among those children were Adelyn and Arabella. The man was bold, walking with confidence directly up to two little girls dressed for the weather in coats, hats, and mittens. They sat crouched looking at something in the grass.

They looked up as he approached. They both peered at him with their father's serious jade eyes, not afraid, more… curious. They leaned in as the person seemed to briefly drop to their level and, for just a moment, the camera lens lost sight of them. Then the man was standing, panning the camera down to show the girls. Jesus Christ. They were holding a snake. A dead fucking snake.

"Do you see that?" Lucas asked. "Are you watching? See the red head? The blue stripes? That's a blue Malaysian coral snake, Thomas. They handed my children a snake that could kill every last one of those children in minutes."

Thomas was shaking. In the video, a woman shouted somewhere in the distance. The teacher, perhaps? Then the person behind the camera was taking the snake back and walking away, leaving the girls behind.

"It's so easy," they chided in a creepy, hissing whisper. "I could have ended them right there. I want my money. Time is running out. I'll be in touch."

Then the video shut off.

"They went after my children," Lucas said, voice thick with rage and tears. "My babies. They're not even two. They walked right up to my little girls in broad daylight and handed them a dead fucking snake."

"I—" Thomas started.

"What the fuck is going on? What the hell is this all about? Your dead family? Is that what this is about? Who is after you? Why do they want money? Why do they think you killed your fucking family?"

Thomas understood Lucas's anger. "I'm—"

Lucas cut him off once more. "If they harm one hair on my children's heads, I swear on everything that is holy, Thomas, I will go full-on scorched earth. I will burn it all down. I will flay the fucking skin from their bones, and if, somehow, you brought this down on my children's heads, I'll fucking kill you, too."

"Calm down, *umnishka,*" August said from somewhere close by.

"Don't you dare tell me to calm down, August Mulvaney. They're babies. They are my babies. They're still in diapers. They were holding a goddamn poisonous snake in their tiny hands. They had to be so confused. They don't understand any of this. This was never supposed to fall back on them, remember? You promised. You said the lines between our real lives and our fake personas would never cross until they were old enough to understand. You all promised me."

"We're coming home," Aiden said before Thomas could think of anything to say. "We're coming home and we're going to fix this. As a family. Okay?"

"Oh, now, you want to be a part of this family?" Lucas snapped. Aiden said nothing. After a taut moment of silence, Lucas said, "Sorry. I didn't mean that. I just... They went after my children, Aiden."

"I know, man. I know. We're going to get to the bottom

of this shit, and when we do, I promise, you can have the kill if you want it. Okay?"

Aiden sounded like he was asking Lucas, but he was looking directly at Thomas, who nodded.

"Yeah, okay," Lucas said finally.

"We'll be home soon and we'll explain everything," Aiden assured them, holding eye contact as if to make sure Thomas understood he was telling him, too. "Family meeting. Tonight. Everybody needs to come and bring whatever they need. We're all staying together at the mansion until this is over. There's safety in numbers."

"Everyone?" August asked.

Aiden eyed Thomas sharply. He cleared his throat, forcing himself to finally speak up. "Everyone. Cricket, too. You as well, Calliope. I know you're eavesdropping somewhere. Dimitri and Arlo. Everyone. If Jericho feels the boys aren't safe, he can bring them, too. It's time for everyone to come home."

"I'll let them know," August said, voice dangerously calm.

When Aiden disconnected, Thomas fell back against the pillows. He thought he'd have more time to prepare himself for the wrath of his children, but now, their children were in danger, too. Somehow, it had never occurred to him that whoever this bastard was would go after the most vulnerable in the family. His granddaughters. His babies. His heart and soul.

They were worth losing everything. Keeping them safe, even if it meant him losing everything else, was worth it. They were going to find this fucking piece of shit and they were going to put him down…as a family. Whatever the family wanted to do with him after that…

As long as they were safe, he'd accept it.

TEN
AIDEN

Thomas sat in the passenger seat, ashen and fidgeting, likely distressed over his impending revelation to the family. Aiden was stressed, too, but not over Thomas's confession. No, Aiden's brain wouldn't stop focusing on something else entirely. Something most people would find rather insignificant in the grander scheme of things.

Sex.

More to the point, the sex he'd had with Thomas. Possibly the only sex Thomas would ever let him have with him. And he'd lasted barely five minutes. Five minutes. He was almost positive he'd lasted longer than that when he'd lost his virginity. It had been over so fast. Had Thomas noticed? Had it upset him? Had Aiden taken advantage of his fragile state? Had Thomas fallen asleep to avoid talking about it?

Aiden made a noise of frustration, earning a confused look from Thomas. He gave him a tight smile, but Thomas's frown only deepened before he turned to stare out the window once more.

Aiden shook his head. Like…what did the man expect? Aiden had been fantasizing about having sex with him for two decades, picturing it in painstaking detail. Often. So fucking often. Embarrassingly often. And it had felt better than he'd ever fucking imagined it could. Was it really Aiden's fault it had been over so quick?

No.

It was Thomas's fault.

It was his fault for dragging it out, for building that level of anticipation, for feeling so fucking good Aiden had barely even had time to enjoy it before it was over. He hadn't even grabbed a condom. Not that they'd had any. But still, when it came to Thomas, Aiden was an idiot in every sense of the word. He lost all control.

By the time they pulled into the mansion's drive, there was barely enough room to park his Jeep. While his brothers had opted to park in Thomas's airplane hanger-sized garage, others—like Jericho's kids—had parked their cars along the sand-colored pavers. Most of the cars were beaters, junk cars abandoned at Jericho's garage and fixed up by his boys. Despite their appearance, Aiden knew most of them could beat Asa's Audi R8 in a street race. Jericho's kids might not be rich, but when it came to cars, they might as well be wizards.

Aiden exited the Jeep, expecting Thomas to follow. He didn't. He just continued to stare straight ahead until Aiden went around and opened his door, taking his arm and pulling him to his feet. Thomas gave Aiden a look of dread, like he was walking the green mile to the electric chair.

Aiden wanted to tell him he was being dramatic, that his children would never abandon him, that they certainly wouldn't blame him for what happened with Shane. But Thomas wouldn't believe him. No matter how high his IQ was, he lacked the capacity to see people's motives like Aiden did. He believed in his heart he would lose his children after his confession, no matter how absurd the idea was. It was real to him.

Aiden opened the front door, rolling his eyes when he realized they'd left it unlocked. What good was asking the family to come home for safety if they were just going to roll out the welcome mat for whatever lunatic they were dealing with. One would think a family filled with serial unalivers, would take security more seriously, but with a lack of remorse or guilt came a heavy dose of hubris and audacity. This family really thought they were invincible.

When Thomas once again didn't budge, Aiden pushed him through the door. Thomas fought for a brief moment, then fell into the foyer, eyeing the potted palm in the entry just long enough for Aiden to fear he might vomit in it. Aiden closed the door and locked it, relaxing only once the automatic lock engaged. Anybody they wanted inside had the code for the front door.

It wasn't hard to find the others. They followed the cacophony of voices to the large drawing room deep within the house, stopping short in the wide doorway. There were people everywhere, more than Aiden had ever seen in one place at the same time. He did a mental headcount. Zane sat in Asa's lap on the sofa, Felix sat on the arm, Avi by his side. Noah and Adam stood with some of Jericho's kids. The blue-haired boy was Arsen, the one beside him was…a number. Seven. They called him Seven. He couldn't remember the name of the one sucking on a lollipop, but the quiet boy with the long hair was Cree.

Jericho sat in one of the armchairs, hypervigilant. His husband, Atticus, slumped in the other, chin on his hand, surveying his family like a bored prince surveying his subjects. Lucas and August were missing, but Aiden had seen their SUV outside. They were probably in the nursery settling the girls in their mini-palace.

There were no women in the room. Had Calliope refused to come? Was it that important to keep her identity a mystery? It seemed a weird hill to die on. They knew her son, they knew his last name. Twenty-five dollars and a Google search could have found her.

He shook the thought away. That was a problem for later. Thomas was his current problem. Slightly hungover, sweating and rooted in place, refusing to move farther into the room with his family. A blur broke from the sea of bodies and launched themselves into Thomas's arms. Noah. It was always Noah. If ever there had been someone meant to be Thomas's biological child, it was him. Nobody— possibly not even Aiden—loved Thomas as much as Noah did. Like a father. A father who could do no wrong.

"Why did you leave?" Noah asked, his muffled voice accusatory. "You wouldn't have let us run away."

Thomas stood as still as a statue, not hugging Noah back, not doing anything at all. Just staring at his children while they stared back at him, all with varying degrees of confusion, hurt, and betrayal etched on their faces.

Thomas shook his head. "I—"

Before he could finish whatever he was about to say, a female voice echoed throughout the marble halls. "Hello?"

Noah stepped back, his expression going from misery to excitement far faster than any sane person could manage. "Calliope?" He looked to the others, bouncing on the balls of his feet. "Calliope!"

Then he was gone—they all were—rushing back towards the main entrance, all desperately curious about Calliope's true identity. Aiden was curious, too. He followed the others, dragging a near catatonic Thomas along with him. "You really need to get it together, Tommy. You're scaring the shit out of the kids."

Thomas nodded but said nothing, letting Aiden pull him along. By the time they made it back to the entrance, there was a weird stand-off of sorts happening. A woman— Calliope, presumably—stood flanked on either side by Dimitri and his boyfriend, Arlo.

Over the years, Aiden had pondered what Calliope might look like. He'd imagined her to be a blonde woman in her fifties, quirky but matronly, maybe a lot of makeup and teased hair, a bit rough around the edges. He'd been wrong. Dead wrong.

If Calliope was over forty, Aiden would eat his left boot. She had long black hair with a shock of white framing her face. She was taller than average and curvy in an hourglass figure kind of way. She wore ripped jeans, a *Ramones* t-shirt, a leather jacket, and a pair of black unlaced Doc Martens like she had just stepped out of a nineties teen drama.

"Calliope's…" Noah started, then trailed off like he wasn't sure what to say.

"Young," Jericho supplied, his surprise evident.

"Goth," Seven added.

Aiden rolled his eyes as the twins chorused, "She's hot."

Dimitri took a threatening step forward, glowering at the twins. "Fuck off."

"It's okay. Relax," Arlo cautioned, rubbing the younger man's arm until his shoulders sagged.

"No wonder you didn't want us to meet her," Asa said under his breath but loud enough for everyone to hear.

Calliope ignored them all, scrutinizing Thomas beneath false lashes before marching up to him and slapping him hard in the face. "Snap out of it."

The gasp from the group was audible, like something out of a movie. Nobody moved, not even Aiden. He could have defended Thomas from one of the boys, but what was he going to do to Calliope? It was…Calliope. And, honestly, he agreed with her. Thomas needed to snap the fuck out of it.

"What?" Thomas muttered.

She put both hands on her hips in a stance that looked weirdly maternal on a woman who looked like a roadie for a metal band. "I said snap out of it. I don't know what you did or why you did it, but not a soul here believes you to be capable of killing children. You're not that kind of person. You never have been and you never will be."

"You don't know that," Thomas said.

"Of course, we do," Noah said, like the idea of Thomas as a bad man was ludicrous.

Thomas shook his head adamantly. "You don't. You really don't."

"I, for one, don't care who you killed," Asa said with a shrug.

"I do."

Everyone turned to see Lucas and August coming down the stairs. It was Lucas who had spoken.

"Lucas..." Thomas started, trailing off when Lucas raised his hand to silence him.

"I don't care about your excuses. If you killed children, you'll be dealt with per the code." Thomas nodded, but Lucas wasn't done. "But none of us believe you killed children. Not by accident or on purpose. We do think you're being uncharacteristically cowardly about this."

"That's super harsh, Lucas," Felix said.

Lucas's gaze cut to Felix. "A man with a grudge against our family handed a dead snake to my children in broad daylight. It's not harsh enough." Once more, he turned his attention to Thomas. "You need to get your shit together."

Thomas blinked at him. "What?"

Lucas's lip curled, and he shook his head. "You're Thomas fucking Mulvaney, the head of this fucked-up little family. Start fucking acting like it before something happens to my children and I have to fucking kill you myself."

"This is stressful," Zane muttered. "I think I'm gonna be sick."

Felix flung an arm around his shoulders, patting his head in a gesture that contradicted his next words. "If you throw up on my fifteen-hundred dollar sneakers, I'm not speaking to you for a week," Felix promised in his sweetest tone.

"This place looks like a museum," Arlo said, turning in a circle, very much sounding like he was trying to appease a crowd about to turn violent.

"Yes," Arsen said in heavily accented Russian. "That's why we came. The others didn't believe only one person could live in a house this big."

Thomas ignored the boys and looked to Calliope, who cocked her hip, nodding towards Lucas. "I'm with him. We need the old Thomas back. The 'fuck around and find out' Thomas. I'll smack you again if I have to."

Thomas blinked like he was coming out of a trance, then heaved a heavy sigh, scrubbing his hands over his face. "That won't be necessary. Just give me a few minutes to shower and I'll explain everything."

"Fine," Calliope said as if she was doing him a favor. "While you're up there, look for your big boy panties so we can figure out who threatened your grandbabies."

"She's mean," Arsen whispered. "I like it."

When Thomas turned towards the stairs, Aiden said, "I'll go with you."

"Oh, no, you won't," Calliope said, catching him by the ear.

What the fuck? Not even his mother had ever done that. Why the fuck did it hurt so bad?

"Ow," Aiden growled.

Calliope scoffed. "You will not be distracting him with your pelvic sorcery."

Aiden blinked at her. "My what?"

"He definitely doesn't have TikTok," Felix said to Zane, his stage whisper conspiratorial.

"Of course not," Atticus sniffed. "He's an adult."

Adam folded his arms and sneered. "We all know your cat has a TikTok, Freckles."

"What? He does not," Atticus protested, his face turning as red as his hair. "And don't call me that. Only my husband can call me that."

Calliope pushed Thomas towards the stairs, ignoring the others. Aiden watched until Thomas was out of sight before turning back to the clusterfuck that was his family.

Jericho chuckled. "Ignore them, Freckles. We have bigger fish to fry."

"What does that even mean?" Arsen asked. "Like, what does a fish's size matter?"

"Don't let them lie to you," the boy with the lollipop told Arsen. "Size matters. Even in fish."

"Oh. Right," Arsen said, his face a mask of confusion even as he nodded. "So, what bigger fish do we need to fry?"

"Let's ask our new stepdad," Adam crowed. "Can we call you Dad? On that note, do you still call Thomas Dad or is it Daddy now?"

Aiden launched himself towards Adam, his fist flying, a grunt of satisfaction leaving him as it connected squarely with the younger man's jaw, sending him stumbling backwards.

Adam laughed and rushed forward like he was ready for a brawl, but Noah stepped in front of him, jabbing a finger into his chest. "Enough. You had that coming. Leave him alone."

Aiden's fist throbbed, but if the little shit wanted a fight, he was more than happy to beat his ass. It would be a pleasant distraction from worrying about Thomas, who hadn't been out of his sight in days.

"It's not my fault he can't take a joke," Adam muttered.

"You're the joke," Aiden snapped.

"Oh, great comeback. Are you a comedian?" Adam asked, giving Aiden the finger.

"Oh, my God!" Calliope shouted. When they all gaped at her, she gave them a deceptively sweet smile that matched her sickly tone. "Mouths shut, ears open, eyes on me," she said, like she was talking to a bunch of toddlers.

Miraculously, it worked. They all stood still and quiet, waiting for her to say something, but before she could, Zane floated forward, almost like he couldn't help himself. He didn't stop until he was just in front of Calliope, studying her through his thick lenses. "Wait…I know you."

She gave him another patient smile while he seemed to try to place where he'd seen her before.

Finally, he said, "Yeah, you were at our wedding. Dad said you were a business acquaintance."

She shrugged. "Am I not?" She looked at them all in turn. "Did you think I would miss any of your weddings?"

The twins rushed forward, stopping short when they were just behind Zane, leaning over him to get in her face like she was a slide they were studying under a microscope. She didn't so much as flinch.

"No fucking way," Asa muttered, reaching up without thought like he was going to touch her hair.

"If you so much as lay a finger on my mother, I'm going to remove your lungs with a rusty fucking spoon," Dimitri promised, voice a low purr. "Honestly, I don't even like you breathing that close to her. Back up."

Avi scoffed. "Easy, Benjamin Button. Nobody is going to touch your mommy."

Dimitri's lips curled into a snarl, but Calliope held up a hand. "Boys. We have shit to do." She looked at Zane. "Be a doll, would you? Take Felix and my boys and show them to the war room. I need to set up."

"Set up?" Felix echoed, stepping forward.

Calliope gestured to four black metal cases, similar to the black boxes musicians used to move equipment. "I don't go anywhere without my babies."

"You carry your pets in those?" Lollipop boy asked.

Adam frowned, still rubbing his jaw. "Why the war room?"

"Yeah, Atticus's trash goblin is in the laundry room," Noah said.

"How dare you?" Atticus said imperiously. "Boots is not a trash goblin. Besides, she smells better than the gassy bio-weapons you keep pilfering off our dead clients."

"I meant trash goblin in a good way," Noah said to Adam, pouting.

"I know, baby," Adam said. "Freckles's bowtie is just on too tight."

Atticus moved like he was going to attempt to punch Adam in the face when Jericho snatched him by the arm. "Easy, killer. Just let it go."

"Boots isn't a trash goblin. She's a lady," Atticus muttered.

"I know, Freckles. I know," Jericho said, squeezing his arm.

"My babies are my computers. I can't do what I do without them." She looked at them all with a dubious expression. "And trust me. You all need me."

Aiden couldn't argue with that. When Zane and Felix had left with Calliope's boys, he asked, "Are the girls okay?"

August nodded, wrapping an arm around Lucas's waist. "They're fine. They're in the nursery with Cricket. We're going to take turns keeping watch. Just in case."

"Do you really think someone would have the balls to walk into Thomas's house and take the children?" Atticus asked.

"Well, it doesn't help that you left the door wide open," Aiden muttered.

"Yeah, someone could be living in here for a year and you'd never know it," Seven said, looking around dubiously.

"Right?" Noah agreed. "That's what I said. Like, this house is too big."

Aiden agreed with them but kept it to himself. It hardly mattered. Thomas would never get rid of the place. But that was an issue for another day.

Those who were left returned to the drawing room. Noah and Jericho took his kids and found snacks, bringing them to the ornate coffee table in front of the antique sofa. It seemed absurd but also weirdly accurate to see Fritos and

Funyuns sitting next to cheap beer and expensive whiskey on a table that had probably belonged to a king. If that wasn't some kind of metaphor for their whole fucked-up family, Aiden didn't know what was.

When Thomas re-entered the room, Aiden's heart tripped behind his ribcage. Thomas wore white linen pants and a navy sweater, and his hair was dry and styled, his face clean-shaven. That was the man he knew. The man he loved.

That was Thomas fucking Mulvaney.

ELEVEN
THOMAS

The war room was bursting at the seams. Thomas had given talks to thousands of people—CEOs, heads of state, politicians, hell, even royalty. But he'd never been so nervous as he was facing down his own family. He fought the urge to fidget, to wipe his sweaty palms on his pants or shift his weight. He couldn't fall apart again. His family couldn't function without a leader and that was him.

For better or worse.

He looked around as they all settled into their respective groups, some of them forming surprising little sub-units within the space. It was no surprise that Jericho's kids all huddled together on the floor, but it was when Arlo and Dimitri settled comfortably in their midst, clearly all familiar with each other.

How had their paths even crossed? That was a question for another day.

His sons, along with Jericho and Lucas, had opted for the office chairs, taking up their usual seats around the immense table. But, unlike the others, Zane, Felix, and Noah sat directly on the conference table, careful to avoid Calliope's elaborate set-up while keeping as close to Thomas as possible without standing beside him.

The trio held hands like they were at a candlelight vigil. These three were the ones he feared hurting the most. In the forty-eight hours or so he'd been with Aiden, he'd come to realize that he'd wrongfully painted himself as a villain. That he hadn't allowed himself the same grace he'd easily given to others…even Shane. But that didn't make what he was about to do any easier. Hell, if anything, it made it harder. Admitting he was fallible and not some kind of superhero like Noah imagined him to be was going to be much harder than just being a killer.

"I guess we should get started," Thomas said.

Just as he was about to gesture to Calliope that he was ready to begin, the door to the war room burst open and Archer and Mac all but fell inside, Archer frowning at Thomas. "Did you start without us?"

Start without them? Thomas hadn't even known they were in town. When he hadn't seen them among the others, he'd assumed they couldn't get away or that they just hadn't been notified. "Why aren't you in Vegas?"

Archer formed a heart with his hands. "Aww, I missed you too, Dad."

Thomas sighed. "You know what I mean. Who's minding the school?"

Archer and Mac exchanged amused looks before looking back at Thomas. "You know we don't actually run the whole school, right?" Mac said. "Boone and the others do the day-to-day toddler taming. We just pick the assignments and teach the occasional defense class."

"So, there really is a school for baby psychos?" Seven asked, though not to anybody in particular.

"We prefer the term neurodiverse," Thomas said, giving Seven a stern look. "Psychopathy is a spectrum."

Asa scoffed. "I, for one, prefer psycho. Neurodiverse makes us sound…soft."

Thomas gave his son a baleful look. Nobody had ever looked at any of his sons and thought they were soft. Well, maybe Atticus, but he was only that way for Jericho. His sons had been called many things from "nerd" to "drunk," but they'd never been called soft.

"I like neurospicy. Makes us sound tasty," Avi said, winking at Felix, who rolled his eyes so hard Thomas feared he might injure himself.

Archer dropped into a chair beside Calliope. "Also—to answer your question—we've been here since Aiden kidnapped you. We got the SOS and took the jet back ASAP."

"Five minutes working on a military base and he only speaks in acronyms," Adam mused out loud.

Archer gave him the finger without bothering to look in his direction.

Aiden glowered at Archer. "I didn't kidnap him."

Thomas found himself fighting a smile at Aiden's grumpy face. "You kind of did…but just a little."

Aiden's gaze cut to his and, for a moment, Thomas forgot they were in a room full of people. Aiden was beautiful and forceful. And when he looked at Thomas like that—like he wanted to eat him alive—Thomas lost his ability to think of anything but the man before him. Aiden was bad for business. Whenever he was near, Thomas got lost in him.

"I didn't hear you complaining," Aiden murmured.

Especially when he said things like that, while looking at Thomas like he was a slab of meat. Heat flooded his system as memories of their earlier encounter filled his head, temporarily rendering him mute.

"Oh-kay, I am not comfortable with this," Noah said, looking at Aiden. "Stop flirting with my dad. It's weird."

"That's not what you said yesterday," Aiden reminded him.

Had Aiden talked to Noah about Thomas? That was new information. What the hell was happening? When had Thomas lost total control of this family?

"Hey, he's Aiden's dad, too," August reminded Noah, lips twitching.

Aiden pointed a finger in his direction. "Don't fucking start, August. I swear I will punch you."

"Color me terrified," August said, tone bored.

"Color me terrified," Aiden mocked in a pretentious tone that made the others chuckle.

"Oh, yeah," Seven said in a half-whisper. "I forgot he's, like, Thomas's…son? Awkward."

"More like awesome," Arsen challenged, grinning as he watched the back and forth.

"Careful, August," Atticus said. "You don't want to piss off Dad's favorite."

"Yeah, he might ground you," Avi crowed.

"I hate all of you," Aiden said.

"Our new stepdad's kind of abusive," Adam said, then snickered.

Aiden looked at Thomas. "Control your children."

August laced his fingers together on the conference room table. "Hey, I don't know what you're complaining about. You just moved up the rank from son to husband. I'm the one who's going to have to explain to my children how Uncle Aiden went to Grandpa Aiden."

It was clear to Thomas that August was not at all upset about it. He didn't even have the capacity to be truly upset. Aiden, however, seemed to be rendered speechless at August's casual rebuttal. His gaze darted to Thomas like he half-expected him to bolt from the room.

But Thomas wasn't going anywhere. He didn't know where any of this was going, but he was tired of running. Now that his worst fears had finally come to fruition and everything was about to come to light, Thomas was hit with this weird sense of relief…and a newfound clarity. Nothing good came from keeping secrets from family.

He'd spent the last two decades playing this scenario over and over in his head, the day he might have to finally reveal his past to his children. He'd revealed his past in a million different ways, imagining their reactions, but whatever Thomas had expected from this confrontation, it wasn't this.

The good-natured teasing, the knowledge that his feelings for Aiden hadn't been as hidden as he'd thought they were all this time. He thought he'd feel embarrassed or ashamed of those feelings, but instead he just felt…relieved. No matter what happened later, at least—when it came to his relationship with Aiden—they all appeared to approve.

But there was still this one final matter to deal with.

He looked to Mac, who was the only one still standing. "Sit down, please. I want to get this over with."

"And then you two can explain where you've been for the last twenty-four hours," Atticus said, looking at Archer and Mac pointedly.

Mac dropped into Archer's lap beside Calliope's chair, taking her hand and kissing it. "Looking lovely, as always."

Noah whipped his head around, expression mutinous. "No fucking way did you already know Calliope in person."

Mac's expression was smug. "She works for Elite, too, remember. Our paths have crossed. Though, it took me an embarrassingly long time to put two and two together. She doesn't look quite like this when she's in the office."

"This is such bullshit," Noah muttered to himself.

"Enough, *please*," Thomas begged, wishing he had a drink. But it was better that he remained clear-headed.

Archer waved his hand in a dramatic *go-on* gesture. "The floor is yours."

"The whole house is," Levi said under his breath.

Thomas stifled a small laugh, then looked to Calliope, who tapped a few keys. The screens behind him lit up. He didn't look at the photos. He couldn't. He didn't want to see it. Not again.

"This is my family," he said, knowing Calliope would

handle the reveal of the crime scene photos. "When I was fifteen and away at boarding school, my cousin, Shane, drugged and strangled them all before turning the gun on himself."

"Whoa," someone said from the floor.

Thomas didn't look to see who it was, just scanned the sea of faces, hoping to gauge how they all received the news. Noah, Zane, and Felix looked shocked, Lucas seemed… resigned, almost like he'd known. Maybe he had. Lucas had most definitely seen something the day they'd first met, but he was respectful enough to keep it to himself.

But his sons stared blankly, expressions inscrutable.

"That's really fucked up," Noah said. "But what does that have to do with you? Why does the blackmailer think you killed your family?"

"Because, in a way, I did," Thomas said hesitantly. He didn't want to have to slog his way through the entire story all over again. Just telling Aiden the details had almost killed him.

"What? How?" Felix asked, his disbelief evident.

Thomas rested his palms on the conference room table, closing his eyes. "Because I told Shane I wanted them dead. And he wanted to make me happy. So, he made my wish come true."

"Your cousin killed your family because you asked him to?" Noah asked, voice dull, like he couldn't believe what he was hearing.

"It's not like that," Aiden said, voice dangerously low, like he was prepared to defend Thomas with extreme prejudice. It eased something deep inside him.

Still, there was no time for half-truths. "Isn't it?"

Aiden shot to his feet. "No, it's really fucking not."

"You wanted me to tell them everything. So, I am," Thomas reminded him.

"No, I wanted you to tell them the truth."

"That is the truth," Thomas said.

"No, that's a small, distorted part of the truth," Aiden snapped.

"So, why don't you tell us what the whole truth is?" Jericho asked, like he was ready to play mediator if he had to.

"Shane was a psychopath who groomed him, assaulted him, and somehow convinced him that it was love. He didn't ask him to kill his family—he said he hated his mom and dad and he wished they were dead. And he should have because they were abusive fucking monsters." To Thomas, he said, "Tell the story right or don't fucking tell it at all."

There was a moment where the entire room froze. Even Thomas. Aiden had trauma dumped Thomas's entire life on an unsuspecting audience and they were all fighting to process his claims, even Thomas. And he'd lived it.

"He…raped you," Noah said, tears forming in his eyes.

"It—" Thomas cut himself off. What was he going to say? It wasn't rape? Wasn't it? Would he have called it rape if it was one of his sons who'd been the victim? Yes. Undeniably. "It's complicated."

"Your parents abused you?" Zane asked quietly.

Thomas sighed. Why was this so fucking hard? His parents had been horrible people, but talking about them now to a room full of people seemed unnecessarily cruel. What was wrong with him? Why was he still protecting them?

"My mother was a narcissist who used her 'love' like a reward system for doing as I was told. My father followed along, probably so he didn't become a victim himself. Nobody physically beat me or assaulted me at home, but I was made to feel invisible in a house filled with people. It wasn't…good," Thomas finished lamely.

"Shane was your cousin?" Noah asked. "I don't remember hearing about him."

"He was my cousin by marriage. My uncle married Shane's mother when Shane was fourteen. We went to the same school. We became…friends."

"You weren't friends," Aiden muttered. "You were barely thirteen and he was almost sixteen. He groomed you. For two years, he played with your feelings."

Thomas shook his head. "He was sick. He was a psychopath. He needed help. If his parents had just acknowledged what he'd done and gotten him help, maybe…maybe none of this would have happened."

"That's why you did it," Seven blurted, like he'd just been handed the last piece of a puzzle. "That's why you adopted them. Right?"

Thomas nodded. "Yes. At first, I hated Shane for what he'd done. Then I hated myself. But beneath all of that, I realized that maybe if someone had just intervened, this could have all been avoided."

"But you taught us to kill," Adam said, not sounding upset about it. More like he was asking for clarification.

This was going off-topic, but Thomas owed them some

kind of explanation. "I had a chance to kill Shane myself that day, standing there in the cabin surrounded by the bodies of my parents, my siblings. He handed me a loaded gun and asked me to kill his parents."

"He wanted you to kill his parents, too?" Felix asked, looking to his brother almost like he just wanted the comfort of his presence, the reassurance he was near.

Thomas nodded. "I could have taken him out myself, but I ran. Luckily, he decided that he'd rather go out on his own terms and put the gun to his own head, but it made me think, what if he'd run? How many future deaths would be on my head? That was when I realized…it was my job to help those I could and put down those I couldn't. There's a line and once it's crossed, there's no going back. I believed—wrongly—that all psychopaths needed a target for their rage, so I made it my mission to give them one and clean up the mistakes made by a far too fallible justice system. I thought it would be my penance."

Silence stretched as those in the room seemed to process Thomas's reveal until Jericho finally broke the silence. "I'm still confused about why this blackmailer thinks Thomas killed his family. It doesn't make any sense."

"What do you mean?" Atticus asked.

Jericho leaned back in his chair. "I mean, what Shane did was obviously covered up. The world thinks that they died in…what, a gas leak? Carbon monoxide poisoning? Some freak accident, right?"

Thomas nodded, frowning.

Jericho waited for a moment, like he was hoping someone

would understand his confusion, before shaking his head. "Okay, so Shane's dead. Everyone involved in the cover-up knows the real story. Right? They must. They know that Shane killed everyone and then himself."

Aiden's brows raised. "Right. So, what's your point?"

It was Cree who spoke. Thomas had almost forgotten the quiet boy was there. He was always so still. "So, whoever is blackmailing you clearly doesn't know the whole story. They couldn't. Or they'd know it wasn't you who did it."

"Exactly," Jericho said. "They somehow had access to crime scene photos that no longer exist, but they're pinning the blame on you. Why? Why do they think you killed your family? How do they even know this happened? This is obviously personal because they went after Adi and Ara. But why? And how do they only have half of the story?"

"Maybe they just need money?" Nico said. "Maybe they're just trying to, like…incentivize Thomas into giving him what he wants faster? Could they be a family member of a cop or someone at the crime scene?"

"Maybe," Jericho said. "But, it's risky, no? Thomas could just expose the truth. It might be a little bit of a scandal but nothing that would destroy an empire. If anything, it would make him more sympathetic. Not less. Whoever is doing this believes in their heart that Thomas killed his family."

"Which means they either don't know the whole story or they do," Noah said.

"What do you mean?" Adam asked.

"Well, we know Thomas didn't kill his family. But Shane believed that was what Thomas wanted. So, whoever this is, has to know Shane killed Thomas's family for Thomas. Right?" Noah asked.

"What about Holly?" Aiden asked suddenly.

Thomas froze. "Holly? No. I don't think so."

"Who's Holly?" Lucas asked.

"She was Shane's ex-girlfriend," Thomas said absently.

"Another victim," Aiden clarified. "Shane liked to pit Thomas and Holly against each other to try to entice the other to play his games."

"But…surely, she wouldn't be on his side. Right?" Lucas asked.

"People who've been abused often side with the abuser, though," Mac said.

"She filed rape allegations against Shane. I don't think she'd blackmail Thomas," Aiden said. He looked at Thomas.

"It's not Holly," Thomas said definitively, hoping that would be the end of it.

"How do you know?" Archer asked.

Thomas sighed. "Holly's dead. She died of ovarian cancer fifteen years ago."

Aiden moved to Thomas's side, placing a hand on his back. "Tell them the whole story. All of it. Start to finish. Just like you told me."

"I-I don't know if I can do it again," Thomas admitted. Just thinking about tearing open that wound made him feel a hundred years old.

"You have to, Tommy. It's the only way we're going to figure this out. Calliope, take notes. We'll go over everything once it's all said and done."

TWELVE
AIDEN

It took about an hour to explain it all. Aiden stood beside Thomas, holding his sweaty palm, as he did his best to get through all the painfully intimate details of his childhood with a somewhat clinical efficiency. It was like he hoped he could spare his sons some of the horror if he could just get through it without any type of emotion.

But that wasn't the case. It never would have been the case. Noah and the rest of the feelings faction were in tears. Jericho's boys were quiet, attached enough to Thomas to be sad for him but not enough to have any overt reaction to the story. Besides, they all had similar trauma and were far closer to it than anyone else in the room.

But Thomas's sons...they were seething. Aiden hadn't expected that. He had expected a level of anger at Thomas for lying to them, but the fury was palpable. They wanted to kill. If Aiden had learned anything over the years, it was what his former brothers looked like when they smelled blood in the water. They were ready to go to war.

"Do you have any questions?" Thomas asked, looking two seconds away from collapsing.

Hands shot up around the room, but Aiden shook his head. "No. No questions. It's after midnight. We'll pick this up in the morning." To Thomas, he added, "You need to go upstairs and see the girls. Then go to bed."

Thomas opened his mouth like he was going to argue but then nodded, expression grim. Before he left, he said to Noah, "You'll make sure everyone has a place to sleep tonight?"

"Yeah, of course," Noah promised. Thomas gave another heavy nod, then left. When he was gone, Noah asked, "Did you just send Dad to his room?"

Noah was still calling Thomas Dad, just as Aiden had expected he would. It was clear that Thomas's childhood trauma had only solidified their bond, not broken it. Well, it was clear to Aiden. Maybe not so much to Thomas.

Aiden sighed. "He's exhausted and he can see how upset everyone is." Turning to Jericho's kids, he said, "Can I talk to the Mulvaney clan alone for a bit?"

As they all stood, Arsen looked to Noah. "Are we still going to the basement?"

Noah nodded. "You can start setting up."

They left, taking Arlo and Dimitri with them. Calliope stayed seated, giving Aiden a stubborn look. It was fine, he hadn't meant her anyway. She was family, too.

"What's happening in the basement?" Aiden asked, unsure he wanted to know.

"Mario Kart tournament," Noah answered.

The level of compartmentalizing in this family was staggering. Their family was under attack. Someone was literally threatening to expose them as killers, and yet, Aiden had no doubt Noah was about to lead the others in a Mario battle that would last long into the morning. Maybe it was how the feelings faction blew off steam? Whatever it was, it was clear that the neurotypicals held no ill will towards Thomas for doing what he had to do to survive.

"Oh-kay," Aiden said before turning on the others. "Look, he can feel how pissed you all are, you know. He doesn't get that it's *for* him, not at him."

"Why would we be angry at him?" Atticus asked. "He's literally the victim. One of many, it seems."

Aiden began to pace. "He's been building this moment up in his head for decades. Two days ago, he'd convinced himself you guys were going to kill him for violating the code. He's been punishing himself for this for years. And right now, he thinks you all either pity him or hate him."

"But why?" Avi asked, clearly confused.

"He doesn't feel like a victim," Noah said. "He feels like a willing participant."

"What do you mean?" Adam asked.

Noah let go of Felix's and Zane's hands, hopping from the table and going to his fiancé, sitting in his lap and dragging his arms around him like a seatbelt. It was a comfort thing. Any time Noah brought up his past, he needed Adam there to…anchor him somehow. The thought of Adam being anyone's anchor was astonishing to Aiden, but it was right there, impossible to miss.

"When you're resisting your abuser, it makes you feel like you're doing the right thing, like you're still…the wronged party. But eventually, fighting gets too hard, especially when it changes nothing. So, you give in. You give them what they want without fighting, maybe you even pretend to like it. It doesn't make it easier or less painful, but it does allow you to mentally check out."

"But that doesn't mean you're not a victim," Lucas said.

"It doesn't," Noah agreed. "But when you stop fighting, sometimes—in your head—a voice whispers that you're not fighting because you like it, because you want it, because, deep down, you deserve it. And you start to feel like a willing participant. You start to think you really do deserve it. That really you and your abuser aren't that much different, just two people locked in a relationship you can't escape. Sometimes, you even feel sorry for them."

"Feel sorry for them?" Felix echoed.

Noah nodded. "I know it sounds crazy, but there were times when I felt sorry for my d—for Holt. He said he couldn't help the things he did to me. Said it was a compulsion, a sickness. I was a kid, I didn't know any better. I thought he was my father." Noah shook his head like he was trying to keep himself from being dragged back down into a nightmare. "Thomas was a kid, too. Nobody should blame him for what happened."

"We don't," Archer said. "At all."

"We're going to kill this guy, right?" Felix asked. "Like, we all get a piece of him when we find him. Right?"

"Obviously," Asa said.

"Yeah, we have a whole list of ideas we can't wait to try out on this fucking freak," Avi agreed, rubbing his hands together.

"I get first crack at him," Lucas recalled. "They went after our children."

Lucas's sudden bloodlust was both worrisome and impressive. Up until the girls were born, he'd been the level-headed one who somehow quieted August's somewhat volatile moods, but after they arrived, Lucas became the unreasonable one, the paranoid one, the mama bear. Except, in this case, he wasn't being paranoid or unreasonable. Someone had threatened his children. What would Aiden do if someone threatened his kid? If he had a kid. What would he do with a kid?

"Don't worry, mindhunter," Asa teased, pulling Aiden back from the ledge. "We got you. You can have the scalpel first."

Avi's eyes lit up. "Are we finally going to skin someone? I really want to skin someone."

"Ew, count me out. That's a hard pass for me on the skinning, thanks," Zane said, lip curling.

"I'll go," Noah said.

"Me too," Felix said.

"Well, if you guys are going, I don't want to *not* go," Zane said, deflating. "I just hate all the screaming."

"I have excellent ear plugs," August offered. "I'll bring you a pair. You won't hear a thing."

Zane's eyes went wide, clearly shocked at the offer. "Oh… thanks."

"See, family bonding time. Yay," Adam said.

Noah turned, putting a hand over Adam's mouth. "Never say that again."

"But it's true," Adam said, words muffled behind Noah's palm.

"The family that slays together stays together," Calliope murmured.

"Focus," Aiden said, trying to drag them back to the point. "Yes, we'll find this douche, and yes, we'll catch him, but in the meantime, you all just need to be…nicer to Tommy, okay?"

"Tommy, oof," Avi said, then shuddered. "Make it stop."

"He's Tommy to me. If you don't like it, maybe August can get you some of those fancy ear plugs." He leaned towards the twins. "But listen very carefully. It's taken me twenty fucking years to get to this point with your father. If you make him feel weird about our relationship, I will put every single fucking one of you through a goddamn woodchipper. Got it?"

August laughed, but Atticus frowned harder. "Nobody's going to make him feel bad. We've known about you two for years now. But it's gonna take some getting used to. We've had twenty plus years of thinking of you as our weird, loner brother, and now, we have to think of you as our weird, loner…stepdad?" Atticus did a hard, full-body shiver like Avi. "Yeah, no. Can't do it. That's just fucking weird. You can marry our dad, but I'm not calling you anything but Aiden."

Aiden made a *bring it on* gesture. "Get all the jokes out

of your system now," Aiden warned. "But you will be nice to him."

"We totally will," Noah promised. "We'll be so nice to him."

"Uh-uh. Not you three," Aiden chided, sweeping his finger from Zane and Felix to Noah. "You three keep your bleeding hearts to yourselves. You just maintain the status quo. I want him to feel better, not have him spend the next six months swimming in your tears."

"Rude," Felix muttered.

"Beyond," Zane agreed.

"Not for nothing, but we did some actual investigating while you guys were off planning gaming tournaments and thinking up creative ways to torture people," Archer interjected.

"We were keeping two tiny humans alive and working for a living, thank you very much," Lucas said.

"Not you two," Archer clarified benevolently.

"And?" Aiden asked when he didn't elaborate.

"And we found some stuff about Thomas on the internet," Archer said.

"He's a billionaire. There's stuff about all of us on the internet," Adam said, rolling his eyes.

"No, we were deep, *deep* into the internet. Like flat-earthers, 9/11 was a hoax, JFK Jr. is still alive level deep."

Calliope frowned. "I have spiders crawling all over the darknet. There's no way I missed a Mulvaney conspiracy theory."

"Okay, not that deep," Mac admitted. "But still, we

found this really innocuous-looking thread that, on its face, looked like it was about pet-sitting. But deep within those threads are some really weird posts between a number of people talking about murder…and Thomas Mulvaney."

"Like, killing him?" Noah asked.

"No, like him being a killer. And a hypocrite."

"Which is ironic because these very same people appear to be serial unalivers themselves," Archer said.

"Wait, so these people are like vigilantes?" Felix asked.

"Sounds more like something assassins would do," Zane said.

"No, not vigilantes or assassins. Serial killers. Serial killers were talking about Dad. To each other. Claiming he was one of them," Archer insisted.

Atticus frowned. "Are you trying to say that there are people on the internet—people who are our usual targets— who know what we do?"

"They didn't mention us. They only mentioned Thomas," Mac said.

"So, this is all happening because of an internet conspiracy theory where Thomas is a serial killer?" Calliope asked, looking shook.

"No," Archer said. "Well, I don't know precisely, but it seems like this person who calls themselves…what was it?"

Mac reached for his phone, opening up his memo app. "ALWAYSCHRISTMAS1225."

"Yeah, that. Was trying to use this group of killers to crowdsource information about Thomas's extracurricular activities."

"Did they ever find anything?"

"Not sure. The thread died three years ago, and we couldn't find any trace of these people anywhere else on the net," Mac said.

"Always Christmas…as in Holly?" Noah asked.

"But Holly's dead."

"But what if she had a kid?"

"A kid who somehow blames Thomas for killing his dad? But Holly filed rape charges. Surely, she wouldn't raise a kid to think her rapist was a good guy, right?" Felix asked.

Mac shook his head, gesturing helplessly. "Hard to say at this point."

Aiden's head hurt. "Okay, this is getting us nowhere. It's late. Everyone's tired. Give Calliope whatever information you got from that site and we'll pick this up in the morning like I said."

Everybody nodded. People stood and stretched, talking softly to each other as they filed from the room. Calliope stayed where she was, her dagger-like nails flying over the keyboard. Aiden couldn't imagine how anybody could type with those talons, but she seemed unbothered.

"You need to get some sleep, too," Aiden said.

"Fuck that. If these guys were on the web—*my* web— talking shit about *my* family, I'm not sleeping until I find them. Go take care of Thomas. I've got this."

"You need to rest," Aiden prodded gently.

She shot him a mutinous glare. "I need to figure out who handed two toddlers a venomous snake. Go. I'm good. I never sleep more than four hours a night as it is."

"What? How are you alive?"

"Sheer force of will," Calliope promised.

Aiden snorted. "Don't you need your beauty sleep?"

Calliope put a hand under her chin and fluttered her lashes. "Oh, darling. Petty keeps me pretty."

Aiden shook his head. "Good night, Calliope."

"Night, Aiden," she sang as the door closed.

Aiden made sure all the doors were locked and alarms engaged, then texted the others so they knew as well. The last thing he needed was the whole house at defcon five because someone decided they wanted some fresh air. He thought about checking on Thomas in the nursery, but decided to give him some time with the girls. They always soothed something in him, even if he was just watching them sleep.

Instead, he went to his room and checked his email before deciding on a quick shower. Standing beneath the scalding water, it was impossible not to think about Thomas. Was he in bed already? If Aiden made his way to his room, would he reject him? The boys already knew about them. They clearly didn't give a fuck. Was that enough? Would it finally be enough for Thomas? He needed it to be. How much longer could he be expected to stay away from him? He was already going insane trying not to touch him every time they were alone in a room together.

Thomas was Aiden's favorite drug and he was close enough

to have him clawing at the walls, so close but not close enough to satisfy. Fuck. He turned off the faucet, toweling off quickly before throwing on a t-shirt and sweatpants just for the sake of decency, then headed out the door before he changed his mind.

He paused outside Thomas's room, hand poised to knock. He expected he'd find Thomas in bed, but that wasn't the reason he didn't want to knock. He didn't want to give him a chance to refuse him. He knew how fucked up that sounded but he was fucked up. Thomas had fucked him up, had tugged at his sanity year after year until Aiden didn't care what was right or wrong anymore. He just… wanted. He needed Thomas, needed him like he needed air.

He dropped his hand to the knob, relieved when it turned without issue. He hadn't locked him out. Something unknotted within him. He stopped short just inside the door when he realized nobody was in there. All he could see was the soft amber glow of a lamp in the corner.

He frowned. Where the hell was Thomas? There was no way he was still in the nursery; it was after one in the morning. He was about to turn and leave when he heard something from deeper within the room, opposite the bathroom. Thomas's closet. He padded closer, his footfalls silent on the carpeted floor. When he reached the doorway of the sprawling walk-in, his heart stopped.

Thomas stood to the left of the door, facing a low dresser against the mirrored wall, a gun in his hand, so focused on the weapon he didn't even see Aiden in the reflection. Aiden's first instinct was to rush to him and snatch the weapon from his hand. But he pushed the thought back, watching as Thomas just stared at it. What the fuck was he thinking? Surely not the worst, right? He wouldn't ever be so cruel as to try to take himself out of the equation. They couldn't do this without him. Any of it. Aiden couldn't go on without him.

He was crossing the room before he could stop himself, wrapping his arms around Thomas from behind, gripping his hands. Thomas sucked in a sharp breath, his startled gaze meeting Aiden's in the mirror. That was when he realized there was a mirrored wall behind them as well.

Thomas stiffened in his arms for just a moment, then sort of melted against him, his bare skin warm even through Aiden's t-shirt. He gently took the gun from Thomas and set it down, but kept him pinned where he was against the dresser, watching Thomas's face in the mirror as he gave into his needs and trailed open-mouth kisses along his throat.

"Fuck, you always smell so good," Aiden murmured, dropping his hands to his waist, then splaying fingers across his chest and belly as he sucked a red mark onto his neck.

"What are you doing?" Thomas asked, pressing his ass against Aiden's half-hard cock.

"Requesting a do-over," Aiden said, his fingers finding Thomas's nipple and tugging it until he sucked in a breath. "I love when you make that sound," Aiden admitted. "I love that I can *make you* make that sound."

Thomas flushed but said, "A do-over?"

"Mm, a do-over," he murmured, letting one hand slide up into Thomas's hair and twisting his head to capture his mouth in a dirty kiss that lingered. "I didn't take my time with you last time," he said as he let him go, returning to exploring Thomas's bare skin with his mouth.

"You didn't?" Thomas asked, tilting his head to give Aiden better access.

Fuck. Aiden felt high. High off the feel of Thomas's skin beneath his hands, the tang of his skin, the masculine scent of his shampoo. Aiden just wanted to drown in Thomas. He was already so fucking hard. There was no way Thomas could miss it. "No, something I'm going to rectify right now."

"Here?" Thomas managed, glancing around the closet.

Aiden glanced around, then smiled, filthy fantasies suddenly filling his head. "Yeah. Why not? You can watch."

Thomas's lips parted, his tongue darting out to lick over his lower lip. "Watch what?"

Aiden bit Thomas's shoulder, then dropped to his knees, his fingers catching in Thomas's pajama bottoms on his way down, dragging them lower, then off. "This."

He bit Thomas's ass just hard enough to leave teeth marks. "Open your legs for me," he coaxed, then tugged his hips back. He wished he could see what they looked like. How many times had he thought about this? Pictured it in his head? He spread him open, then gave a broad sweep of his tongue from his balls to his hole, smiling a bit when Thomas's knees gave out.

"Fuck," Thomas muttered.

"Oh, I'll get there," Aiden promised, then buried his face in the heart of him, spearing his tongue against his entrance, then licking over it once more. Thomas tasted like soap, and Aiden's cock was already leaking, tenting his sweatpants. Thomas's hands grasped at Aiden blindly, like he just needed something to hold onto.

"Fuck. Fuck. Fuck," Thomas muttered, pushing back on Aiden's tongue like it just wasn't enough.

Aiden curled his hands around Thomas's hips, dragging him back until it felt like he might suffocate. He didn't care. If this was how he died, it was totally worth it. Thomas's blunt nails dug at his shoulders as he moaned and swore under his breath whenever Aiden did something he liked.

When Aiden finally relinquished his hold on him, it was only to wrap a hand around Thomas's aching cock, stroking him slow enough to have him cursing his name. Aiden sat back, massaging a finger against Thomas's hole before pushing inside to the second knuckle. Aiden groaned. Thomas was so hot and tight. He wanted to bury himself in that heat immediately.

"Christ," Thomas muttered, pressing himself back on Aiden's finger. "Enough. Just fuck me already."

"You're so fucking tight. This is why it was over so quickly last time," Aiden said accusingly.

"Are you seriously complaining right now?" Thomas asked. "Lube's in the top drawer of the bathroom. Are you going to get it or am I?"

Aiden slapped Thomas's ass, then stood. "Always so bossy," he muttered.

It took two tries before he found the right drawer, but when he returned, Thomas was facing him. That was fine with Aiden. He captured his mouth in a kiss, finding

Thomas's tongue and sucking it into his mouth as he pushed slick fingers into his crease, teasing only a moment before forcing them inside, relishing Thomas's surprised grunt.

"What's wrong?" Aiden murmured against his lips. "You were the one in such a hurry."

Thomas bit Aiden's lip hard, then sucked it. "Smartass."

Aiden wanted to take his time, had planned to open him up slowly, fuck him lazily, but Thomas was refusing to play ball. He was shoving at Aiden's sweatpants, using the lube to slick his hard cock. That alone was almost enough to have Aiden coming.

Fuck it. If this was how Thomas wanted it, why was he fighting it? They had plenty of time to take it slow. Aiden wasn't letting Thomas go. Not ever. Never again. He picked him up, setting him on the low lip of the dresser. Thomas braced his hands against the top. It was the perfect angle.

He crashed their mouths together as he slid home, both of them moaning. Christ, he felt so good. So hot and tight and perfect. Had anything in the world ever felt as fucking good as this? Aiden didn't think so. He caught Thomas's knees over his elbows, pulling almost all the way out before slamming back home.

Thomas threw his head back, gripping the edge of the dresser for dear life as Aiden gave into his instincts, driving into him again and again. "Touch yourself," Aiden begged.

Thomas looked at him, gaze hazy, lips parted, then took himself in hand, stroking himself in time with Aiden's thrusts. Aiden stared, riveted, watching his hand move, addicted to the breathless gasps and the low moans. It was perfect. Thomas was perfect. This was everything Aiden had wanted last time.

He squeezed his eyes shut, certain if he kept watching he'd finish before Thomas. But that was worse. With his eyes closed, all he could do was focus on the perfect squeeze of Thomas's body around his cock. And he was already so fucking close. He was reaching the point of no return, where his body wasn't going to let him slow down and wouldn't let him do anything but let him chase his own pleasure.

"Fuck," Thomas muttered, then cried out, his nails once more digging into Aiden's skin, his upper arms this time. Would it leave marks? Aiden fucking hoped so. He'd let Thomas maul him like a goddamn tiger and wear the scars proudly.

He opened his eyes just in time to watch Thomas spill over his hand, his expression shocky and blissed out. That was it. Aiden gripped him harder, his eyes finding the image of them in the mirror on the far wall. The picture they made was more than enough to finally push him over the edge.

He watched their reflection in the mirror, watching himself fuck Thomas, every thrust forcing another grunt from him until Aiden couldn't hold back anymore, finally emptying himself inside, waves of pleasure literally throwing his whole brain offline.

He didn't pull free, just clutched at Thomas, trying to drag breath into his lungs, praying he didn't have a sudden change of heart and kick him out. "I'm sleeping with you tonight," he said, making sure he knew it wasn't a request.

Aiden's stomach dropped when Thomas said nothing, but then lips brushed his forehead. "I know."

"I'm sleeping with you every night from now on," Aiden said, his body forcing him to slide free of Thomas's.

"I know."

Aiden hadn't expected Thomas to give in so easily. He didn't know what to say other than, "Good."

"We should try to get some sleep. It's late."

"Okay," Aiden said but made no move to release Thomas.

"Are we sleeping here in the closet?" Thomas asked, amused.

Aiden sighed and stepped back, helping Thomas down. "It's not my fault your bed is so far away."

"Are you saying you want to put a mattress in the closet?" Thomas asked, helping Aiden right his sweatpants but forgoing his own pajama pants on the floor.

"No," Aiden said. "Well, maybe. Or we could just put mirrors over the bed."

"Nothing screams class like a mirrored ceiling," Thomas said, climbing into bed and rolling onto his side.

Aiden lost his sweatpants then climbed in, curling himself around Thomas. "Fuck class. Don't tell me you didn't watch me on my knees for you."

"I plead the fifth," he said. "Now, go to sleep."

"Uh-huh," Aiden said. "That's what I thought."

He buried his face in Thomas's neck, kissing over his pulse. "Good night."

Thomas's hand reached back, curling around Aiden's bare thigh. "Night."

THIRTEEN
THOMAS

Thomas woke to find Aiden lying on his side, head propped on his hand, studying him, expression inscrutable. A shock of warmth bled through Thomas at just the sight of Aiden's face. Was this what he'd been denying himself for so long? How many times had he imagined a life where he woke up to that face every morning?

When Aiden didn't acknowledge Thomas, he frowned. How long had he been watching him? What was he thinking about? Was he sleeping with his eyes open? Almost as quickly as the thought came, Aiden reached down and cupped Thomas's chin, turning him so he could look at him more thoroughly.

Thomas smiled to hide the surge of lust that shot through him. "Should I be concerned about you watching me in my sleep?"

Aiden continued to hold his chin as he leaned down and pressed their lips together before saying, "I've heard it's considered romantic."

Thomas grinned. "Did you read that in *Serial Killer Monthly*?"

Aiden snorted. "Quarterly, actually. I can't afford the monthly subscription on a PI's earnings."

It was a joke. Thomas knew—for obvious reasons—that Aiden was worth a fortune. He lived like a hermit in the middle of the woods in a cabin he'd built himself. He drove a Jeep that was over ten years old. Every dime Thomas had paid him over the years had gone into a separate account that Aiden used to donate to people who needed it and to fund his somewhat disturbing hobby of building medieval torture devices.

This knowledge didn't stop Thomas from saying, "You know I'd give you anything, right?"

Aiden's smile fell, his expression becoming guarded. "Except you."

Thomas had walked right into that one. Aiden was right. All he'd ever asked of Thomas was this…was them. And he'd wasted years torturing himself. Torturing them both, really. But Thomas had been so committed to spending his life alone, to paying for his sins, that it now seemed insane to just change his mind. Wouldn't that be the shittier thing to do? Did he even deserve Aiden after dragging him over broken glass all these years?

Thomas didn't know how or why, but in the last seventy-two hours or so, this thing, this one event in his life that had seemed like a mortal sin, now seemed…insignificant. Maybe it was knowing his children didn't hate him. Maybe it was knowing Aiden was still there after everything. But the fear Thomas had spent years choking on had evaporated.

But that was worse somehow. Knowing he'd denied himself and Aiden a lifetime together felt like a far worse sin now. And it had happened in the blink of an eye. He didn't deserve Aiden's love. He didn't deserve Aiden's forgiveness. It didn't matter, though. Because Aiden had told him last night he wasn't leaving and Thomas had acknowledged it as fact.

Somehow, Thomas had been dragged kicking and screaming to the finish line and he was still getting to walk away with the only prize he'd ever wanted. It hardly seemed fair. Thomas shouldn't still win.

He pulled himself from his thoughts to see Aiden looking morose. Aiden hadn't posed his last response as a question, but looking at him now, Thomas knew it was. Aiden was practically holding his breath waiting to see if Thomas would disappoint him for the millionth time.

Thomas was waiting, too. Was he a coward like Aiden said? Or was he as brave as his sons believed him to be? Was being with Aiden selfish? Had Thomas earned Aiden? *No.* His heart slammed against his ribs. Every fiber of his being was telling him to run away…again. But he couldn't. He wouldn't.

"You have me, Aiden. Even when I'm not right next to you…you have me. There's only ever been you."

"I don't care if you're pining for me from a distance. I need you next to me," Aiden said. "I'm done giving you chances."

The lightning-sharp pain in his chest was so acute Thomas

thought his heart might have stopped beating. What the fuck was that supposed to mean? Aiden had said months ago that he was giving up on Thomas, had told him not to call, not to text, to just leave him be. He'd said he was sick of him constantly martyring himself. But Thomas had thought they'd gotten past all that.

Was he wrong?

"I'm not leaving you. And I'm not letting you leave me. I can't," Aiden said. "I know myself. And I know if you deny me again, it will literally become my villain origin story. I will go full-on scorched earth, Tommy. I'll become the monster you feared your sons would be."

It wasn't said as a threat, more like a dire prediction. Thomas knew Aiden meant what he said. For better or worse, Aiden always told the truth. Thomas had admired that about him. Aiden knew himself, knew what he was capable of. That was how he was different from all the others.

Before Aiden, Thomas had thought that the essential element of psychopathy was a lack of empathy. When psychopaths killed, they did so with a clinical detachment that allowed them to play with their victims *because* they lacked the ability to put themselves in the victim's place.

But Aiden had taught Thomas there was something far more terrifying than a psychopath…and that was a dark empath. A rather gimmicky new age buzzword that hid a very real, very twisted darkness. Aiden was empathetic. He felt things deeply. Hurt, sadness, guilt, remorse. He felt them so deeply in fact, that he easily picked up on even the subtlest of tells in others. He was practically a human lie detector. It let him hone in on the things that scared people most. The things that scarred them deeply. It let him look into others' psyches with an almost Lucas-like level of insight. But while Lucas used this gift to create profiles, Aiden used it for a much darker purpose. He used it to create a weapon, one custom-made to inflict maximum physical and psychological damage on his victim before he ended their life.

Aiden exercised impeccable restraint on most days. But Thomas believed him when he said he would become the monster Thomas created. Because that was what Thomas had set out to do all those years ago. Create monsters to do his bidding, just for good instead of evil. And, for the most part, he'd succeeded.

But he couldn't let Aiden off his leash. He loved him too much. The Mulvaney code was unbreakable. Kill without permission and you die. But Thomas knew he could never kill Aiden, no matter how bad he got. In that way, Aiden was like Shane. Thomas didn't know what that said about him. Nothing good. But Thomas was only human.

"Don't say that," Thomas begged.

"You know it's true. Are you going to turn me away again? Send me back to Washington? Pretend none of this ever happened? Was what you said last night a lie?"

Thomas shook his head. "I wasn't lying. I'm not sending you away. I'm not. I *should*. I don't deserve you. I don't deserve this. But, this time, I'm going to be selfish. I'm going to be selfish with you. I'm going to keep you. Here. With me. Forever."

Aiden's gaze went wide, like he'd expected he would have to fight like hell for Thomas to agree to be with him. But there was no sense in fighting the inevitable. And they were inevitable. They were destined to come back to each other again and again because the truth was nobody could ever truly understand them but each other.

Aiden ducked under Thomas's arm, his cheek pressing against Thomas's chest, directly over his heart. It took a full thirty seconds for Thomas to realize Aiden was just… holding him. Tightly. His arm locked around his waist, one leg thrown over both of his. He hated how natural it felt, how right it felt. Aiden and him just fit, like torn paper, edges frayed, but still perfectly matched.

Thomas swept his knuckles along Aiden's bare back lazily, content in the silence. He was almost dozing again when Aiden asked, "Why were you holding that gun last night?"

Thomas opened his eyes, glancing down at the top of Aiden's head. He took a deep breath and let it out. Why *had* he been holding the gun? "I just needed to feel like I could protect my family. Like I'd called you all home to keep you safe, not to use you as human shields to protect myself. I guess I was just feeling…vulnerable."

"There's nothing wrong with calling your family home to protect you. We protect each other. That's what family is for. You've been saving those kids their whole lives. Let them do the same for you. It makes them feel better. Especially the feelings faction. If they had their way, you'd be tucked away in a panic room, swaddled in a blanket burrito and forced to listen to nature sounds or monks chanting."

"A blanket burrito?" Thomas echoed.

Aiden nodded against Thomas's chest. "Yeah, it's like a straitjacket, but fuzzier and full-body. Like thunder jackets for dogs."

Thomas sat in stunned silence, imagining his children holding him hostage in blankets. "Aiden?"

"Yeah?"

"Please don't let my children put me in a fuzzy straitjacket for dogs."

Aiden snickered. "I'll do my best, but they're hard to resist when they're all heart eyes and Care-Bear stares."

Thomas chuckled. "I always wanted one of those."

Aiden craned his head back to look up at Thomas. "Heart eyes?"

Thomas shook his head. "No. A Care-Bear. My father said they were for children."

"Weren't you a child?" Aiden asked.

A deep sadness settled over him. "No. I really never was."

"Is that why you built a palace for the girls filled with toys they're far too young to even enjoy yet?" Aiden asked.

Thomas smiled thinking of the two girls sleeping peacefully in their beds.

"Yeah. Maybe so," Thomas agreed. "I just want them to have time to be children. There's going to come a time when we all have to decide whether we let them in on our family secret, tell them who we are—who we *really* are—or hide it from them and pray they don't find out."

"Those are August's children. There's a chance that no matter how good August's and Lucas's parenting skills are, they may be predisposed to their father's psychopathy," Aiden said.

Thomas nodded. "But we now know not all psychopaths kill. Especially those raised in loving and nurturing homes. I could have just tried to protect them when they were little instead of stealing *their* childhoods. My boys. I could have given them therapy and…burrito blankets…and maybe they would have never wanted to kill at all. I… Maybe I ruined them."

Aiden sat up, turning to face him, legs crossed to tuck himself against him as closely as possible. "Sure, you taught them how to shoot and fight and kill. But you also let them swim, let them play sports, let them be mathletes and drive race cars."

"As a cover," Thomas said, shaking his head.

"They had a blast. And look at them now. They're all married, all successful, all thriving. The only one who doesn't truly enjoy what he does is Atticus and he was smart enough to fall for a man who not only enjoys killing but who also brought along his own school of murderous muppets to join the party. There's a whole school full of psychopathic Gen-Zers who are proving that your theories—though slightly self-serving—have merit. You didn't ruin anyone or anything. Someone has to take out the trash society can't. That's us."

Thomas sighed. "I just want Adelyn and Arabella to have a normal childhood. The same with any other grandchildren I have."

"Did you want more?" Aiden asked, studying Thomas's

face intently.

"More? Grandchildren? Not really my call. But I hope so. I love when the girls are in the house. Just knowing they're there is…a relief, I guess."

"I meant children…of your own?" Aiden asked. "Of *our* own."

Thomas felt like he'd been sucker-punched. "Our? Children…"

Before Thomas could formulate some kind of intelligible response, Aiden's phone began to silently vibrate its way along Thomas's side table.

He picked it up and looked at it before saying, "Hello?" There was a female voice on the other side. "Did you find something? No, don't tell me yet. Let me get the rest of the group together and I'll FaceTime you—Nobody cares if you have on makeup—or a bra—Fine. Fine. Thirty minutes."

Thomas chuckled when Aiden hung up, happy to shelve their current topic of conversation before he had a panic attack. "Lola found something?"

"I guess we'll find out. Archer and Mac were doing some digging last night and found some stuff, too," Aiden said, climbing over Thomas, making sure to drag himself against him as he stood.

"Like what?" Thomas asked, taking Aiden's offered hand and allowing him to pull him to his feet.

"I'll fill you in while we shower."

"We're showering together?" Thomas asked, not resisting as Aiden tugged him towards the bathroom.

"Yes. Do you have a problem with that?" Aiden asked,

giving him a stern look that went straight to Thomas's dick.

"No, sir," he said, voice low with just the slightest hint of mocking.

The heated look Aiden gave him showed him he was choosing to ignore the teasing and focus only on the dirty suggestion in his tone.

Thomas had spent a lot of time wondering about what Lola looked like ever since Aiden said they were...close. But nothing could have prepared him for the woman who was now staring out over a sea of strangers with a look of both curiosity and confusion.

She was tall, at least six feet, but currently wearing brown suede boots that went to her thighs, tight jeans that hugged her curves, and a sweater that looked like it had been painted on under a brown leather jacket. Gold jewelry adorned her neck, her ears, her fingers, and her wrists, highlighting terracotta-colored skin that looked like it glowed. Lola was stunning and probably scared the shit out of insecure men. Thomas liked her immediately.

"Am I doing a debriefing or a TED talk?" she asked.

There were some snickers from around the room. For the most part, everyone had returned to their seats from the previous night. The only exception was that Thomas and Aiden sat across from Calliope at the conference table, chairs turned towards the large screen where Lola currently loomed.

"Lola, my family. Family, meet Lola," Aiden said, amused by the varied expressions on their faces. "Where are you?"

She ignored his question, then plopped herself up on her kitchen counter, legs swinging as she grabbed a mug of what Thomas could only assume was coffee.

"Charmed, I'm sure," she said with a heavy fake Southern accent.

"She's a goddess," Seven said in wonder.

"She's a badass," Noah said.

"Have you ever thought of modeling?" Felix asked.

Lola pretended to push back her wild hair, smiling and preening. "Stop," she said in a tone that clearly said *go on*.

"No, seriously," Felix said. "Call me. You'd be killer in my spring line."

"Can we focus on the task at hand?" Aiden asked, sounding exasperated.

Lola tsked. "Don't be mad 'cause I'm prettier than you."

Asa's eyes lit up. "I like her so much. Let's adopt her. We need more girls in this family."

Cricket, who had left the girls with the nanny, gave Lola a flat stare. "Don't fall for it. It's a trap. They'll just try to use you for breeding purposes."

"We would have gorgeous babies," Felix said, giving Lola an appraising look.

"Easy, kitten," Avi said. "Let's at least meet her face to face before we start trying to mine her girl parts."

"Did you actually find anything?" Aiden said loudly.

"Well, maybe?" she hedged. "But when I say I had to go way back, I mean way, *way* back. Most of the people who were involved in the 'accident' are long dead."

"Why are you air-quoting accident?" Aiden asked.

Lola took a sip of her coffee, eyeing him over the brim. "Like you don't know? It wasn't an accident. It was a murder-suicide. It was a cover-up. A really good cover-up, but a cover-up nonetheless."

"If it was a good cover-up, how did you figure out it wasn't an accident?" August asked.

"Since the deaths occurred at the lake house, which is in an unincorporated part of the community, it was handled by the local cops. There were only three of them and to say they were ill-equipped to handle a mass murder is an understatement. The sheriff was Methuselah old when it happened, died not long after the crime itself, one deputy took over as chief but died in a car crash five years later. The third deputy moved far away. I finally chased down the third deputy who was no longer a cop but a politician. He was…uncooperative."

"Uncooperative?" Jericho parroted.

Lola nodded. "Yeah, implied that there are a lot of ways nosey people tend to go missing."

"He threatened you?" Aiden snapped.

Lola teetered her hand back and forth. "Meh, nothing as overt as that but I was definitely picking up what he was putting down. He was telling me to just forget about it."

"And did you?" Thomas asked. "Forget about it?"

Lola's gaze snapped to him, giving him a hard once-over, eyes locking on where Aiden's fingers threaded with his own on the arm rest. "I see you've finally decided to stop being a dumbass."

"Whoa," Seven whispered. "Did she just call a Mulvaney a dumbass?"

Noah's spine straightened, his expression turning stormy. "Don't talk to my dad like that."

"Yes, he's stopped being a dumbass," Calliope said. "For now, anyway. Can we just not do the male posturing today? Too much testosterone gives me a headache."

Lola gave Calliope a once-over of an entirely different kind, biting her full lower lip before smiling. "Me too. I can only take men in small doses. Women, though...that's entirely different."

Thomas turned as Calliope rocked in her chair, giving a smile he had never seen on her before. She held up her hand in a *call me* gesture.

"What is happening?" Zane asked, looking back and forth between the two women.

"I'm pretty sure Lola is hitting on my mom," Dimitri said, not sounding even remotely bothered by this turn of events. "Happens all the time. She's hot."

"Your mom is so cool," Nico whispered.

"Can we focus?" Atticus asked. "I have research to get back to and I can't do that until we figure out who's after Dad."

"I was entirely focused," Asa said. "In case anybody was wondering."

"We weren't," several people chorused.

"Rude," Asa muttered.

"What did you find, Lola?" Aiden asked, his exasperation

obvious.

"Like I said, most people were dead or scattered to the far reaches of the Earth, but then I found something. The coroner. I figured if there was something weird going on, like a cover-up, he'd know all about it."

"And did he?" Adam asked.

"Yeah, did you talk to him?" Lucas asked.

"No. He has dementia. He's in a care facility and they wouldn't let me talk to him because I'm not family." Thomas watched as people all around the room seemed to deflate with disappointment.

"So, how did you find out it was a murder-suicide if you didn't talk to the coroner?" Calliope asked, leaning forward, sounding excited.

"I talked to the nurse. She mentioned that nobody ever comes to see the patient, even his family because he was a real asshole and apparently a bit of a hoarder. She then casually mentioned that they disliked him so much that they had pretty much just locked the door to his house and never went back."

"But you did?" Calliope prodded. "You went to his house, didn't you?"

"I did. It was just like the nurse said. Filled to the brim with boxes and papers and notebooks and photographs. Including the real Mulvaney crime scene photos."

"We need to get our hands on everything in that house," Aiden said.

"I figured as much," Lola said before hopping from the counter and grabbing her phone. She panned the camera around the room, showing dozens of boxes. "He lived about an hour away from you. I'm already here. I'll drop a pin with the address."

"Aren't you worried people will ask questions if we all just swarm into some old guy's house?" Cree asked.

"The man lived alone on six acres," Lola said. "His nearest neighbors are livestock. Trust me, nobody is gonna notice." She gave the boys and then Thomas a look. "I'd leave the Prada at home, though. This place isn't going to win any good housekeeping awards. Dress accordingly."

"Is she saying those are her casual clothes?" Felix asked, then looked at Avi. "She's perfect. Seriously. Hot, smart, stylish. Can we keep her?"

Cricket snorted, then looked at Lola. "Girl, run."

Lola cackled. "See you soon, Mulvaneys and assorted Mulvaney associates."

FOURTEEN
AIDEN

Thomas and Aiden rolled to a stop just outside of a sagging aluminum gate and a fence made of chicken wire which now sat flat enough to drive over. Once upon a time the gate had probably served as a deterrent to anyone who dared to trespass, but now—like the fence—it was barely clinging to its post. Aiden hopped from the passenger seat and gripped the free end, grunting as he hauled it from the rut it made in the ground to drag it open. How had Lola opened this herself?

Once the gate was swung wide, Thomas drove inside, the other vehicles trailing in behind them like a convoy. Not everyone had come along. There was no need. The coroner could only provide a very narrow scope, if any at all. He was clearly not the man they were looking for and there was no guarantee they'd find anything to even tie him to the blackmailing. But Lola seemed to think it was important for them to at least see the mess with their own eyes.

So, they'd decided to divide and conquer.

Jericho and Atticus had stayed behind with his boys in case they needed to run down any leads. Adam and Noah were at Calliope's beck and call as she tried to digitally run down this AlwaysChristmas character Mac and Archer had stumbled upon to see if it was all a bizarre coincidence, another fucking problem, or the man they were looking for.

The twins—along with Felix and Zane—had all but insisted on coming along. Aiden feared Cricket was right, that Felix and Zane were already wondering if maybe parenthood was something they *were* interested in, and if so, could Lola be the one. It was all too weird for Aiden. For a thousand reasons.

Lucas and August were there as well at Aiden's insistence. Lucas's gift would be invaluable. It had practically taken an act of congress to get him to leave the girls; he only said yes when Mac and Archer agreed to babysit.

Aiden smiled to himself. For a group of psychopaths, they were surprisingly gentle with the girls. It was like when a gorilla was given a kitten. The boys were both fascinated with them and overly gentle, fearful of accidentally injuring them. Well, all but Adam, who played with them like they were puppies, rolling around on the floor until they were squealing with laughter that echoed through the house and made Thomas smile. Aiden was grateful for anything that made Thomas happy like that.

And he was relieved Lucas had acquiesced, reluctantly or not. They needed him. They'd all have targets on their backs until this was solved. And this house felt important. While the coroner wasn't the blackmailer, whoever that was must have been there at some point. How else could he have gotten a hold of the photos?

Aiden hated this shit. It felt like the answer was…right there, just out of reach. This vague notion like they had all the pieces but not the picture on the box.

The coroner's house was just as Lola described, a ramshackle Victorian-style farmhouse that looked as if it had fallen from the sky into the middle of a desolate nowhere. Which was good for them. No prying eyes to watch what they did.

Aiden scanned the dead ground and the trees in the distance. What had this place looked like twenty years ago? Had there been green grass or livestock? Or had it always been patches of brown weeds, puddles of stagnant water, and muddy gravel that crunched underfoot as you walked on it?

Off to the left was another old building, a shed or barn, maybe? The paint—once a brick red—had long since given way to time, leaving the wood weathered and gray. There was a vintage Mercedes Benz sitting just outside that looked just as unkempt as the grounds and house. This man's family must have really hated him to leave a car like that just lying around.

Lola waved from the front porch, a cup of coffee in her hand. How many of those had she had already? Before Aiden could even open his mouth, Zane and Felix were flying past him, holding out their hands to her.

"I'm Felix—I'm Zane," they said in tandem, sticking out their hands.

They were close enough to make a lesser person painfully uncomfortable. These two were a different kind of neurodivergent. They had zero sense of decorum. "Boys. Maybe don't start sniffing her hair like creeps five seconds after meeting her," Aiden said.

Lola cut her eyes at him. "They're fine. Do I look like I can't speak for myself?"

Felix and Zane both gave him a smug look that had Aiden rolling his eyes. Why did he bother? The Mulvaneys were like a circus rolling into town wherever they went. He'd missed the chaos. Even if he would never admit it out loud. There was safety in that chaos.

He shook the thought away and stepped inside the home, stopping short just inside the door. "Fucking hell," he muttered under his breath.

The inside was exactly what Aiden had anticipated, but his stomach dropped just the same. There were floor to ceiling boxes, not just in the living room but the dining room, the kitchen, strewn along stairs, and spilling from the hallway. There was room to walk—and to sit if one wasn't picky about ruining their clothes—but the options were limited. How had nobody known how mentally unwell this man had been?

"Don't worry," Lola said, stepping behind him. "I've made good use of my time. I've managed to isolate the few boxes that deal with the Mulvaney murders to the dining room table."

Aiden nodded towards the boxes and the rest of the family—minus Thomas—descended on them like locusts, quickly finding a chair and digging in. This would take all night if Lucas couldn't do his thing.

Aiden gave her a doubtful look. "You couldn't possibly have looked through all these boxes."

"Of course not," she said, "but not all of these boxes can pertain to the Mulvaneys. The guy was a hoarder, not a historian. He knew about the cover-up, so he clearly didn't have any reason to dig any deeper. He wasn't trying to Sherlock Holmes his way through a mystery. He was someone mentally ill who couldn't stop collecting things."

"How do you know that?" Aiden asked.

Lola side-eyed him once more. "I've been in this house for two days. The Mulvaneys make up a small part of his interests. It looks like, somehow, the evidence came up for grabs and he just…took it. Maybe he'd told them he would destroy it and they were dumb enough to believe him."

"You don't know the whole story. Someone is blackmailing Thomas," Aiden said. "They're threatening to tell the world that Thomas killed his family, even though they know the truth."

"Well, it wasn't this guy," Lola said. "He's in a locked unit due to his severe dementia."

Aiden groaned in frustration. "Fuck. I know. How can someone know the whole story and still think Tommy is the guilty party? How can they still be offended? None of this makes any sense."

"It does if the wounded party has a connection to Shane," Thomas said gently.

"Or *is* Shane," Zane called from the dining room. When

they all stopped to look at him, he shrugged. "I mean, I can't be the only one thinking it, right? He was practically unrecognizable. Maybe he had a contingency plan just in case Dad didn't play along with his delusional fantasy?"

Thomas shook his head. "No. Absolutely not. It was Shane, trust me. This isn't a movie. He's…he's dead."

Aiden put a hand on Thomas's lower back, gently pushing him into the dining room with the others. Lola followed close behind. Zane and Felix took things from the boxes, took pictures with their phones, then handed them to Lucas, the only one who hadn't taken a seat. Instead, he stood looming over the table, taking what they handed him and pressing his hand to them, eyes closed.

"All the people who cared about him are dead, too," August said. "At least, those we know about. Are you getting anything, *umnishka*?"

Lucas tilted his head, his facial gymnastics almost comical as he seemed to rifle through the impressions left behind. "These photos passed through a lot of hands. People in uniform, people in suits. The man who lived here. And another man…someone who didn't belong here."

"That is so freaky," Lola whispered. "But it's so cool."

"What does he look like?" Thomas asked.

Lucas grimaced, then shrugged. "I can't tell you that. I can only see from his point of view, I can only *feel* from his point of view… and he's pissed. He's vengeful. He…hates you, wants to destroy you like you destroyed him."

"You destroyed him?" Felix questioned. "How could he do that if Thomas didn't know he existed? And how did he even know about this? About any of this? This has to be Shane…centric. It's the only thing that makes sense."

"Relax, kitten," Avi said. "We'll get there."

August pulled a large, coffee-stained manila folder from a box. It was brimming with papers that were folded and worn at the edges. When he opened it, he stopped short. "It's Shane's medical records."

"This guy had his medical records?" Avi asked. "How does that make any sense?"

"Maybe it was part of the initial investigation? Before they decided it was easier to just cover it up and pretend it never happened," Asa supplied.

"Or maybe this guy was trying to 'Sherlock Holmes' his way through an investigation," Aiden said, giving Lola a superior look that was completely lost on her.

Thomas met August's gaze. "Can you?"

August scoffed like it was a stupid question then began to run his finger along the page, reading and absorbing faster than any human had a right to. He flipped page after page as they all watched.

"This is crazy. Is he reading those?" Lola asked before taking a sip of coffee.

"Yeah, he's…unique," Aiden said, fumbling to describe his brother, who loved his husband, his kids, pop divas, and murder.

Lola rested her hip against the wall. "They're kind of a power couple, huh?"

"So, we know this guy has it out for Thomas and we know it has to do with Shane. That screams family," Aiden said. "Like, it's personal. Did Shane have siblings? Cousins, maybe? Anyone who might have the same fucked-up psychopathy as him?"

"Get Calliope on the phone," Thomas said to Asa.

Asa took out his burner phone and hit a button, then set it on the center table.

"This is Cassandra, your all-seeing, all-knowing prophetess. How may I serve you?" Calliope chirped.

"Is she always like that?" Lola asked with a smile.

"Yes," they all chorused.

"Calliope, dig deep. Is there *anybody* in Shane's family tree who could somehow not have known about his mental illness? I can't even imagine who, but step-siblings on his father's side, maybe that came after his death? Someone who maybe romanticized what happened?" Thomas asked.

There was a slew of typing, and after about three minutes, Calliope said, "As I'm sure you know, his mother and your uncle both passed without having any children between them. Shane's father remarried and he had three more children." Once more, there was a long pause. "Two daughters and a son."

"We know the blackmailer is a man, so focus on the son."

"Roger Graves—Graves? Yikes," Calliope said. "Married to a…Vanessa Slaughter—Jesus, imagine getting an invite to the Graves-Slaughter wedding? No, thank you, I'll pass," she muttered to herself.

"Calliope," Thomas said sharply.

"Yeah, yeah. Roger and Vanessa have been happily married for nineteen years, have two children, and are currently living in Okinawa, Japan where he's a lieutenant general. I don't think he'd be able to pull off any major crimes from across several continents and this required planning. Years if the message boards are to be believed."

Aiden's heart sank. Fuck. The message boards. For a brief moment, he'd forgotten about them. The random strangers on the internet who believed Thomas Mulvaney was a serial killer like them. "Did you find out anything more?"

"Yeah, were there any more messages claiming Dad's a serial killer?" Zane asked, still flipping through pages.

"A serial killer?" Lola said, taking a step back, not out of fear but more like she was assessing him. She gave him a thorough once-over and then snorted, dismissing the idea. "Hardly."

Calliope chuckled. "I found another dead thread, but I can't tell if these are the same players or different ones because their handles have changed. All but one. That AlwaysChristmas handle was still calling the shots. If this is tied to blackmail, I would bet money he's our guy."

"Why do you think that?" Asa asked.

Calliope sighed. "Because he's still feeding the others tidbits of information, riling them up, telling them you're like them but that you're hunting your own kind. That you're some kind of betrayer."

Lucas slammed his hand down on the table. "What the fuck? So, is this about Shane or isn't it? Why is this sick fuck going after my kids?"

August didn't stop reading and flipping. "Relax, my love. We will find them and we will make sure you get your revenge."

That seemed to placate Lucas slightly, but Lola was now leaning against the wall, watching them in a way that made the hairs on the back of Aiden's neck stand on end. It was only a matter of time before she realized the real Mulvaney secret. And then what?

Felix jumped up with a Sharpie he'd found on the table in hand. "Okay, let's just take a second. Right now, we have two issues, right?" He drew a line down the wall. "On the one hand, we've got this random Christmas guy, who is claiming that Thomas is a killer killing killers. Right? On the other hand, we have someone who knows the truth about Thomas and Shane and still blames Thomas."

"What else is being said by Mr. Christmas?" Zane asked Calliope.

There was the familiar sound of nails flying over keys. "He's organizing them, helping them kill better, essentially building a little…hub of killers."

"How many?" August asked suddenly, looking up from his work.

"How many what?" Calliope asked.

August glanced at Asa and Avi, then asked again, "How many killers are in his little hub?"

Calliope made a vague sound, then said, "The names have changed, but there are seven in both threads. I can't tell you if they're the same seven people, but we could posit that's the case."

Asa's expression grew grim. "He knows about us."

"What?" Thomas asked.

Asa's voice was dangerously quiet. "They're both the same man. And he knows what we do."

"What do you do?" Lola asked.

"We kill people, really bad people," Felix said, earning a wide-eyed look from Zane. Felix shrugged. "What? If Lola is going to be part of the family then she needs to know."

"That should have been Dad's decision," Lucas said. Felix stood firm, his expression unapologetic.

"Well, she has to be family now," Zane said. "I don't want to kill her."

Lola snorted. "Kill me? Good luck, little one."

"We only kill really bad people…if that helps," Zane said, uncertain.

Lola smirked, then looked at Felix, who nodded his head quickly. "Really, *really* bad. The worst of the worst. Someone's gotta do it, right?"

"I mean, it doesn't hurt," Lola said, surprisingly calm about the situation. "It actually explains a lot."

"Can we focus?" Lucas said. "If Asa's right, that means this guy isn't just trying to destroy you, he's trying to… counteract you. Create new players on the board anytime we take one out. Christ."

"Have we totally ruled out Holly?" Avi asked out of nowhere.

"I mean, she's dead so, yeah," Zane said.

"Yeah, I know, but what if she had a child? A secret one nobody knew about? Maybe when she died, he learned about his dad and went digging?"

"There's no record of her having any children," Calliope

said. "But I can do some digging."

With that, she was gone.

"What do you say we take these boxes to go?" Thomas said. "We can have more eyes on these files at home in the war room." To Lola, he said, "You're welcome to come home with us. There's plenty of room."

"Please?" Felix said, eyes glinting.

Aiden arched a brow when Lola locked eyes with him. "Are we gonna have a problem now?" he asked. "I really don't want to have problems with you. You're my only friend."

Lola snorted, then shook her head, crossing her arms over her chest. "Do you have any idea how many times I've wanted to put a bullet into a pedophile's head instead of throwing them in prison for the fifteenth time? I'm more mad that you didn't let me help than that you did it at all."

Aiden's shoulders sagged, then he hugged her.

Lola stiffened in his arms and patted his back like he was a stranger. "Okay, that's enough of that," she said, pushing him away. "So, are you taking me to the Mulvaney mansion?"

"Looks like we are," Aiden agreed.

Aiden had worked so hard to create a life that ran parallel to Thomas but never intersected, but now, those world's were colliding, collapsing into each other at an alarming rate. If this ended badly, he'd have no safe spaces left.

Anywhere.

FIFTEEN
THOMAS

Thomas was on edge. It felt like they were barreling closer to the truth and he wasn't sure how he should feel about it. No matter the answer, it wouldn't be anything good. There was no peace to be found from this. Whoever was out to destroy him knew everything.

But why were they stalling? Thomas hadn't paid. Why didn't the blackmailer just release what they knew? Because it wasn't about that. It was about revenge. Revenge for Shane? But why? Fuck. It made no sense. Part of Thomas just wished the asshole would go public already. It had to be easier than carrying this giant fucking secret forever. What was the worst that could happen? The public learned his family wasn't perfect?

Or would people dig deeper?

That was the real fear. That once they knew the truth, people would want to know more and more and they might eventually realize that his family's past wasn't even the tip of the iceberg in the grand scheme of shocking secrets. Not by a long shot. Covering up a murder/suicide? Scandalous, for sure. A family of homicidal vigilantes? A death sentence. A real one.

Aiden studied his profile from the passenger seat, his worry evident. Thomas could practically hear him trying to figure out how to make it better, how to make it right. And Thomas wanted so badly to let him.

That was the other problem. When Aiden was with him, it was so much easier to just let him fix things. Aiden was good at fixing things. He was good at managing crises. He was good at managing Thomas.

Too good.

Before Aiden, Thomas had spent years solving his own problems. That was who he needed to be now. For the family. He needed to be the leader. It was what was expected of him. It was what was right.

But now that Aiden was there—right there beside him—Thomas had a hard time letting go of this pull to just let him take care of everything. But he had to stop relying on him so much. That was the right thing to do. He should be taking care of Aiden, not the other way around.

Fuck.

Thomas had let the others leave the coroner's house first, ensuring they were far out of sight before he stepped on the gas and eased onto the barely-there road. He thought about turning on the radio, just for something to take his mind off his thoughts, but couldn't bring himself to lift his hand off the wheel long enough to reach for the button.

He jumped when Aiden's hand landed on his thigh,

squeezing gently. "You good?"

Aiden's voice slid over him like silk. That low timbre just did something to his insides. How did he do it? How did Aiden carry himself like he knew all the secrets of the universe? Like he always knew the right thing to do? There had never been a time—not even when he was eighteen—that Aiden hadn't walked with the confidence of ten men.

"I'm fine," Thomas managed, even though it was obvious he wasn't.

Aiden smirked at him, eyeing his semi-hard erection, his hand sliding farther up Thomas's thigh at a pace designed to torment. "You sure?"

That level of ego was intoxicating. Thomas's kink was competence, it seemed. And Aiden did everything well. Thomas took a shuddering breath as Aiden's thumb traced the outline of his now rigid cock.

Yeah, everything.

He let his knees fall open as much as he could while driving, letting Aiden know he wasn't opposed to whatever he had in mind. His tongue darted out to wet his lower lip, and he stole a glance, only to find Aiden looking at him like he was about to tear him apart.

Fuck, how did he do that? How did he make Thomas's heart hurt and his cock ache at the same time? He shifted in his seat, wanting more of Aiden touching him, but Aiden refused, teasing his thumb along Thomas's zipper in a light touch that made him squirm.

When Thomas groaned, Aiden chuckled, then leaned into his space, his other hand landing on the back of his neck to hold him steady while he traced the shell of his ear with his tongue. "Eyes on the road."

"They're on the road," Thomas said, once more trying to coax Aiden's hand on his dick to do something.

"What's wrong?" Aiden teased, applying just enough pressure to make Thomas grind against his palm.

"You're distracting me," Thomas chastised. "We could get into an accident."

"Mm," Aiden agreed. "Should I stop, Tommy?"

"You should stop being such a fucking tease," Thomas murmured.

Aiden sucked at his earlobe, squeezing the back of his neck and his cock in tandem. "Okay, I can do that. But you need to pull the car over. Safety first."

Thomas didn't pull over, just hit the brake and threw it in park, turning to press his lips to Aiden's. He let him kiss him but didn't deepen the kiss.

"Tell me what you want," Aiden said, licking over the seam of his lips.

"This. You," Thomas answered, unable to verbalize what it was he needed as he chased Aiden's lips.

"You have me," Aiden promised, repeating the words Thomas had said to him the other night. "You've always had me." With that, he used his thumb to tug down Thomas's jaw, fucking his tongue into his mouth in a way that made Thomas's head spin. Then, he pulled back to say, "And you can *have* me whenever and however you want."

Thomas blinked at him. Was Aiden saying what he thought he was saying? It shouldn't have shocked him.

They'd been to bed a few times now and there hadn't been any thought to the roles they'd fallen into. But now, Aiden was looking into his eyes like he was trying to make sure Thomas understood what he offered.

"What are you saying?" He needed to be sure. Or maybe he just wanted to hear those words on Aiden's lips.

"Fuck me, Tommy," he said against his lips, once more working his tongue over Thomas's.

Thomas pulled back, looking around the car and the semi-wilderness beyond. "Here?"

"Why not?"

Lube? Room? Strangers seeing their bare asses through the window of the SUV and it ending up on fucking TMZ? "It's not like we came…prepared," Thomas said lamely.

Aiden's hand groped him persistently through his jeans. "Thomas Mulvaney not prepared for something? Gasp," Aiden said, still sipping from his lips. "The scandal."

Maybe it was his teasing tone or maybe it was the way he was kneading his aching cock in a way that was making him see stars, but whatever it was, Thomas lost his ability to see reason. He turned, sealing their lips together in a kiss he hoped conveyed all the words he was currently choking on. Of course, he wanted him, wanted to fuck him. Anytime, anywhere. Who wouldn't?

Aiden slipped his tongue into Thomas's mouth, making a sound of approval when he sucked on it.

"Does this mean you want me?" Aiden asked, biting at his lower lip.

"You know I fucking do," Thomas managed.

Aiden's hand was already on the button on Thomas's jeans. "Then say it. Tell me how bad you want to fuck me."

Thomas made a noise of frustration, biting at Aiden's jaw, then his throat. "I want to fuck you. I want to be inside you. I want to feel you clenching around my cock. Good enough?"

Aiden made an appreciative sound, plunging his hand into Thomas's underwear and stroking him a few times. "But the question now, Mr. Mulvaney…is *how* do you want to fuck me?"

"You're pushing your fucking luck, Aiden. I have an alphabetized list of all the ways I've thought of fucking you, but if you don't let me get on with it, it won't matter. Your hand feels too fucking good."

Aiden laughed, releasing him. Then he was squirming his way into the backseat, reaching back to drag Thomas with him. Neither of them were small men, leading to an awkward tangle of limbs, but as soon as Thomas's ass hit the seat, Aiden was on him, climbing into his lap. Then nothing was funny anymore.

Thomas captured Aiden's mouth, fucking his tongue between his lips, his hands going for the buttons on his shirt. But he quickly lost patience, yanking the fabric off his shoulders to drag his mouth along whatever skin he could reach. Fuck, he felt so good.

Thomas licked and sucked at Aiden's nipples, even as he rolled his hips down, grinding against Thomas's cock, using the back of the seat to create friction and pressure that had them both panting.

Thomas wanted to slow down, wanted to savor every single moment, but then they were both tearing at each other's clothes, their mouths clashing, teeth bumping, until they were skin on skin with not a stitch between them.

Aiden's hand found his cock again, jerking him roughly, almost painfully.

"If you keep doing that, this is going to be over before it starts," Thomas said against his lips.

Aiden took Thomas's hand, lifting it to his lips and sucking two fingers into his mouth obscenely. Thomas hissed, his hips rutting against Aiden's now leaking cock. He rose up on his knees, guiding Thomas's hand back, until Thomas realized what Aiden wanted.

Thomas might come from just this alone. He gripped Aiden's ass with one hand, two spit-slick fingers sliding into the crevice, rubbing against his hole. Aiden didn't give him the chance to push inside, just pressed himself back until Thomas's fingers were buried in the tight squeeze of his body.

They both moaned. Thomas leaned forward, kissing any part of Aiden he could reach as he rode his fingers, biting at his ribs, his hip bones, reveling in the way Aiden pulled and tugged on his hair, guiding Thomas's mouth where he wanted it next.

After a minute or two, Aiden tugged at his hair, making him look at him. "I'm good."

Thomas nodded, withdrawing his fingers. Aiden once more used his spit, this time to slick Thomas's cock, then lined himself up. When he started to lower himself, Thomas grabbed his hips at the last moment. "Are you sure about this? I don't want to hurt you."

Aiden studied him, his hands cupping his face. "I don't mind hurting for you. I've been doing it for years. It's who we are. It's who we've always been. But this is the kind of hurt I want."

Before Thomas could even formulate a response, Aiden was sinking down on him, encasing his cock in the most exquisite heat. Fuck. Fuck. Fuck. How did that feel so fucking good? He gripped Aiden's ass, spreading him open, rising up to meet every downward motion, wanting to get as deep as he could, wanting to leave him as full as possible. Aiden gripped the back of the seat once more, his expression pinched as he worked himself on him.

Maybe Aiden was right. Maybe this was just who they were, never allowing themselves pleasure unless it came with some level of sacrifice. Not that this felt like any kind of…penance. It was a little raw, a little painful…there was no smooth glide, just a sort of disjointed catch and slide that ached even as it shot jolts of delicious heat along his nerve endings.

Aiden grabbed Thomas's hand, licking his palm and guiding it to his cock. Thomas jerked him in time with his motions, both of them too far gone to do anything but hold onto each other as they chased their own orgasms.

Thomas tried to hold off, tried to wait until Aiden was there, too, but he couldn't. The heat, the friction, the smell of their sweat, the panting grunts of Aiden working himself on his cock…it was all too fucking much. He couldn't stop himself. When he came, he bit down on Aiden's chest, something that was wholly unlike him, but he just needed it, needed to feel his flesh between his teeth, needed to leave some mark, some visual reminder that this was all real. That he had been inside him.

Pleasure rolled over him in waves, his blunt nails digging into Aiden's hips even as his teeth dug into his skin. Aiden cried out, and Thomas pulled away just in time to watch his release spill over his fist onto Thomas's belly. He continued to work him in his fist, fascinated as he just kept coming. Finally, Aiden batted his hand away with a full-body shiver.

They both sat there, trying to drag in breaths, while Thomas attempted to will his heartbeat back to a normal rhythm, an almost impossible feat with Aiden clinging to him, his forehead resting on his shoulder.

Thomas wasn't sure how long they sat there, but when Aiden finally shifted his weight, his muscles were stiff and they were both sticky, covered in sweat and cum. "This was hotter during the sex," Aiden said, looking down at them with a grimace.

"There are wipes in the kill kit under the floorboard in the back," Thomas noted. Aiden was up on his knees once more, then leaning over the back row, ass in the air as he rifled through the hidden compartment, giving a triumphant cry when he found what he was looking for. Thomas slapped his ass a second before Aiden settled back into the backseat, beside him this time.

They took their time cleaning each other up and getting dressed, at one point having to leave the vehicle to do so.

When they got back in the front seat, Aiden insisted on driving. Thomas was content to let him. When he took his hand, threading their fingers together on the center console, Thomas closed his eyes, enjoying the unfamiliar feeling spreading through his chest.

What was it? Not love. He *did* love Aiden, but he loved a lot of people, so he knew what that felt like. This was something else, something soothing and…quiet. Contentment. He was content. When was the last time he'd ever felt completely at ease? And why now? Things were not settled by any means. Maybe he was just cum drunk. But it didn't feel that way.

Whatever it was, he didn't want to lose it. He didn't want it to go away. He didn't want Aiden to go away.

"I can hear you thinking from here," Aiden said, squeezing his hand. "We're so close to figuring this out. You just have to hang in there for a few more days. Okay?"

Thomas nodded. "It's not that. I mean, of course, it's that, but it's not just that." He spared a glance at Aiden, who was now frowning at him. This time, it was Thomas who squeezed his hand. "Now, I can hear *you* thinking," he teased.

"Well, you have a bit of a track record," Aiden said, sounding slightly huffy. "Whenever you get all broody, it usually means I'm about to be dismissed…again."

It was true. Twenty years of push and pull. For nothing. So much time he wasted. He owed Aiden a million apologies, but that would never be enough to undo the damage, to get back the time lost. So, instead, he just said, "I love you."

The car veered dangerously towards a grove of trees before Aiden recovered, giving Thomas a wide-eyed look. "W-What?"

Thomas shrugged. "I love you."

"But…" Aiden said warily.

Thomas shook his head. "No buts. I love you. And I think it's time you come home. Forever."

Aiden's eyes darted from the road to Thomas and back again, like it was suddenly him having the crisis. "Where is all this coming from? Is this the orgasm talking?" Aiden shook his head. "You know what? I don't care why. Yes, I'll come home. Forever. But if you wake up tomorrow and say you've changed your mind, I'm going to lock you in the fucking basement and keep *you* there forever."

That feeling of warmth continued to spread through Thomas until he felt almost giddy from it. "I won't change my mind. Not this time."

Aiden grinned and, for a full thirty seconds, they just smiled at each other like idiots. But then Aiden's smile suddenly disappeared. "Fuck."

Thomas frowned. "What's wrong?"

"One of us is definitely going to fucking die now, for sure," Aiden muttered.

"What?" Thomas asked, amused.

"This isn't how we do things," Aiden said. "We pine, we fight, we fuck, then we yell at each other, then we hate each other, and then we ignore each other…until it gets to be too much and we do it all over again. We're not the type who get happy endings. That's not for people like us.

Now you've gone and said you love me with no qualifiers afterwards and that for sure means the universe is going to fuck us."

Thomas blinked rapidly, then laughed. "I had no idea you were so…superstitious."

"It's not about superstition, it's just my bad luck," Aiden muttered. "I'm not allowed to have something I want. Ever."

Even for all of his opining, he still hadn't stopped holding Thomas's hand. Aiden didn't really mean what he was saying. He was just…venting. Scared. Thomas knew that. Because he was scared, too. Loving Aiden meant having something to lose. And while Thomas had always loved Aiden, it felt like some cursed, fairy tale, Greek tragedy kind of love. There had been safety in knowing you couldn't lose what you never had.

But they definitely had something to lose now. They probably always had. "I promise I won't die on you. And I won't let you die on me."

It was a ridiculous thing to say and optimistic considering their current situation, but Aiden's shoulders sagged. "Promise?"

"I do."

SIXTEEN
AIDEN

Aiden and Thomas entered the parlor to the knowing stares of Calliope, Cricket, and Lola. They sat curled up on the sofa, wine in hand, chatting like they'd known each other all their lives. Well, Calliope and Lola had wine in hand, Cricket was drinking mineral water. Weird. Not that she was a drinker, but Aiden had seen her drink at more than one wedding.

He filed that information away for later. He envied how women could just bond so easily. Maybe not all women but definitely these women. None of them had ever met a stranger. Something about them just seemed to put people at ease. Nobody had ever said that about him or any of the Mulvaneys.

Aiden liked maybe three people he didn't share a last name with and they were all present in that room. What would Aiden do without Lola? Tommy wanted him to come home…permanently. That meant closing up shop on his PI business, but it also meant giving up Lola.

"Where've you two been?" Cricket asked, giving them a thorough once-over.

"Car trouble," they both said in unison.

Shit.

Calliope snorted. "Something need to be lubed?"

"Calliope," Thomas said, her name more a warning than a plea.

"Thomas," she mocked in the same stern voice.

Aiden tried to hide his smirk as Thomas easily gave in, shoulders dropping. Aiden didn't know why Thomas even bothered. Calliope was the only person Aiden knew who had no fear of Thomas. Maybe it was their years of friendship? Maybe Calliope had just vowed never to fear anyone. Either was a very real possibility.

"Where's everybody else?" Aiden asked, breaking the staring contest between the two.

Cricket sighed. "Team A is in the conference room going over the stuff in the boxes Lola found, Team B is playing Mario Kart, and Team C is on babysitting duty, which just means they're also playing Mario Kart but with two toddlers in their laps."

Thomas and Aiden exchanged glances before Aiden said, "What?"

Lola shrugged. "There are too many of them. We can't keep naming them all. So, we just separated them into teams. It's just easier that way."

"Who's Team A?" Aiden asked.

"August, Lucas, Mac, Archer, Jericho, Atticus, and the twins," Cricket said, listing them off on her fingers.

"Team B?" Thomas asked, amused.

"Adam, Noah, Felix, Zane, Arsen, and Seven," Calliope listed.

"And before you ask, Team C is Lake, Cree, Nico, Levi, Arlo, and Dimitri," Lola said.

"You got August and Lucas to agree to leave the girls with a group of Gen Z gamers...on purpose?" Aiden asked.

"As opposed to the vigilante killers who are their parents and uncles?" Calliope asked.

She had a point. The girls were safe, especially with the feelings faction guarding them. Jericho's boys were the best of both worlds, truly. They could kill when they needed to but somehow managed to keep all their humanity intact. Maybe that was just the resilience of their age. Or maybe that was what life was like when you had faith that what you were doing was justified.

"They're waiting for you in the war room," Cricket said, waving her hand vaguely in the direction of said room.

Thomas frowned at Calliope. "Are you coming?"

Calliope looked at Lola and Cricket. "Yeah, I'll be along shortly."

Thomas eyed her wine glass. "Sober?"

Calliope's brows went up, her expression...frosty. Oof. Thomas needed to tread lightly. They couldn't afford to lose Calliope. She was literally the backbone of the entire operation. Without her, they'd be crippled indefinitely. Also, she scared Aiden just a little. He could probably beat her in a fist fight, but she could tank his credit score in two strokes of a keyboard. Hell, she could make him disappear like a black ops agent if she wanted, making it so Aiden never existed at all. Yeah, no, thank you.

"Drunk or sober, I can still get the job done," Calliope said. "Besides, who are you to lecture me about responsible drinking? You're half in the bag whenever you and this one"—she pointed her thumb at Aiden—"have another fight. Which is often."

"She's got you there," Cricket murmured.

"I—" Thomas started, looking comically offended.

Aiden chuckled, grabbing Thomas's forearm. "Come on. Let's go downstairs before you piss off your only friend."

Thomas gave him a huffy look. "I have other friends."

"Do you?" Aiden asked, tilting his head.

"Do *you*?" Thomas asked, tone mocking.

Aiden really didn't. He didn't trust people. He hadn't really trusted Lola when they'd met but then, somewhere along the way, she'd just sort of snuck in. He didn't know when it happened. Maybe it was all those nights she spent listening to him drunkenly whine about Thomas. She'd more than proven herself as a friend. Aiden wasn't sure she would say the same of him, but he hoped so.

"Just Lola. And you only have Calliope. So, be nice." Aiden bumped their shoulders together, tone teasing as he said, "You just got laid, you should be relaxed."

"I am relaxed," Thomas muttered as Aiden opened the door to the war room.

Team A were exactly as Cricket said, hunched over paperwork strewn over the conference table. August was still scanning the papers in the thick manila envelope, and

Lucas was running his hands over the papers, reading as much as he was trying to get impressions. Asa and Avi sat on the table, passing papers between them, Mac and Archer sat in chairs segregated from the others, using their phones to look up whatever information was on the notes in front of them, while Jericho and Atticus studied what looked like autopsy photos.

They all looked up from their tasks upon his and Thomas's entrance. "Took you two long enough," August said.

"Car trouble," Aiden muttered.

Asa snorted. "Yeah, those brand new luxury vehicles can be tricky."

"Where's Calliope?" Atticus asked, looking behind them like she might be hiding.

"Upstairs drinking with Cricket and Lola," Aiden answered.

Lucas glanced up sharply. "Cricket's drinking?"

Aiden frowned. "No, she's watching them drink."

"Why do you care if Cricket is drinking? She's your baby mama not your daughter," Jericho said.

"Because she's pregnant," August said, not looking up from his task. "Alcohol increases the risk of birth defects, developmental delays, low birth weight, miscarriage, and even stillbirth."

Aiden's eyes went wide. He glanced at Thomas, who started to smile. God, this man really loved babies. Did that mean he actually wanted babies of his own? Would that be weird? They were both much older than most new parents. Also, their grandkids would be older than their aunts and uncles. That would be bizarre. But the idea of a baby with Thomas's blue eyes made Aiden a little breathless. Christ, he was so far gone.

"You could have just stopped with she's pregnant, babe," Lucas said, still running his hands over pages in the file.

"Congrats," Mac said before returning to his phone.

"Yeah, *mazel tov* and all that," Archer agreed, raising his water bottle in a mock salute.

It would never not be weird to Aiden to see a sober-acting Archer. After years of finding him sleeping in bathtubs and alleyways, it was damn near impossible to believe it was all fake. In the news, they spun it as him sobering up for the love of his life, which to an extent was the truth. He hadn't sobered up, but he had stopped living a double life. Working at that school provided enough plausible deniability to keep their more unseemly activities at bay.

"You guys are having *another* baby?" Avi asked. "Why didn't we know that?"

August finally looked up, frowning. "Are we supposed to tell you whenever we're attempting to conceive a child?"

"No but you could tell us when you've managed to do it," Atticus said stiffly. "Don't you think there are enough kids running around?"

Lucas gave Atticus a superior look. "You don't get to talk. You have six children."

"Mine are all old enough to drink," Atticus said, earning a surprised look from his husband. When Atticus noticed, he said, "What?"

"That's the first time I've heard you acknowledge that

they're your kids as much as mine."

"I mean, technically, they're neither of yours," Avi said.

"Regardless," Lucas said, "you don't get to lecture us. You took the easy way out and just unofficially adopted fully-grown humans."

Atticus scoffed. "If you think corralling those kids is easy, you've never tried to herd cats before."

"You think that's bad?" Archer said. "Try over a hundred homicidal twenty-somethings with access to military-grade weapons and the department of defense discretionary budget."

Aiden couldn't imagine attempting to wrangle that many psychopaths in one place, much less keep it organized enough to carry out kills that, if done wrong, could start international incidents, even wars. The fact that Thomas thought Mac and Archer were prime for the job spoke to how little Aiden knew either of them.

Lucas, however, was unimpressed. "You can talk to me when you have two eighteen-month-olds simultaneously projectile vomiting on you or finger painting with their own poop," Lucas said.

Avi pulled a face. "Ew. Why the hell are you having another one?"

Lucas and August exchanged a look that made Aiden feel like he was intruding, then August sighed. "You just won't get it until you have one."

"Which, if Felix has his way, might be sooner rather than later," Jericho said.

"Yeah, laugh it up, grease monkey. You're the one who's

going to end up a grandfather in his thirties," Asa said. "All your kids are old enough to breed and half of them aren't super picky about gender, so…may the odds be ever in your favor."

Jericho flicked him off.

"Enough," Thomas said. "Congratulations on the baby, Lucas."

"Why just Lucas?" August said, frowning.

"Because he's the only one who cares about formalities," Thomas said, his tone soothing.

"True," August said. He pointed to the manila folder in front of him. "I've been going through Shane's medical records. Seems his parents knew he was prone to violence from a young age. He'd already hit the McDonald triad before he was ten. He killed some neighborhood pets, set fire to the pool house. Attacked a housekeeper with a screwdriver."

Thomas dropped into a chair, rubbing a hand over his face. "How did nobody know about this?"

"You know how," Asa said. "The same way nobody knows about us. Money. His mom is an heiress. She just kept paying off his victims."

"He wasn't like that in school," Thomas said, almost like he needed to believe it. "He was popular, likable. Most people thought he was good-natured."

"Come on, Dad. How many times have we heard that about Ted Bundy? That's part of their cover. Hell, it's part of ours," Archer asked.

"He just wasn't violent like that," Thomas said, sounding

lost.

"Wasn't he?" Aiden asked, placing his hands on Thomas's shoulders.

It was crazy how Thomas could still be so deeply ensnared by Shane. He had to know, on some level, that everything he and Shane had shared had been a tactic, a ploy to get Thomas to trust him, to let him abuse him freely. Nobody should know that better than him, but he was blind to it. Maybe it was the only way he could cope, but it was still frustrating. Aiden didn't want him thinking about anybody but him.

"It didn't seem like it at the time," Thomas said. "He was manipulative, sure. But…"

Aiden squeezed his shoulders. "But what? He was a narcissist and a rapist. Just because you loved him doesn't make him any less of those things. It just made it easier for him to manipulate you."

Thomas scrubbed his hands over his face. "This is getting us nowhere. None of this is helpful."

"Holly is a dead end," Atticus said. "We can at least scratch her vengeful love child off our list."

"Why's that?" August asked.

Atticus held up a stack of papers. "I requested a copy of her autopsy report. Luckily, they did one. The coroner notes she never had children."

"Wouldn't the coroner just be going off of her medical records? Maybe she lied?" Asa asked.

Atticus shook his head. "There are osteological markers that show a woman has or hasn't had kids. She hasn't.

There's no secret love child stalking Thomas for revenge. I suppose she could have had someone close to her who sought revenge, but it still doesn't make sense why they'd go after you instead of Shane unless Holly lied. Which is hard to believe. Would she protect her rapist?"

"I did," Thomas said quietly.

Aiden squeezed his shoulders once more. He wished there was some way to quell his fears but the only ways he could think of required them being alone.

"Maybe this has nothing to do with Shane at all," Thomas said suddenly. "Maybe Shane was just a means to an end. Maybe this person has just had it out for me from the beginning. Someone who is pissed we killed a partner? Someone looking for people to kill with to replace that partner? It would explain the online activity."

"Well, we need Calliope if we're going to chase the rabbit down that black hole," Jericho said just as the door opened. "There's no way we can run those leads down without her."

"Ask and ye shall receive," Calliope said, breezing in, wine glass still in hand. "Despite my relaxed, vacation-like demeanor, I've been on top of our little band of psychopathic misfits. I tagged all of the names and have lots of little bots scrubbing the web, both dark and light. Whoever they are, I will find them. Fear not."

"So, we're giving up on the Shane angle entirely?" Atticus asked.

"Not entirely," Thomas said. "Maybe I just pay them and see what happens? Maybe it all goes away."

"No. We don't negotiate with terrorists," Asa said.

"Yeah, we're not giving this dick our inheritance money," Avi said. "Besides, he'll just come back for more or release the story anyway."

"We could release it first," Lucas said. "Let Zane write it. Get ahead of it and put our own spin on it."

"You're forgetting something," Calliope said. "If this AlwaysChristmas guy and the blackmailer are one in the same, they don't just have you dead to rights on that family secret, they know you kill people. All of you. What if they can prove that, too?"

"So, what do we do? Go back to the beginning?" Mac asked.

Thomas closed his eyes and leaned back in his chair. "Let's just call it a night. Come back to it in the morning with fresh eyes."

The others looked like they wanted to protest but Calliope gave them a subtle shake of her head. Once all of them had filed out but her, she sat on the table beside Thomas's chair. "How you holding up, buttercup? You don't look so good."

"I'm fine," Thomas said warily.

"Anybody with eyes knows you're clearly not fine. But are you okay? Can you handle this?" Calliope asked.

That was a good question. All the strain couldn't be good for him. He had too much heart. Aiden never worried about Thomas's physical health before. Thomas was always the fittest one in the family. He went to the gym nearly every single day, ate clean, and didn't smoke. Hell, his only vice was liquor and even that was only after a fight with Aiden.

But Aiden would be lying if he said he couldn't see the

strain was taking a toll on him. Aiden needed to take better care of him. And maybe, for once, Thomas would actually let him.

Calliope gave Aiden a hard look that seemed to convey that she expected him to take care of this…of him. "Why don't you guys go take a shower…or a bath? Yours is probably big enough for ten people."

"What are you going to be doing?" Thomas asked.

Calliope shrugged. "Well, first, I'm going to work my magic on those keys and see if I can't dig up some more information on our Mulvaney counter-strike serial killers. Then, if I'm lucky, I might get to do Lola."

Thomas coughed in surprise. "Calliope."

Calliope laughed. "What? You asked."

"And on that note…" Aiden said, letting his words trail off as he tugged Thomas to his feet.

"Good luck," Aiden said in lieu of a farewell.

"When you look like me, honey, you don't need luck," Calliope said.

"I meant with the computers, but I admire your confidence," Aiden said, shaking his head.

"Night, boys."

SLOTH SLOTH
SLOTH SLOTH
SLOTH SLOTH
SLOTH SLOTH
SLOTH SL
SLOTH SLO

SEVENTEEN
THOMAS

Thomas had never been one for baths. Showers had always seemed far more efficient and he rarely had time for languishing in lukewarm water. But now, lying back in the tub with Aiden straddling his hips, massaging his chest with soap-slick hands, he was thinking maybe he'd been too hasty.

Aiden was taking it slow, almost too slow, digging fingers into the muscles of Thomas's shoulders, his arms, his chest. He ran his fingers through the hair there, running his thumbs over his nipples, teasing until he was half-hard and squirming beneath him. He couldn't help himself. When Aiden continued his exploration, palms running lower to his stomach, Thomas arched up into his touch.

Aiden's thumbs traced the ridges of his abs. "You have a very nice body, Mr. Mulvaney. Has anybody ever told you that before?"

Thomas's blood rushed from his head to his dick so fast it made him dizzy. He'd barely been able to resist Aiden just existing in a room, but now that he was no longer bound by Thomas's rules, he was lethal. "Nobody who mattered."

Aiden looked at him hungrily. "Good."

"Good?" Thomas asked, amused.

"Mm," Aiden said, pitching forward to slowly lick from his chin to his lips. "I don't want anybody to matter but me. Not when it comes to this body anyway."

Thomas ran his hands up under Aiden's ass, dragging him against him until they both groaned, a finger playing at his entrance. "And what about your body?"

"What about it?" Aiden teased, sliding his tongue into Thomas's mouth, retreating just as quickly.

"Who does it belong to?" Thomas asked, gripping the back of Aiden's head with his other hand and dragging him back in to plunder his mouth thoroughly.

"Like you don't know?" Aiden said, pulling away to continue his exploration, biting at Thomas's chin, his earlobe, whatever skin he seemed to find enticing enough to risk the taste of soap.

"Maybe I just want to hear you say it."

"It's yours," Aiden said, rolling his hips again, sending jolts of electricity along Thomas's spine. "It's always been yours."

"If you keep talking like that, we're never going to get anything done for the rest of our lives," Thomas said, pushing a finger inside.

Aiden sank back on it, lids going half-mast. "I'm good with that. Noah can take over and you can just live out the rest of your days as my sex slave."

"I think I'm a little past my prime," Thomas said.

Aiden looked down at Thomas's cock, gripping it in a tight squeeze and stroking him in a way that made him groan. "I don't know. It's been working just fine so far."

Fuck, this felt good. Not just Aiden's hands or his body, but the lack of tension between them. The ease of it all. It felt surreal. Never had Thomas allowed himself to imagine a time when this could be his reality. Where Aiden was his—fully his—without having to push him away.

Aiden gripped his face hard. "Hey, where'd you go? Don't do that thing where you start thinking too much."

Thomas shook his head. Aiden knew him so well. "Yeah, okay."

"Let's go to bed," Aiden said, giving him another hungry kiss, before hastily rinsing the soap from Thomas's chest.

He didn't argue. When Aiden exited the tub, he followed. They didn't even towel off, just fell onto the mattress still wet. Thomas rolled Aiden beneath him, coming up on his forearms to look down at him.

Thomas wanted to say something, something big and profound, but when he opened his mouth, nothing came out. Aiden smiled, lifting just enough to capture his mouth in a kiss. "I know," he said.

Thomas nodded, hoping it was true. But he didn't want to have any big conversations right now, conversations that were probably long overdue. So, he distracted himself, dipping his head to lick over Aiden's nipple, tugging it with his teeth until he hissed, bucking up against him.

Thomas smiled, giving the other nipple the same

treatment, before sliding lower between Aiden's legs, burying his face in the crease of his leg, inhaling deeply. Was it weird how much he fucking craved that scent? He sucked at Aiden's balls before running his tongue over the underside of his heavy cock.

Aiden was breathing heavily. He tangled his fingers in Thomas's hair, trying to drag his mouth where he wanted it, but Thomas ignored him until he growled in frustration. Only then did he swallow him down, sucking him from root to tip, teasing at the crown, before making his way down once more.

"Christ," Aiden muttered, writhing beneath him like he was trying to stop himself from fucking up into his mouth.

Thomas took him deeper, letting him cut off his air supply as he swallowed around him. Who needed air? Thomas would gladly go without just to hear Aiden panting his name.

Thomas pulled off as something hit his arm. The lube. Aiden certainly hadn't gained any subtlety. Thomas laughed, slicking up two fingers, positioning them at Aiden's entrance, taking him back in his mouth as he worked his fingers inside.

Aiden's hands once more found Thomas's hair and twisted. But he wouldn't be swayed. He sucked him slowly, worked his fingers in and out slowly, finding that spot inside Aiden that made him fucking whimper—actually whimper.

God, that sound was addictive.

"Enough, Tommy," Aiden said, tugging at Thomas's hair hard enough to make his point. "Fuck me already."

Thomas sat up on his knees between Aiden's legs, using the lube to slick himself, swiping some over Aiden's hole. Thomas knew, the minute he slid inside, he was going to lack the patience to go slow.

He dragged Aiden down the mattress until he was where he wanted him, watching as he pressed inside Aiden's body. Thomas could have come just from that alone. It should be illegal for anything to feel as good as sliding into him felt. It was better than any drug.

When he was all the way inside, he pulled free, then slammed home again. Fuck, he took it so well. He caught Aiden's knees over his elbows, leaning forward, practically bending him in half so he could kiss him as he drove into him. Aiden's hands found his ass, spurring him on, like he needed even more.

"Oh, fuck."

"That what you wanted?" Thomas managed.

"Mm, for most of my life," Aiden admitted in a gasp.

Fuck. Thomas kissed him again, his tongue spearing into his mouth with every thrust. Aiden's blunt nails were all but clawing at his skin. Thomas would wear every fucking mark like a badge of honor. He'd spent so much of his life fantasizing about what it would be like to have Aiden in his bed, underneath him, letting him use his body.

Fuck. He was already so close. Aiden just did it for him. Would there ever come a time when this seemed mundane? He didn't think so. He sat back a bit so he could reach for Aiden's cock, but he batted his hand away. "Uh-uh," he said, dragging Thomas back to him and locking his legs around his waist. "I'm going to finish inside you. Once you come, it's my turn."

Jesus. Had Aiden always been so fucking blunt? Probably, yeah. Thomas had just never given him the opportunity. Still, there they were. Aiden contented himself with licking and sucking at whatever skin he could reach. It would leave marks, but he didn't care. He just didn't care what anybody thought about them anymore. Maybe it was his impending orgasm talking? Maybe he was drunk off the tight squeeze of Aiden's hole milking his cock. "Fuck, I'm gonna come."

"Do it," Aiden panted against his ear. "Fill me up. I want to be inside you with your cum still painting my insides."

Thomas flushed. What a dirty mouth he had. But he was too far gone to give it much thought, driving inside Aiden a few more times before his hips stuttered, his release slamming into him like a truck as he emptied himself inside.

He was still panting when Aiden gently pushed him off of him. "On your stomach."

That wouldn't be a problem. Thomas did as Aiden asked, perfectly compliant. Aiden kissed his neck even as he worked wet fingers into Thomas's hole. He hissed at the slight intrusion, but more from instinct than actual discomfort. Aiden's exploration was perfunctory, more making sure Thomas could take it than attempting to pleasure him with his hand. Almost as quickly as they arrived, they were gone, replaced with the blunt head of Aiden's cock.

His body had a much more visceral reaction to that invasion. He hissed at the slight burn of it, tensing before remembering that would only make it worse. Besides, he wanted this invasion, liked the way his body made accommodation for Aiden, like he belonged there.

Aiden didn't stop until he was buried as deep as he could go. His fingers found Thomas's hair once more, tugging his head to the side to mouth at his cheek, his ear, his throat, as he rocked lazily in and out of Thomas's body.

"You feel so fucking good."

"So do you," Thomas said.

And it was true. He wasn't able to get hard again, but that didn't mean he didn't like it. There was something soothing about Aiden's weight on top of him, using him for his own pleasure. Aiden deserved to use Thomas after the years he'd made him wait. He deserved everything.

Aiden's breath was panting in his ear, his fingers twisting in his hair, his cock filling him just right. If Thomas could have gotten hard again, he absolutely would have. It was all too perfect, it felt too fucking good.

"I love fucking you," Aiden growled into his ear.

Thomas's cock did stir at Aiden's words. How could it not? "I like when you fuck me," he said, breathless.

Aiden's weight lifted, disorienting Thomas for a moment, before strong hands gripped his hips, pulling him back until he was where Aiden wanted him. His breath left him as Aiden pulled almost all the way free before driving home again in a way that had Thomas's toes curling.

Fuck. Fuck. Fuck.

Aiden was strong—strong enough that Thomas was certain he'd have finger-shaped bruises on his hips in the morning. The thought stirred something deep inside.

Aiden used him hard and well until Thomas was half-hard again. Then Aiden cried out, dragging Thomas back against him one last time before collapsing on top of him, the heavy weight of him pressing Thomas back down into the mattress.

Aiden's dead weight should have been too much, but it wasn't. It was perfect. So perfect that Thomas started to doze off.

"I'm pretty sure I fell in love with you the day we met," Aiden said out of nowhere.

Thomas closed his eyes, still able to perfectly picture Aiden when he was younger. Hair bleached blond, hoodie up, feet on the table, mad at the world.

Thomas gave a low chuckle. "You were so hostile towards me."

"I was hostile towards everybody, but you were different. It killed me when you sent me away," Aiden admitted.

Was that what Aiden thought? That Thomas had banished him? It wasn't like that. It had never been like that. This was a conversation they should have had a long time ago.

Thomas sighed. "I didn't send you away to punish you. I wanted you to find someone your own age. I wanted you to see that it was just a crush. That you were just going through some kind of…transference. Hero worship, maybe."

Aiden snaked his arms under Thomas's, resting his cheek on his shoulder blade. "Yet, here we are, all these years later. Do you still think it's a crush?"

How could Thomas explain it to Aiden in a way that didn't sound selfish? That didn't sound like an excuse.

Thomas had had a million reasons for refusing him, not the least of which was his age. He'd loved Aiden but not like that. Never like that. He'd been a child. It wasn't until later, when he finished college, that Thomas really saw him as a man. But that hadn't changed anything.

"No, but if I hadn't sent you away, things would have gotten…complicated. I wanted you to be happy. I know having me would have made you happy short-term, but you were a kid. I could never prey on a child that way. Besides, look what happened when you came home. How long did I manage to refuse you?"

"I was twenty-two years old, by then," Aiden said. "I was very much an adult."

"Only in the eyes of the law. I was thirty-six," Thomas reminded him, heart aching. "I was thirty-six with seven children, one of which was you. Do you know what the press would have done to us had we somehow started a relationship? The scandal would have broken us."

"And now?" Aiden asked.

Thomas could feel every deep breath Aiden took, like he was just waiting for Thomas to say something that would break his heart again. "And now, we take the risk. We're adults. All of us. We can all weather the scandal together. Especially if we get ahead of it. But none of that will matter if we don't find this fucking blackmailer."

Thomas's lids fluttered as Aiden pressed a soft kiss to the back of his neck. "I think we should tell people the truth."

Thomas's heart skipped a beat. "Define the truth?"

"The truth about Shane. It will be one less thing for

people to blackmail us over in the future," Aiden reasoned.

"Will it? Or will it just entice reporters to dig deeper into the family?" Thomas asked.

"Not if we let Zane do it. Let Zane write a tell-all about the entire fucked-up Mulvaney family. If people think there's no other skeletons in our closet because Zane told them all, they'll lose interest. People like snooping, but once they find the answers, they get bored and look for a new mystery. Just…just think about it."

Thomas nodded.

Maybe Aiden was right. Maybe the best way to keep the family safe was to expose all of the darkness, all the abuse, the suffering, everything. Once and for all. Compared to his family's past, his relationship with Aiden would barely seem like a blip on the radar.

Thomas just needed his family to be okay. He needed them safe and happy and free. He needed to find this fucking blackmailer so they could put him down…and figure out if he'd really made a hub of serial killers. The thought chilled him more than a little bit. Not just one monster, but a collective of them. They would all have to be dispatched before they revealed too much.

"Go to sleep," Aiden said, slipping free of Thomas's body and rolling them both onto their sides.

Thomas let Aiden manhandle him into little spoon, his fuzzy thigh pressed between Thomas's knees, his arm an iron bar across his waist.

"Shouldn't we clean up first?"

"No," Aiden mumbled, already half-asleep.

Thomas smiled despite himself. Aiden was nothing if not decisive. Thomas loved that about him. He shook his head. He loved everything about him.

EIGHTEEN
AIDEN

Breakfast was organized chaos. Per usual, an army of staff members descended on the house to make breakfast before Thomas dismissed them once more. As soon as the food was set out, Jericho's boys and half the Mulvaneys fell on it like ravenous vultures, piling food onto their plates then disappearing down into the basement. After watching them all pushing and shoving, jockeying for position in line, it occurred to him that maybe Mac and Jericho were right— maybe toddlers *were* the way to go.

Outside was cold and miserable, but inside was toasty warm, making it easy to forget it was still winter. As Aiden helped himself to food, he watched Thomas, who was sitting between Ada and Ari, cutting up strawberries and dropping them into their plates. They snatched them up greedily with their tiny sticky hands and popped the offerings into their mouths. They looked like angels compared to the horde of heathens who'd just demolished a buffet in less time than it took a school of piranha to eat a fish.

Lucas had said they seemed to shoot projectiles from both ends, but he was still about to have a third. It couldn't be all bad. What was a little puke from something that looked like a tiny version of the person you loved? Hell, Archer had puked on Aiden more than once—something they were going to have a very stern talk about now that the truth was out. It couldn't be worse than that.

Lucas and August sat on opposite sides of each child, feeding them eggs and tiny bits of vegetables. Noah sat in Adam's lap at the end of the table, essentially doing the same to him, forking random bites of his own breakfast into his mouth. Archer and Mac were having a conversation amongst themselves by the fireplace. They'd opted for black coffee in lieu of real food. Lola and Calliope were also at the table with Cricket, talking in low tones about something to do with proxy servers. Girls were weird.

When Thomas glanced up and saw Aiden watching him, he smiled. It felt like he'd been kicked in the stomach. He really had loved that man most of his life, from the moment he'd laid eyes on him. Christ. He was so far gone on Thomas. He always had been, but he'd never let himself have this before. This sense of…ownership. Aiden wanted the world to know Thomas belonged to him, something that was less tacky and more permanent than the hickeys he currently sported, peeking out from beneath a pale blue button-down that made his eyes as silver as his hair. Would their kids have Thomas's blue eyes or Aiden's?

He shook the thought away. He was getting far too many ideas watching him with the girls. He took his food and sat opposite Thomas, whose bare foot was suddenly snaking up Aiden's pant leg all while he pretended nothing was happening.

When the plates were empty and Cricket had taken the girls to the nursery, Thomas finally asked, "Did you find anything helpful in the files? Anything that might lead us somewhere other than Shane?"

August shook his head. "No, unfortunately not. I went over the case files, had Calliope run down every person who had so much as touched the case. Even the politicians Shane's mom had used to force the locals into silence. There are no red flags."

Jericho threw down his napkin with a sigh. "I was sure it was going to be Holly's secret love child," Jericho said. "It made perfect sense."

"Yeah, until she didn't have one," Lucas lamented.

August twisted his fingers, something he rarely did as an adult but had done frequently as a child. "I find it hard to believe that someone just randomly stumbled onto Dad's family secret and then sided with Shane, no matter how much of a psychopath this random stranger might be. If it was about money, he would have already outed Dad when he didn't pay, or he would have kidnapped the girls to force his hand…but he didn't. It's almost like he *wants* a confrontation. He wants us to find him. That screams personal and that screams some kind of attachment to Shane."

It was infuriating. If the guy wanted something, why didn't he just make his move already? Had he not anticipated Thomas would tell his family? Had he not anticipated him closing ranks? If he didn't want revenge, what the fuck did he want?

Aiden sighed. "It's staring us right in the face but, somehow, we still can't see it."

Thomas took a sip of his orange juice, then glanced down the table to Calliope. "You didn't manage to find anything on any additional family Shane may have had?"

She gave him a pained look. "Now that we know his stepbrother is definitely in Japan and his sisters are living their best suburban mom life on the opposite side of the country, I'm out of options. I mean, short of a DNA sample that I could run through a database that may or may not pinpoint some random secret family members we don't know about, Shane's family is a dead end. Literally."

Like Jericho, Aiden had been banking on it being Shane's secret child. It made the most sense. Well, it made no sense, really, in the grand scheme of things, but it did in the fucked-up mind of a psychopath. And nobody knew psychopaths better than the Mulvaneys. All roads had led to Shane.

Aiden had seen first-hand how his brainwashing could leave someone with mixed feelings about what had happened to them. While Thomas would never paint Shane as a hero, he still frequently made excuses for his actions and worked hard to put the blame on them both equally. As if they'd both been in the wrong. It wasn't hard to imagine Holly spinning a fairy tale for her baby to try to fool herself. Denial like that was common.

Aiden was temporarily pulled away from his thoughts

when Asa and Zane appeared, both of them looking smug enough for everybody at the table to know exactly what had kept them from breakfast.

Atticus rolled his eyes. "Where's your doppelgänger?"

"Avi?" Asa asked reflexively.

"No, your other twin brother," Atticus quipped.

Aiden felt his whole body go hot then cold as the answer he'd been searching for crashed into him like a big yellow school bus. Jesus. He was right, it was staring them in the face the whole goddamn time. "It's the other one."

They all turned to stare at him, their confused expressions almost comically similar. "What?" Mac asked.

"It's the other one," Aiden said again, nodding as he got more confident that he was correct. "We were right. Well, not a hundred percent right. Right theory, wrong fucking person. It was the fucking other one."

"What is he babbling about?" Avi asked, entering the room with Felix.

"He does this," Lola said with a wave of her hand. "He's had some kind of epiphany but you're just gonna have to let him talk it out."

Aiden was right. He knew he was fucking right. "Shane. Fucking Shane. We were right, but we were wrong."

Lola twisted in her chair, giving him a dubious look. "Are you trying to say that Shane had a twin or something because that's a little too fucking soap opera if I'm being honest."

Aiden huffed out a breath through his nose, trying to gather his patience and his thoughts so he could explain it to them. "No. Not another Shane. Another Holly."

"Holly had a twin?" Felix asked, looking at the others like it was news to him.

"Another victim," Thomas said, finally seeming to catch on.

"Yes," Aiden said, a little too triumphantly considering it was just a theory. "There was another girl who reported being raped by Shane after Holly, right?"

Thomas looked dumbstruck. "It was the reason I broke things off with him. How could I forget about her?"

"Because of the fucking handle on the internet. AlwaysChristmas equaled Holly, but what if it didn't? What if it's just a significant date to this guy? Something that mattered only to him? We had the right concept, we just had the wrong victim."

"Well, shit," Jericho said. "Do you know the girl's name?"

Thomas frowned. "No. The school protected her identity because she was a minor. I don't know if she ever went to the police."

Aiden made a frustrated noise. "Fuck. I cannot believe we don't have her name."

"I do," Lucas said. "At least, I think I do. When I was going through the boxes last night, aside from this guy's hatred of Thomas and women in general, I was getting a T name."

"That's about as helpful as a psychic hotline," Asa said, earning a dark glare from August.

Lucas sighed. "Terry? Tara, maybe?"

Thomas rocketed forward. "Theresa? Could her name

have been Theresa?"

Lucas nodded. "Yeah, definitely."

"Shane was constantly staring at this girl on the quad. Whenever I would ask about it, he would just say she was some girl he'd been asked to tutor but had refused. It always bothered me how he never stopped…tracking her with his eyes."

"Do you know her last name?" Calliope asked.

"No, but I'd probably recognize a photo," Thomas said. To Calliope, he asked, "Is it enough?"

"In the hands of a lesser man, no. But for me, definitely." She stood, chucking Aiden under the chin as she passed. "Let's go see if you're right."

They all filed down to the war room, falling into whatever chair they came into contact with first. Except Aiden. He couldn't sit down. He needed to move, needed to do something with the adrenaline coursing through him. Thomas gave him a worried look but said nothing, opting to sit beside Calliope as she worked.

Aiden passed behind her, glancing at the screen, but it was all hieroglyphics to him. There was no way anybody would understand the streams of code flying past but Calliope, so he continued his pacing. After about fifteen minutes, he couldn't stop himself from asking, "Did you find anything?"

"If I had, don't you think I would have said something?" she chided. "I'm using the same data frame as I did to pull Holly's police report, but I'm not getting anything for a Theresa."

Aiden hit the table with his fist. "Shit."

Thomas gave him a patient look. "She may not have gone to the cops. She may have just reported it to the school. That's what Holly tried first, too. But the school protected him. Just like people always did, I guess."

"I won't have access to those files," Calliope said, tapping her nails on the desk.

"What about yearbook photos?" Lola asked. "If the school is still open, most of them have digitized and archived their old yearbooks. Surely, you could hack into a school's system."

"Of course, I can," Calliope said, giving Lola a smile that they most definitely didn't have time for in Aiden's mind.

"Flirt later," Aiden muttered.

"Boy, if you don't sit down and stop pacing, I'm going to tie you to a chair," Lola said. "And I *will* do it."

Aiden opened his mouth to speak, but Lola raised a brow. Whatever, it wasn't worth arguing over. He sat in the chair closest to him, folding his arms across his chest as he waited impatiently.

Calliope's nails on the keys were usually a soothing sound to Aiden, like shit was getting done, but right now it was nails on a chalkboard, working over every nerve ending until he wanted to fucking scream. He just needed a name to put with the face of this motherfucker so he could kill him once and for all.

"We've got three Theresas in the school during that time," Calliope finally said, throwing up three photos of girls that looked far too young to ever be mothers. Do you know which one she is? Do you have anything that might help us?"

"The second photo," Thomas said, voice dull.

It was likely jarring for him to see how young they'd all been when Shane had happened to them. It was jarring for Aiden. It made him want to go back somehow and protect Thomas from all of it. Even if it meant they never would have met.

Calliope nodded. "We have a winner. Theresa Jeffries."

"What do we know about her?" Asa asked.

"She didn't finish high school. She's listed on the birth certificate as the mother of Nathan Jeffries. Father unknown. The time frame adds up, age wise. Definitely could be Shane's kid."

"Do we know anything else? Can you find anything on this Nathan character?" Avi asked.

Calliope typed for what seemed like another hundred years. "Police reports," she said, sounding sad. "CPS was called to her house several times for child neglect and endangerment. Seems she had a drug problem. The boy was removed from her care when he was eleven on…"

"On…" Aiden snapped.

"On Christmas day."

"Always Christmas!" Avi yelled like it was the final answer on a quiz show.

Aiden's tension left him in a whoosh as he fist-pumped mentally. He'd been right. This had to be it. It couldn't all be a coincidence.

"So, we have an abused and traumatized child with

possible genetic markers for psychopathy undergoing years of chronic abuse before losing his abusive mother to go into a foster system which probably only abused him further," Lucas said. "I'm going to say this is our guy."

Thomas clasped his hands together. "Tell me the system didn't lose track of him, Calliope."

Calliope went back to her lightning-speed typing. "Nathan Jeffries was in and out of the system, managed to finish high school—good for him—did two years of community college before he dropped out to…start his own business."

"Doing what?" Mac asked.

Calliope sat back in her chair. "Construction."

"Ah, yes, the preferred cover of both the mob and killer clowns," Avi said.

"So, this is our guy, right?" Adam said. "Now we can go fucking kill this guy?"

"But how do we know for sure?" Thomas asked.

"Why don't I just ask him?" Calliope said.

"You want to just tell this guy we're onto him?" Noah asked.

Adam nodded. "Yeah, doesn't that seem counterintuitive to us murdering this dude?"

"He wants this confrontation," Calliope said. "I get it now. It's all been a game. Some culmination of a master plan. Possibly even a suicide mission. He wants to see Thomas face to face. Let's just invite him for a sit down."

Aiden snorted. "You think I'm sending Tommy in to face down a serial killer alone? Besides, what if you're wrong about his motives and you tip him off?"

"What if *you're* wrong and he's not the right guy?" Felix asked. "Then we just all but admitted to a stranger who might also have beef with Dad that the family is being blackmailed."

"What if you're right and he kills us all?" Adam offered.

"Send it as Thomas but don't frame it about the blackmail," Zane said. "Just tell him that you have information about his birth father and want to meet. If he's the guy, he'll know what it's really about. If he's not, it seems like a harmless enough message."

"We're not wrong," Aiden said. "Lets just go fucking kill this guy."

Calliope looked at Thomas. "What do you want to do, boss?"

Thomas sighed, leaning back in his chair, fingers steepled. When he looked at Aiden, he shook his head. It was a bad idea.

Thomas gave Aiden an apologetic smile. "Send the message."

SLOTH SLOTH
TH SLOTH SLOTH S
SLOTH SLOTH S
SLOTH SLOTH S
SLOTH SL
TH SLOTH SL
SL

NINETEEN
THOMAS

Thomas hadn't been expecting an expedient reply from the blackmailer, but as the hours stretched with no response, he started to think they had it all wrong. The others moved about the house, hovering near enough to respond immediately to any news. But Aiden stayed glued to Thomas's side as if Jeffries might appear like the boogeyman and snatch him away.

"I'm fine, you know," Thomas told him when he followed him into the kitchen.

"I know," Aiden said, a little defensively. "I just want to be near you."

Thomas turned on him, backing him into the counter. "We were very near each other just a few hours ago."

Aiden hopped onto the counter, opening his legs and drawing Thomas forward. "I just want to make sure you're okay. You know…mentally."

Thomas gave a small laugh. "I'm as okay as I've ever been."

"Not a ringing endorsement," Aiden said, kissing his

forehead.

Thomas tipped his head up, running his hands along Aiden's jean-clad thighs, sighing when Aiden kissed one cheek and then the other, then his chin, his nose, and finally his lips. Nothing soothed like Aiden's touch.

"Oh, God," Noah yelped, entering the kitchen then promptly turning away as if he'd caught them naked. "This will never not be weird."

"Noah," Thomas said patiently. "We're just standing here. It's not quite the scandal you think it is."

"Talk to me when you find *your* brother kissing your father," Noah said, flushing to the tips of his ears.

"Former brother," Aiden teased. "Soon to be your stepfather."

"Affection, gross," Adam said, entering the kitchen, hooking a brow upwards when he saw Aiden perched on the counter, Thomas between his knees. "Are we interrupting something?"

Only a conversation Thomas feared he and Aiden would be fielding for the rest of their lives. They would have to publicly address it eventually, but they'd jump off that bridge if they survived this one last trial.

Before Thomas could reassure him that he was not, in fact, interrupting something, Calliope made a strange noise from the living room like someone had just stepped on a cat's tail, then called out, "He responded. He responded."

It was a mad dash to the war room with everyone doing their best to get there first. Nobody even tried for seats, all of them standing as Calliope double clicked on the message.

Dear Thomas,

Looks like you were as smart as my father thought you were. You're right. I think it's time we meet. How about at the lake house? Where it all began…or ended, I suppose. Either way, it has a nice symmetry to it. I'd tell you to come alone, but I know you won't. So, bring who you like. I do so love the attention.

Nathan McAvoy

Thomas stared at the message, a thousand questions running through his head at once.

"I thought the lake house blew up," Adam said.

"I thought his last name was Jeffries," Arsen added, confused.

"I thought you guys were smart enough to recognize a trap when you see one, so clearly we're all wrong," Calliope barked, fuming. "Fuck this guy."

While Thomas agreed with the sentiment, it wasn't conducive to fixing the problem. His insides shook at just the thought of setting foot on that property again. "I had the remains of the lake house razed and another home built there. But I could never bring myself to sell it. It's just a rental property now."

"Who's renting it?" Noah asked.

Calliope worked her keyboard magic, then shook her head. It's empty. It's listed as for rent."

"Using his father's last name in the message is a bold

move," Asa said. "I don't like it. It screams end game."

Thomas had picked up on that, too. Blackmailers—especially ones who appeared to also moonlight as serial killers—didn't sign their name to things. Nathan had a plan and they were playing into it somehow.

Avi nodded. "This is a suicide mission."

"But for him or us?" Felix asked.

"I think I should go alone," Thomas said. "It's safer for you all."

His sons began to angrily talk over each other until Thomas had no idea what they were saying. It was only when a loud whistle shrieked through the space that they all fell quiet, looking at Calliope with wide eyes, August particularly irritated.

"One at a time. Arguing helps nobody," Calliope instructed.

"There's no way he's going alone," Noah said.

Before Thomas could respond, Aiden was nodding. "Yeah, no, that's not even remotely a possibility." He pointed a finger at Thomas. "I'll tie you to a fucking chair first."

Thomas didn't bother to argue. There was no point. He might have been able to convince them one on one, but as a group, he was clearly outnumbered.

"Well, we can't all roll up on this lake house, twenty plus men deep. It will trigger whatever final sequence this guy has planned, and like he said, he loves an audience," Mac said.

"If we could just figure out his motive, maybe we'd know

how to prepare," Noah muttered.

"He wants to put on a show," Lucas said. "This whole thing has been...performative. He's trying to prove something, either to you or himself. He's a narcissist. He wants you to know he's smarter than you are. He wants to show off. If he is a serial killer, as Calliope expects, he's going to want to show Thomas what he's done."

"But why?" Zane asked. "Why go through all of this just to confess? He has to know he's not getting out of this alive."

Lucas shrugged. "Like Avi said, it's a suicide mission. There's a very good chance he's going to have an exit strategy. The kind that involves bodies. Mostly ours."

"How would he accomplish that?" Zane asked.

"Blow us all up in the same house his dad died in?" Archer suggested. "Symmetry, remember?"

Was that really Nathan's end game? If so, Thomas couldn't, in good conscience, let them go with him. He wouldn't allow his family to die for him. That just wasn't going to happen. Even if he had to sneak off when they weren't looking. He just had to find a way to slip free of Aiden.

Noah shook his head. "How do we combat dynamite? It doesn't seem like the kind of thing we'd have just lying around."

"C4 most likely," Archer said offhand. "TNT is far too unstable."

Noah frowned. "It alarms me that you know that off the top of your head. And it still doesn't answer my question."

"Depends on how he plans to detonate said bomb," August said. "If he's wearing it and holding a trigger, we have a better chance of surviving the blast, but fewer chances of stopping it."

"Is that what you would do?" Felix asked August. "'Cause I'd plant the explosives around the house at key joists to cause a collapse and I'd detonate with a cell phone, something remote on the off chance I make it out."

"Felix has a point," Asa said. "If he wants to take us with him, he's going to leave that house as rubble."

"A cell phone to detonate would be ideal," Archer said. "Easy fix."

"How so?" Arsen asked.

"Signal jammer," Mac said. "If he plans on using a cell phone, it would block the call until we could disarm the bomb, supposing there is one."

"Who knows how to disarm a bomb?" Atticus asked. "Dad taught us a lot of things but not explosives."

"I can do it," Mac said. "I'm trained in explosive ordnance disposal. Building and deactivating bombs is part of my military training. It's also one of the many skills we teach at the Watch."

"I'm starting to think the Watch isn't a real place, like Hogwarts, or Dr. X's academy for mutants," Adam said. "Tell the truth, you're just living in the desert getting high all the time and spinning these elaborate fairy tales about psychopathic Gen Zs."

"Don't be jealous," Archer said, blowing him a kiss. "You can come visit whenever you want."

"He's just sad he didn't get his owl," Noah said, patting Adam on the head like a puppy.

Thomas would never get over the way Noah handled his son. Of all of them, Adam had been the hardest. He was the baby, the spoiled one. The one who had a hair trigger and the least control of his murderous impulses. Yet, Noah treated him like a dog who'd been beaten, combating his blustering by reacting to him like he was an adorable infant.

Adam was like a German Shepherd that had traded in dog fighting for duckie pajamas and flower crowns. Noah had just…quieted something in Adam and Thomas was beyond grateful to him. For that and a million other things he could never fully articulate.

"So, what's the plan then?" Asa said. "And who gets to go? 'Cause I really don't want to miss out on the violence. Lucas said we can try to skin him. Like all of him, like Fukushi Masaichi."

"Who?" Aiden asked, frowning.

"He would skin people of their tattoos when they died then preserve them in a museum," Avi said, barely containing his excitement.

This was the part of the job Thomas hated. Early on, he'd had a certain cruel streak he'd passed on to his children. Not just the need to kill those who were a danger to others, but to punish them in the most heinous ways possible before their deaths. Asa and Avi had taken to it with a relish that Thomas had never been able to quell.

"Yeah, do we draw straws?" Avi said.

"You promised me I'd get to torture this man for going

after our kids," Lucas said. "I'm holding you to it."

Thomas took a deep breath and let it out. He didn't want to endanger any of them. Lucas was right. Thomas could feel it. Nathan Jeffries or McAvoy or whatever he was calling himself was on a suicide mission and he wanted to take at least Thomas with him.

"You can't both walk into a trap," Thomas said to August. "You have children to think of."

"Well, you're not leaving me behind," Lucas said.

August scoffed. "And I'm not letting my husband walk into an ambush alone."

"Okay, then we do it in waves," Thomas said. "I go in alone—"

"No fucking way," Aiden snarled, taking a step towards Thomas.

Thomas raised a hand. "Fine. *We* go in alone. The rest of you can be outside on standby. We will bring the signal jammer because it does seem like a power move to try to take us all out in one go. Once we've subdued our friend, the rest of you can come in and do what you want."

They all looked at each other in confusion.

"You don't want a piece of this guy?" Noah asked. "After the stress and torture he put you through over the last few days?"

Thomas shook his head. He truly didn't. It wasn't that he had any sentimentality towards this man. He didn't. He needed to be put down. But all the fear, all the grief, all the secrets and lies he'd lived with for the last twenty plus years…that was all Thomas. He'd tortured himself. That had nothing to do with this Nathan person or even Shane.

Thomas had been running from a ghost for so long, he didn't even realize nobody was chasing him anymore. He was tired of running. He was tired of it. He just wanted… peace.

Finally, he said, "No. I'm done with Shane. I'm done with the bitterness. Nathan Jeffries went after the children. He likely is a serial killer. He needs to be put down. But he also forced me to finally deal with the ghosts of my past, with my family's secrets. It brought all of you home." He looked at Aiden, taking his hand and squeezing it. "It brought Aiden home. This needed to happen, but now, it needs to end. So, let's go end it."

TWENTY
AIDEN

Aiden kept a close eye on Thomas the whole drive to the lake house. He was looking for some sense of strain or anguish—some semblance of the fear he'd displayed less than a week ago. But there was nothing. Thomas was fine. Eerily calm, even. It scared Aiden. Like Thomas had made peace with dying or something. He didn't like it.

"Tell me you're not going to do something crazy," Aiden pleaded.

Thomas looked over at him and smiled. "Like meet a serial killer in the house where he thinks I killed his father?"

"Like sacrifice yourself for your children," Aiden said, not finding any of this fucking funny.

"I'm not suicidal, Aiden. I'm just…at peace with whatever happens next."

Aiden's heart plummeted into his shoes. What the fuck did that mean? Aiden was not at peace. He would never be at peace while this piece of shit was threatening his family, his future husband, the future father of their children. He needed to know Thomas wasn't going into this willing to die.

"Fuck that," Aiden said. "Fuck all of that. I don't want you at peace. I want you ready to fight."

Thomas took Aiden's hand, threading their fingers together. "I'm not that self-sacrificing. I just have faith that the entire Mulvaney family versus one mediocre serial killer is a fight already won. He's lost his power over me and doesn't even realize it."

Why was he so fucking zen about this? Aiden's insides were shaking. In all his life, he'd never been so scared. He couldn't lose Thomas. Not when the fucking universe had taken twenty fucking years to finally let him have him.

"I need you to take this seriously," Aiden said as they pulled into the long curving driveway that led to the home looming in the distance like something out of a gothic novel.

Thomas gave him a patient look that was so much like the old Thomas he was tempted to slap him. "It's going to be okay, Aiden. I promise."

This was a stupid fucking plan. The stupidest. How could any of this be okay? They should have just had Mac take the dude out with a rifle. What were they trying to prove? Why did they need to torture everyone? To prove a point? They should have just shot him and been done with it.

"You realize you're talking out loud, right?" Thomas said, amused but now also looking a little concerned.

What was wrong with him? He didn't fold under pressure like this. He was the one everyone came to when they needed help, when they needed someone killed. He didn't freak out like this.

"Take a deep breath," Thomas encouraged, still frustratingly calm.

Aiden glowered at him but did as he asked. It didn't help a lot but his heart was no longer slamming against the walls of his chest. It was fine. It was all going to be fine. They were not going to get blown up into tiny little bits. The rest of the Mulvaneys were parking nearby, then cutting through the woods on foot per Thomas's instructions. They didn't want to spook this Jeffries guy.

Aiden rolled to a stop, putting the car in park and scanning their surroundings. They were in the middle of nowhere. There wasn't another soul for miles. Everything was so…still. Even the trees weren't swaying. It all just felt so ominous. He couldn't shake the feeling something bad was going to happen.

There was a late model Ford F-350 in the driveway. When they approached it, Aiden put his hand on the hood. It was cold. Jeffries had been there for some time. He wasn't even attempting to hide his presence.

Hide it from who? he asked himself. There wasn't a soul around. There was no reason to hide his vehicle. Or even his logo on the side. The man was in construction, and that probably gave him all the credibility he needed to be almost anywhere. It had likely helped when stalking his victims.

They approached the house, Aiden peering into the panes of glass on either side of the door to make sure no surprises awaited on the other side. If Jeffries was suicidal, there could be a shotgun or something pointed right at them. But there was nothing. Everything inside seemed cast in shadow, even though there was plenty of light in the sky.

Aiden entered first, keeping Thomas behind him. From the foyer, there was a clear view to a large sitting room with floor-to-ceiling windows, much like the house Thomas and Aiden had stayed at earlier in the week.

But unlike that house, someone had painstakingly blacked out those windows with paper that cast strange shadows on the wall as the sun began to set. They had also pushed all the furniture against the walls, leaving a big empty space in the center. Thomas stopped short. Is this what it had looked like when Shane killed his family?

Lights blazed on all at once, causing them both to lift their hands, blinking rapidly. They weren't particularly bright but surprising in the swirl of shadows. There was a single chair in the center of that room, facing the wall of windows. Aiden could just make out the arms on either side of the chair. One of which dangled a revolver from his limp hand.

"Well, don't just stand there," the man said, his voice sounding almost…frail. Aiden frowned. He and Jeffries had to be around the same age, but he sounded…weak. "You've come all this way. Come on in."

Aiden crept closer, scanning his surroundings, holding Thomas's hand but doing his best to keep him somewhat shielded with his body.

"We're alone," Jeffries assured him. "I am armed, though," he said, holding the gun up so they could see he wasn't bluffing. I assume you are, too."

They were armed. Could Aiden just draw his weapon and

fire a bullet into the man's head?

"You could shoot me. Of course, you could," he said, like he was reading Aiden's mind. A shriek sounded faintly from somewhere in the other man's vicinity and then a phone screen was held up showing a girl bleeding and screaming in what looked like a pine box. Jesus, had he buried someone alive? "But then that poor girl I left out there… somewhere…bleeding in the woods will likely run out of air before you find her. The wilderness is…" He waved a hand. "Vast."

Was he bluffing? Christ, this just got ten times more complicated. Once they stepped fully into the room, they got their first real glimpse of what it was that lined the walls. Pictures. Women screaming. Women bleeding. Women dying. Hundreds of them. On the sofa beneath those photos were dozens of tools, cast red from blood or rust. There were also sealed boxes on the floor.

"What the hell is this?" Aiden asked, his pulse pounding in his throat.

The man gave a wheezing laugh. "My work. Artists like to show their work. I'm quite proud of it. I've been at it for quite some time, as you can see."

They finally came to stand in front of the man for the first time and Aiden saw Thomas stiffen. He didn't blame him. He was what Aiden imagined Shane would have looked like had he been allowed to grow older.

Thomas stumbled back a few steps, which made Jeffries smile. "Have a seat," he said, pointing to the couch pressed against the window directly in front of him. "Let's chat."

Thomas didn't move, just stared. Aiden could feel his palm dampen as he held it. He squeezed it, hoping to keep him from sliding into a full-on panic attack. All that false bravado in the car had just been for Aiden's benefit. He knew it.

Jeffries gave him a frigid smile. "Uncanny, isn't it? My mom hated it. Would tell me every day that I looked just like him. Like the monster who attacked her, impregnated her, ruined her whole life just like me." When nobody responded, he shouted, "Sit down!" Then, in a softer tone, "Don't be impolite."

They did as he asked, sinking down onto the sofa. Doing so let Aiden see him better. There was something wrong with him. His skin had a strange almost grayish cast to it. His eyes looked hollow. The man was sick.

"Your mother was likely suffering from trauma," Thomas said softly.

"Trauma! She was suffering from trauma? She suffered through one assault from a boy she was crushing on and I paid for it every single fucking day. Every day. Beaten. Burned. Hell, one time she stabbed me. That was the day they took me away from her for good. But just when I thought she was the worst, then came the men. My 'foster fathers.' She was the real fucking monster. That's why she was my first victim. I don't think anybody even knows she's dead. By then, she was just another junkie whore."

Christ. This guy was getting it all out. This was his final fucking confession before he did something drastic. "And because of that, you...what? Are somehow justifying all this?" Aiden asked, sweeping his hand around the room.

"No need to be judgey. We're all killers here. Aren't we, Thomas?" Jeffries said. "Sometimes, we let others kill for us, but, sometimes, we do it ourselves. Sometimes, we set up the ones we love to kill for us and then shove a shotgun under their chin and blow their faces off."

"I didn't kill your father. He killed my family and then he killed himself," Thomas said. "He was sick. He needed help. Your grandmother could have helped him—"

Jeffries brandished the gun, silencing him. "I'm sure that's what you told the police. I might have even believed it, if you hadn't then gone on to become a killer yourself. That was when I realized the truth. He killed your family for you and you murdered him to keep it quiet. You wanted your family out of the way so you could take all that money for yourself."

"None of that's true. We were little kids. Your father was sick. He was sick and he killed my family and when I wouldn't kill his, he killed himself. It's as sad and tragic as it is simple," Thomas said.

Jeffries snickered. "Are you telling me your sons don't kill for you?"

"No, I'm not saying that," Thomas said. "But some people—people like you—are too dangerous to live and need to be put down. My sons do that."

Jeffries sneered. "Who died and made you judge, jury, and executioner? Who are you to say who deserves to live and die? The high and mighty Thomas Mulvaney can pluck people from this world at will—people who do the same thing he does. Don't you see what a fucking hypocrite you are?"

Thomas shook his head. "We are not the same. You kill for sport. I kill for necessity. I kill to make sure people like you can't do…this." He waved his hand around.

"We're not that different, you and I," Jeffries assured him. "You've just found a way to transfer your homicidal impulses onto your children and make it seem justified. It appears my father did the same. Too bad he never got to see it."

"We're very different," Aiden said. "You're slaughtering innocent women. We're slaughtering men like you."

Jeffries scoffed. "There are no 'innocent' women," he said. "They're all whores and liars who constantly play the victim. I'm the one doing the public service. Consider it population control."

"Is this why you brought us here? To show off your collection? Your trophies," Aiden asked.

Jeffries smirked. "It's not the only reason, no."

"So, this is some kind of suicide mission then? You don't look well," Aiden said.

Jeffries waved the gun around. "Good eye. I'm dying. Rare genetic disorder. Also inherited from my mother. Nothing good ever came of that bitch, I swear it."

Aiden stared intently at the phone in his lap. So, they had been right. They knew his next move. "So what? You wanted to show us your collection before you blew the three of us up?"

"No, I wanted to tell you that I'm leaving a legacy of my

own. I have my own sons, trained to kill, just like yours. And they're out there, right now, hunting. Maybe hunting your sons."

"If they're stupid enough to come after my sons, they'll get the same thing you'll get. A slow, agonizing death," Thomas growled.

Jeffries studied him then looked at Aiden. "But this one...this one is special, no? This one you definitely don't view as a son. Is he important to you?"

"This isn't about him," Thomas said, swallowing hard.

"Let's not," Jeffries said, hitting the call button on the cell phone. Aiden's blood rushed in his ears when nothing happened. Thank fuck, the signal jammer was doing its job. For now. Jeffries looked up, irritated. "How clever."

With that, he lifted the gun and fired a shot directly into Aiden's chest. It wasn't the first time Aiden had been shot, but he didn't remember much of it. He didn't remember the searing pain or the feeling like he couldn't breathe.

"Aiden!" Thomas shouted.

Aiden felt himself sliding off the sofa just as the window fractured beside them. He heard it more than he saw it. There was a scream, then the gun in Jeffries's hand clattered to the floor next to him, but Aiden couldn't move. He could do nothing but lie there.

He heard everything but couldn't see it. The door bursting open, his brothers' voices.

Aiden fought to keep his eyes open. There was blood everywhere. Christ, this hurt. Someone rolled him onto his back. Archer. He ripped his shirt open, grinning down at him like an idiot, slapping the bullet proof vest right over where the bullet struck. "Hurts like a motherfucker, don't it? Wait 'til you see the bruise you're gonna have."

"I can't breathe," Aiden said. "What's happening?"

"Mac shot the gun out of his hand like something out of an old western," Archer said, looking at someone—he assumed Mac—in the distance. "That bullet knocked the wind out of you. It'll come back in a minute, just ride it out."

"How?" Aiden wheezed. "The windows…"

"We brought all the toys, including our x-ray vision," Noah said, dropping down beside him. "It was so fucking badass. I told you to wear the vest." With that, he was gone once more.

Aiden assumed he was talking about the thermal imager. It wasn't the first time they'd used it. Aiden sucked in a huge breath as his lungs finally stopped seizing. Sitting up, he looked for Thomas, who stood, hands in his pockets as Asa and Avi trussed Jeffries up by his hands, one of which was missing three fingers and a large chunk of palm.

Once he was secured, Thomas strolled forward, stopping inches from the man, giving him a chilling smile. "Now, shall we get started?"

Goddamn, that man was sexy.

TWENTY-ONE
THOMAS

"I told you we weren't that different," Jeffries said, tone smug even as he heaved pained breaths.

"This dude looks like shit," Avi said, disappointed. "Is he even going to survive torture?"

Jeffries made a disgusting sound at the back of his throat. "You brought your whole family to torture me. Tell me again how we're nothing alike."

Thomas shook his head. "No. I'm not wasting my breath on arguments I'll never win. So, how about we turn our attention to the girl you have buried out in the woods somewhere. Tell me where she is, and if she's safe, I won't let my sons skin you alive."

"Ah, man," Avi said, sounding like a kicked puppy.

"Suck it up, babe," Felix murmured, patting him on the head. "There's plenty of time to skin someone later."

Jeffries looked at them all like they were the crazy ones. Thomas supposed they were. He glanced around the room at his children, both patiently and impatiently waiting to find out if they got to torture a man before they killed him. Perhaps Thomas should have been horrified. Disgusted, even. But he wasn't. He was proud of his children, his family. They were everything he'd hoped they'd be and more. And looking at someone like Jeffries just drove home for Thomas the life that might have awaited them had he never found them.

The thought left a pit in his stomach. He couldn't bear the idea of losing a single one of them. He looked at Aiden, still rubbing the bruise on his chest. Jeffries could have shot him in the head. He could have killed him. If he had, this would have gone much differently for Jeffries. It would have been Thomas holding the scalpel.

But Aiden was fine. He was right there. Healthy. Perfect. His. He turned his attention back to Jeffries, who glared at him.

"Do I need to ask again?" Thomas pressed, boredom seeping into his tone.

"Fuck you," Jeffries spit, his ashen skin turning an even more unflattering shade of gray.

"Fuck this guy," Adam said, searching Jeffries for the phone he'd shown Thomas and Aiden when they'd entered. He found it lying on the floor. A different phone from the one he'd planned on using as a detonator. That one was safely out of reach...of anyone. At least until Mac and Archer disarmed the bomb. Once they found the bomb.

Adam picked up the phone, pointing it at Jeffries's face, then tossed it to Noah. "Look for anything that might help us pinpoint where she is."

Thomas bit back a smile as Noah cocked his head, leveling a flat stare at Adam. "A please would be nice."

Adam's eyes went wide and he gave Noah an exasperated look. Noah stood firm. Adam's shoulders slumped. "Please? Please, would you look for anything that could help us save a girl's life?"

Noah flushed, muttering, "Like you even care about some girl's life."

Asa snagged the phone from Noah's hands, playing with it for about sixty seconds before giving a triumphant cry. "I fucking knew it. That video is months old. The sick fuck just wanted you to hear him out and he knew this would be a way to hold your attention."

"How did you know it was old?" Lucas asked.

Asa sneered at Jeffries. "Look at him. You think he could subdue anyone? He doesn't look like he could hold down a full meal, much less a fully grown woman."

Well, that did simplify the task at hand somewhat.

"Excellent. Shall we get on with it?" Lucas asked, wandering along the row of tools laid out on the sofa. He stopped, picking up a tool with a sturdy handle and a lethal-looking spike. An ice pick or an awl maybe.

Lucas stopped before Jeffries, dragging the end of the tool along the squishy underside of his chin. It was clear he'd lost weight, leaving some sagging behind. Thomas might have felt sorry for him if he wasn't surrounded by his victims, if he hadn't gone after his grandchildren, if he hadn't shot the love of his life.

"You. You went after my children," Lucas said.

"You're the psychic, right?" Jeffries said with a pained laugh. "Didn't you used to be in the FBI? You know, before they branded you a lunatic?" If he was hoping to strike a nerve in Lucas, he was in for a surprise. Jeffries leaned in, swaying on his tiptoes. "Let me ask you. If you touched me right now, could you see every girl I murdered? Could you hear their screams, smell their blood, could you feel how much I fucking loved every second of it?"

"You went after my *children*," Lucas said again, enunciating every word, voice eerily calm.

Drool leaked from Jeffries's mouth as he said, "All I did was give them a little gift. You should be thanking me. I could have gutted the little brats."

Lucas drove the tool into the fleshy part of the man's jaw, piercing his tongue and lodging it into his soft palate. He began to make a sickening rattling sound, like something out of a horror movie.

"Hey, we were gonna skin him," Avi whined.

Lucas drove the tool deeper, then spit in Jeffries face. "He's not dead. He's just fucking quiet."

He left the tool where it was, walking away. "He's all yours," he said to the twins as he passed.

August came up and hugged Lucas from behind. "Feel better, my love?"

"I'll feel better when he's dead," Lucas confirmed but gripped the hands around his waist briefly as if to assure him he was okay.

"That's our cue, right?" Asa asked. "Shall we take it from here?"

Atticus grimaced. "I hate this part."

Zane shuddered. "Me too."

"Oh," August said, as if remembering something. "Here."

He handed Zane a set of ear plugs. He gazed at August like he'd given him a kidney. It was rare for him to consider the needs of others, rarer still for him to offer to accommodate those needs. Thomas smiled. His boys were nothing like Jeffries or his…sons as he'd called them.

The boys stood around as Avi and Asa squabbled over what tool to use, how to approach the task, and whether he'd survive long enough for them to enjoy it. Thomas left them to it, finally going to sit beside Aiden, who was slumped into the couch. Thomas brushed his hair from his eyes. He was sweating. "Are you alright?"

"Yeah, I'm fine," Aiden said. "Just having a rough day. Are you okay?"

"I'm not the one who got shot," Thomas reminded him, staring at the bullet lodged in Aiden's vest, imagining the worst.

"The Kevlar did its job, Tommy."

Thomas tried to ignore Avi when he said, "Who gets to start?"

"I'm older," Asa reminded.

"By, like, minutes at best," Avi shot back. "Besides, it was my idea."

Thomas had half a mind to snap at them, tell them to get it together, but before he could say anything, Felix stepped between them, his voice soothing. "Why don't you just do it at the same time. There are two sides of him."

"You're right, kitten," Avi said. "He's always the voice of reason." He turned to Asa. "Should we take the ice pick out of his mouth?"

"No," Aiden said. "He wants to talk. He'll use his last rattling breath to brag about his kills. No matter how much you torture him, he still thinks he's won. He had some grand idea that he was going to go out in some kind of blaze of glory, leave bits of files and photos of dead girls like confetti, create some grand mystery of who killed Thomas Mulvaney and why."

Thomas smiled. Aiden really could read people.

"Can we do it fast, then?" Noah said. "The weird gurgling sound he's making is kind of making me want to barf."

"No," Avi said. "We're going to savor this. Think we could get his skin off in one solid piece?"

"And do what with it?" Felix asked, frowning.

"Yeah, you're not bringing it home," Zane said, pointing a finger in Asa's face.

Asa kissed Zane's cheek. "Easy, Lois, nobody wants to take this guy's skin home. Look at it. It's not even a good color. Besides, like Felix said, what would we even do with it? We're not into arts and crafts like Ed Gein. We just like to try new things."

"Is this what they do at every job?" Thomas asked Felix and Zane.

"Yeah," they said in unison.

"No wonder they always take so much time getting home," Thomas muttered, shaking his head. To Aiden, he said, "I told you he was no match for the Mulvaneys."

"I'll feel better when we're no longer sitting on a fucking powder keg." Aiden winced as Jeffries started emitting a sound like some kind of supernatural creature, letting them know the twins had begun.

Thomas grimaced at the sound of something heavy and wet hitting the floor. "Fuck," Avi whined. "I fucked up already."

"Oh, no," Atticus said, affect flat. "Whatever shall we do."

Jericho chuckled. "Easy, Freckles. Let them have their fun. Why don't you go sit over there? I brought you a granola bar. It's in my bag."

"You treat him like a toddler," Adam said.

"Your boyfriend still has to remind you to say please and thank you, pretty boy, so who's the real toddler?" Jericho shot back.

Adam shot him the bird. Jericho pretended to catch it and stuff it in his pocket. Christ. What the hell was he going to do with these boys?

Archer and Mac appeared from somewhere deep within the house, dirty and sweaty. "So, do you want the good news or bad news?" Mac asked.

"Good?" Thomas said, feeling like neither was going to be encouraging.

"We found the explosives," Archer announced, a huge fake smile on his face.

Thomas's heart sank. "And the bad news?"

"We cannot touch them without blowing us all up in the process." Archer fell back onto the couch dramatically, causing Aiden to list into his side.

"Shit," Aiden muttered. "What do we do, Tommy?"

Thomas looked at Jeffries. Even writhing in pain, his eyes gleamed with triumph. He thought he was going to get his wish. He thought he was going to end up famous one way or another. They either had to alert the bomb squad to the threat or detonate it themselves and give him the show he wanted.

Fuck that. This guy wasn't going to die famous.

"Adam, Jericho, take all of this—the boxes, the tools, all of it—and stow it in the car, everything you can carry. Zane, Felix, get these pictures down, make sure not a single one is left. They're coming with us. Archer, get the tarps out of the back of the truck. We'll need to take him with us and dump him somewhere along the way."

"Dad, what's the plan?" August asked.

Thomas sighed. "We're gonna blow the place ourselves."

"What?"

"We don't have any choice. It's safer than trying to explain why someone broke into our abandoned property and set up explosives around our house, and oh, yeah, they happened to be a serial killer."

"Still, there will be an investigation," Aiden said, looking at Thomas like he was crazy.

Thomas shook his head. "No, there won't be. I'll do what I always do. Call in some favors with Kendrick."

"And say what? Another gas leak?" Asa asked.

Avi nodded. "Yeah, who has that kind of bad luck?"

"We don't have any choice. I refuse to make this shithead famous and we can't take a chance of them starting to put the pieces together. We clean up like we always do, we leave nothing behind. Then after some time has passed, we'll decide if we want to make the real story of my parents' deaths known. But not now, not like this."

"What do we do about the others?" Aiden asked. "His 'sons'?"

"We'll deal with them later. They've been hunting all this time. They're bound to have left some calling cards. We'll dig into Jeffries until we find something." He looked at Jeffries. "And then we'll hunt them down, one by one, and put them down. Just like him."

He snatched the scalpel from Avi and jammed it directly through Jeffries's eye socket. He watched as the man twitched a few times, then sagged.

"Let's get this cleaned up. Clock's ticking."

TWENTY-TWO
AIDEN

Aiden and Thomas were back in the bath, this time with Thomas sitting between Aiden's open legs. There was nothing sexual about it. They were both exhausted. They'd managed to stand under the scalding hot shower just long enough to clean away the dirt and sweat from digging the hole where they'd dumped Jeffries.

They'd been sitting in the tub for the last hour, letting the water grow tepid, then adding more, neither of them in any hurry to leave each others' arms.

Thomas was drifting, his head lulling on Aiden's chest in a way that made him smile. "You were such a badass today," Aiden said, combing fingers through his damp hair. "I've never really seen you in action in the field," he teased.

Thomas snorted. "I didn't do anything."

That wasn't true. Thomas had been in control of that situation from the moment they'd entered. He'd been so calm because he'd already worked through a dozen scenarios in his head before they'd breached the premises. It was impressive. It was hot. Thomas Mulvaney when he was in business mode was a sight to behold.

"You created a plan and an exit strategy for us in ten minutes without giving Jeffries what he wanted. He'll die nameless and faceless. And Calliope will find a way to anonymously make sure the victims didn't die the same way and that their families have some kind of closure. You blew up a fucking house and covered it up with two phone calls. On our terms."

Thomas shook his head. "Yeah, but I had to call in favors with your dad. You know how much I fucking hate that."

"That man is not my father," Aiden said, though not with any particular heat. "Don't call him that."

It wasn't as if Kendrick had ever even attempted to be Aiden's dad. Even as a child, he was never there, far more devoted to his career than his children. Aiden had raised himself and it had been lonely. Until he became a Mulvaney.

"Sorry," Thomas muttered, soothing his hands over Aiden's thighs like an apology.

"It's okay," Aiden assured him. "But what happens now?"

Thomas turned, craning his head back to look up at him. "With what?"

"With us?" Aiden asked.

Thomas studied him for a long moment, like he was trying to gauge what Aiden was really asking. Finally, he said, "Like I said before, you come home...to me. For good." He took Aiden's hands and threaded their fingers together.

Aiden's heart pounded. Those were the words he'd wanted

to hear forever. Thomas had said it the other day, but he'd said a lot of things over the years, had run hot and cold a million times. Some part of Aiden needed more than just words. "And then what…"

Thomas kissed the back of each of Aiden's hands. "And then you marry me."

Aiden sucked in a startled breath. "Are you sure? You know the scandal it's going to cause. We're already going to be dealing with a shit storm if you do decide to tell the truth about your family's deaths."

"I don't give a shit anymore," Thomas said firmly. "I just don't. I am not going to live my life without you. I don't care what the press says, I don't care what the papers say. I'm done putting my life on hold over something that happened when I was a child."

"Okay." Aiden chewed on his lower lip, unsure of what to say next.

Thomas sat up, turning in the tub so the water sloshed over the sides. He was on his knees before Aiden. At first, he thought maybe this was some kind of official proposal, with both of them naked in the bathtub.

Until he grabbed Aiden's face, holding him so he met his gaze. "Can you forgive me?"

Aiden frowned, trying to force his brain to keep up with the shifting conversation. "What?"

"Can you forgive me?" Thomas said again, tearing up.

"For what?" Aiden asked, suddenly lost.

Thomas shook his head. "For everything. For driving you away. For pulling you back in. For using you every time

I had a crisis. For calling you every time I was drunk and alone?"

"I—" Aiden started, only for Thomas to cut him off.

"There's no excuse. None. I had no right to hold your life hostage like that, but I need you to believe me when I say that you've had this hold over me for so long, I don't work without you. When things go wrong, you're the first person I think to call. And I know it wasn't fair to you. It's probably not fair now, after wasting most of your life to ask you to marry me, but I'm asking anyway. Please forgive me. Please marry me. Please let me spend the rest of our lives trying to make up for all the shit I put you through."

Aiden couldn't breathe. How many times had he imagined this conversation? He blinked back tears of his own. "You're right. You did hold me hostage." Thomas's shoulders sagged. Aiden grabbed his face and forced him to look at him. "But not because you called me in the middle of the night or because you were lonely. I told you the other night. I fell in love with you the day I saw you and nobody but you would ever do for me. Even if you hadn't called. Even if you'd banished me and cut me off from the family. I would have still loved you. I would have still waited for you. I'll never stop waiting for you."

Thomas slammed their mouths together in a sloppy kiss, holding Aiden's head with both his hands. They were both crying, both a mess, both clinging to each other while snot ran down their faces. It was hardly romantic. They must have looked ridiculous.

When they finally released each other, Thomas said, "I

need to hear you say you forgive me. If you do, that is."

Aiden sighed, leaning forward to kiss his forehead. "I forgave you the day you told me to come home for good. It doesn't matter how we got here. We're here." He cupped his face. "But if you ever try to leave me, Thomas Mulvaney, I *will* kill you. Slowly. Painfully." He punctuated each word with a kiss on his lips. "Do you copy?"

Thomas smiled, capturing his mouth in a much longer, much filthier kiss, before saying, "Yes, sir."

EPILOGUE
THOMAS

Thomas was still in bed when he heard Aiden enter the room. He wouldn't normally have slept quite so late, but today was his birthday and Aiden had insisted. He stretched, listening to his bones crackle and pop as he watched him approach, hands behind his back and a mischievous look on his face.

Thomas pulled himself up until he reclined on the pillows but made no effort to sit up. "Whacha got there?"

Aiden presented him with a pink bear with hearts stitched onto its stomach and the pads of its feet. Another Care Bear. Thomas laughed, catching it when Aiden tossed it to him, before falling on the bed, laying his head on Thomas's belly.

"Another Care Bear? He's not even born yet and you're already spoiling him," Thomas teased.

"Not a second too soon," Aiden said. "I heard Calliope swearing a blue streak because her laptop doesn't sit right on her belly and she can't wrestle her chair close enough to the desk. He's going to come out with an extensive vocabulary of swear words," Aiden said.

He took the bear from Thomas then pushed it into his face playfully. "Besides, it's not for him, it's for you. From me. For your birthday."

Thomas laughed softly, then leaned down, cupping Aiden's head to lift him for a kiss. "You spoil me."

"Isn't that my job?" Aiden asked.

"Your job is a private investigator," Thomas reminded him.

"It's *pro bono*," Aiden countered. "Is it even a job if you don't get paid?"

When Aiden had come home, he'd brought Lola with him. He'd been unwilling to give up his friend and she was happy to skip town and start a new life, though Thomas suspected that had more to do with Calliope than it did Aiden. The two had been living together since she'd arrived.

It had taken Aiden a couple of months to settle their affairs in Washington and close down the PI practice there. Two long months of Thomas talking to Aiden on FaceTime as he did his best to get his own shit together so they were ready for the inevitable scandal that would be Thomas's and Aiden's official nuptials.

"It's our job to spoil each other," Aiden said. "It was in the vows—"

"No, it wasn't," Thomas reminded.

Aiden ignored him. "It was, I remember. Our vows said I'm going to spoil you and when the baby comes, I'm going to spoil him, too. We both are and you know it."

There was a mini-baby boom in the Mulvaney family over the last few years and Thomas couldn't have been happier.

Lucas and August had a son now, Alastair, and were already discussing having one more. Thomas would have never guessed in a million years that August would be the one who took to fatherhood so well, but he should have. The boy had never failed at a single thing.

Avi and Felix were eagerly anticipating the arrival of their twins. Also boys. Also identical. Lola had graciously agreed to donate her eggs, though not her body. They had hired a surrogate for that. A lovely girl named Genevieve, who was blissfully clueless about the Mulvaneys' secret life of crime.

Asa and Zane said there was no need to have children of their own just yet as they lived with Avi and Felix and were happy to be a second set of hands. Thomas suspected there was more to it than that but didn't look too closely at the relationship between the four. They were all happy and it was really none of his business.

Jericho and Atticus had their hands full with the boys at the shelter next to the shop, but it hadn't stopped them from adopting a four-year-old boy with red hair and freckles named Jett, and a three-year-old boy with brown hair and brown eyes, who they'd renamed Jagger. With the boy's permission, of course.

They hadn't sought out the children, but through some twist of fate, they'd found their way to them anyway. Atticus had insisted on continuing the Mulvaney family naming tradition, but with the twist of all their children having J names like Jericho. It was the best present Atticus could have given Jericho.

Thomas choked up whenever he thought of it. Atticus

had been the one who worried him most. The one who was so fussy and particular and determined to be different from his brothers. Yet, somehow, Jericho had found him and had seen all of Atticus's perceived flaws as attributes. And Thomas had never seen his son so domestic and so content with the messes that came with having two small children.

Mac and Archer were determined to be nothing more than the fun uncles, but Thomas was fine with that. The work they were doing for the Watch was important and, somehow, despite everything Thomas had gotten wrong, the kids there seemed to be thriving.

The government was happy with how the pilot program was working and had even installed a full-time sociologist to study the way the students interacted with each other. Her name was Dr. Sasha Mackey and she said it was fascinating work.

Adam and Noah had finally married in an affair fit for royalty. It had provided a nice distraction after Thomas's book was published, drawing the eye from past family scandals to current family events. While there had been a feeding frenzy after the book went live, reporters lost interest when they realized there was no scoop left.

Especially when the Mulvaneys were willing to feed them a steady diet of weddings, babies, and minor scandals to make it feel like business as usual. Zane had refused to write the book, saying it would only make reporters more curious, not less, thinking that Zane had been coached through the piece. Instead, Thomas had reached out to a world-renowned journalist who just happened to have a child in Project Watchtower. His reputation was impeccable and nobody dared question the book once his name was attached.

Adam and Noah had talked about children, but Noah wasn't sure he'd ever be able to bring himself to do it. The constant stress of worrying something might happen to his child like it did to him would be a near constant strain on his mental health. The boy's scars ran deep. But he was young. They both were. They had plenty of time for babies if they decided they wanted them.

Look at him and Aiden. They were far too old to be raising a child but there they were, waiting for the birth of their son. Calliope had agreed to be their surrogate, though unlike Cricket, she did not provide her eggs. She said she was done parenting kids and if Thomas and Aiden were raising her baby, she'd feel obligated to be more than just Aunt Calliope.

Thomas and Aiden had both understood. Instead, they'd paid for an anonymous donor and fertilized eggs with both their sperm. Three eggs had implanted but only one survived. Their son. Theodore. Theo for short.

Some small part of Thomas had hoped for two, a boy and a girl, like the siblings he'd lost. But real life wasn't like that. And he refused to let any of his children live in the shadow of the Mulvaneys who came before them. Not anymore. Theo would be his own person, even if he was named after his uncle.

"Kendrick asked for a meeting at the end of the week to discuss the project," Aiden said. "Archer asked me to mention it to you since he knows we had plans."

Kendrick. That was how Aiden referred to his father now. No attachment, no anger, no anything. Just Kendrick. In a way, it was the ultimate revenge. Though Thomas's first official meeting with the man after their wedding had been tense, it was Mac and Archer who'd taken the brunt of his fury. But they were used to being yelled at. Angry was his default setting.

"I'll let Noah know to get in contact with him and find a time. I'm not putting off our trip to Bali. It will be our last vacation before diaper duty and formula runs become a thing."

"You sure you don't want to hire a nanny?" Aiden asked again, taking Thomas's hand and playing with his fingers.

"What was the point of retiring if I'm only going to hand over the baby to someone else? Then what will I do all day?"

"I don't know," Aiden said. "What do other retirees do?"

"Move to Florida and die on a golf course. No, thank you. I can take care of Theo and focus on the charity."

"Sorry, I forgot you're a strong independent man," Aiden teased.

Thomas had taken a step back from his company, preferring to work more on his philanthropic goals. The board had appointed a perfectly adequate CEO until Noah was old enough to decide if he wanted to take over those duties himself. But until then, Noah had his hands full coordinating the family's extracurricular activities. There was no shortage of terrible people out there needing to be put down.

Luckily, their network had expanded. Dimitri now worked for them. Jericho's boys, too. It had taken a year for them to hunt down all of Nathan Jeffries's associates, but they'd done it, taking them out one by one, quickly and quietly without anyone knowing there had been numerous active serial killers on the loose for several years, acting as one cohesive unit.

"What are you thinking about?" Aiden asked, turning so he was on his side, eyes falling shut when Thomas combed his fingers through his hair.

He wore it much shorter these days, but he still had the scruffy chin that Thomas couldn't get enough of. "Us. The family. The usual."

"You're getting sentimental in your old age."

Thomas smiled. "I'm just…happy. Aren't you happy?"

Aiden kissed Thomas's stomach. "I can't imagine how I could be happier." He smirked. "Well, I could imagine one way…"

Thomas snorted. "Uh-uh, Casanova. We have too much to do today. We have to deal with that serial predator, meet Lola and Calliope at her doctor's appointment, then we have to swing by school to pick up the girls from Lucas and still be ready for the party tonight by eight. No sex until afterwards."

Aiden huffed, expression adorably pouty. "That's not fair. It's your birthday party. Shouldn't I be able to bed you whenever I want?"

Thomas chuckled. "No, that's on *your* birthday. And only because you never let me throw you a party."

"Yeah, because it gets in the way of me getting you naked," Aiden insisted, sliding his hand up under Thomas's shirt to tease his fingers over his nipples.

"You get me naked almost every day," Thomas reminded, batting his hand away.

"Yeah, *almost*," Aiden lamented. "How am I supposed to live under these oppressive conditions? As your husband, shouldn't I be able to get you naked every day if I choose?"

Thomas laughed. "If I was a woman, I'd call you a misogynist, but I'm not, so I'll just say you're acting awfully entitled."

Aiden buried his face in Thomas's stomach. "I just want to be inside you on your birthday. Or let you be inside me. I'm not picky. I just want orgasms."

Thomas tugged Aiden's hair until he looked up at him. "After the party, you can do anything you want to me."

"Anything?" Aiden asked, narrowing his eyes like it might be a trick.

"Mm, anything. Anywhere—provided we're alone," he added, giving him a pointed look.

Aiden flushed. "How was I supposed to know the housekeeper was cleaning the bathroom?"

"The poor woman was traumatized," Thomas muttered, recalling the look on her face when she'd walked in to find them naked and very much in the middle of sex.

"I think she was turned on," Aiden said.

"Her scream would suggest otherwise," Thomas countered, shaking his head. "Now, come on. Let's get up and go get breakfast somewhere."

Aiden made a face. "Do you really want to be hounded by reporters today? Every time we go out in public, there's another cheesy headline about the billionaire who married his own son. It's obnoxious."

"It gives them something to focus on other than our murdering people. So, I'm all for it."

Aiden huffed out a sigh, letting Thomas know he'd won. "Fine. But I'm holding you to your promise for tonight."

Thomas gave him a dirty smirk. "I certainly hope so."

They were more than a tiny bit tipsy when they fell through the door of the war room, barely managing to close it behind them before they were kissing again, tugging at each other's clothes as Thomas backed Aiden up against the table. "You sure this is where you want it?" he asked against Aiden's lips.

"Yeah, right here, on this conference table. I can't tell you how many times I've thought about you fucking me on this table."

"You can tell me if you want," Thomas coaxed, his hands loosening Aiden's tie and yanking it off before tossing it behind him. Aiden didn't even bother unbuttoning Thomas's shirt—just yanked it open, buttons flying across the room. They'd definitely be noticed later. Most likely by one of the boys. Loudly. In the middle of a meeting. But that was future Thomas's problem.

Thomas did his best to undress Aiden while kissing him

but gave up once his shirt was open. He couldn't help it. Aiden had been toying with him all day, starting with a handjob he didn't finish in the shower and a blowjob in the car on the way to the venue. He'd been edging Thomas all fucking night, and now, it was time for his payoff.

"Lube?" Thomas asked.

"Check behind the whiskey bottle," Aiden said. "I may or may not have stashed some there earlier in anticipation of this event."

Thomas shook his head, retrieving the bottle then returning to push Aiden back on the table, climbing onto it and hovering over him. He looked so goddamn hot like this, like something out of one of Thomas's wet dreams.

He attacked Aiden's lips once more, fucking his tongue into his mouth as he forced his legs apart to settle between them. "This what you wanted?"

"Mm," Aiden said, fingers catching in Thomas's hair as he dipped his head to lick over one flat nipple, biting in a way that made Aiden growl, "It's a start."

Thomas laughed, letting himself taste whatever skin crossed his path. Aiden's jaw with its scratchy stubble, his ear, his throat. "You smell so fucking good," he muttered, nuzzling deeper into the scent.

He teased at Aiden's nipples until he was squirming beneath him, swearing and cursing at Thomas. "Do something before I take over and do it myself."

"Hush. It's my birthday, remember?" Thomas said, sliding off the table and going for Aiden's belt. "Lift up."

Aiden complied, letting Thomas slide his pants and

underwear down then off. Thomas made a noise of appreciation for Aiden's cock, already hard and leaking. He kissed his inner thighs, his hip bones, everywhere but his cock, choosing instead to nose at his balls before yanking him down the table. Once his ass was off the table, Thomas spread him open, burying his face there, tonguing at Aiden's hole with the kind of abandon he only had when he was a little intoxicated.

Aiden was moaning like a whore, his hands all but tearing at Thomas's hair as he tried to ride his face. Christ, he was perfect. He pulled back just enough to press a finger in, watching it disappear, before licking around it.

"Oh, fuck," Aiden whispered.

Thomas laughed, twisting his finger until he found that bundle of nerves that turned his husband into a babbling mess, glancing across it just enough to make his breath hitch before going back in with two fingers and massaging the spot.

"Oh, Jesus, fucking fuck, Tommy. Stop playing, I'm ready. Do we really need the foreplay?"

Thomas rolled his eyes. Drunken Thomas was bold, but drunken Aiden was impatient. Thomas ignored him. He could do this all night. Watch Aiden ride his fingers, feel him contract around his tongue. He ignored his own erection, straining against his zipper, teasing him until Thomas worried if he didn't fuck him soon, it would be over before it started.

When Thomas stood, Aiden looked at him with hazy eyes, lids at half-mast. He watched as Thomas opened his pants, sliding them down and off. When he saw how hard he was, he licked his lips, making eye contact. "What are you waiting for?"

"So bossy," Thomas chided, slicking his cock and settling it against Aiden's hole, giving him a look before slamming home. Aiden sucked in a breath, face contorting. "Better?"

Aiden ignored his question. "Hard. Fuck me hard. I wanna feel it tomorrow."

"Christ, if you keep saying things like that, it will be over before it starts."

Still, Thomas did as he asked, gripping Aiden's legs and bending them back, driving him farther up the table with every thrust.

"Oh, fuck, yeah, like that," Aiden said, eyes closed, lips parted.

Thomas watched as Aiden fisted his cock, jerking himself in time with Thomas's thrusts. When Aiden slipped too far out of reach, Thomas simply climbed back onto the table once more, folding Aiden's legs back and pounding into him hard enough to make Thomas's eyes roll back from the pleasure rolling along his spine.

Once upon a time, Thomas would have tried to go slow, be gentle. But now he knew what Aiden liked, what his body could take, and Aiden liked it hard and fast. He liked to feel used when Thomas was done with him. And Thomas was happy to accommodate.

Who wouldn't be?

Every fucking movement sent heat along Thomas's nerve endings until the base of his spine felt hot and his body spurred him to go faster, harder. Aiden cried out, spilling over his fist. Thomas took his hand, sucking his cum-soaked fingers into his mouth before licking his palm clean.

His orgasm hit hard, waves of pleasure sucking him under until he collapsed on top of Aiden, breathing like he'd just run a half marathon.

"I might be getting too old for this," Thomas said against Aiden's shoulder.

Aiden scoffed. "Sure doesn't feel like it to me."

Thomas slipped free of his body but made no move to get up. "Are you okay? Am I too heavy?"

Aiden's hands combed through Thomas's now sweaty hair. "I'm good. This is good."

Thomas nodded. "This is good. This is the best. This is the best fucking life I could have ever imagined."

"Alcohol always turns you into such a romantic," Aiden murmured, then kissed Thomas's forehead.

"I just want to sleep right here," Thomas said, rubbing his cheek over Aiden's chest, then letting his eyes close with a heavy sigh.

"Okay, but you have a meeting with the boys at seven a.m. Don't blame me if we're still here, naked and covered in jizz when they show up," Aiden muttered, sounding half-asleep.

"Eloquent," Thomas teased, making no move to get up.

He was almost asleep when Aiden murmured, "Happy birthday, Tommy."

"It really is," he murmured.

DEAR READER,

Thank you so much for reading *Maniac*, the final book in my Necessary Evils Series. I hope you guys enjoyed the wild ride that was the Mulvaney clan. If you're worried you're going to miss the boys, fear not. You will see plenty of cameos in the two upcoming spin-off series, *The Watch* and *Jericho's Boys*.

Also, if you want to watch the Mulvaney couples take out the bad guys left behind by Book 7's villain, tune in to my Patreon for the exclusive *Cozy Kills* serial where each couple dispatches a bad guy for a little alone time. And then, who knows?

Maybe more Mulvaneys in 2024?

I know I've said this a hundred times but writing is my therapy. It's what helped me cope with the things I saw while working as a pediatric psych nurse. It's what has gotten me through so many things just over the last three years. So thank you so much for loving my boys and my books. I'm blown away by your support and super grateful for the way you've helped promote me and shown me so much love. You guys have changed my whole life forever.

As always, if you guys are really loving the books, please consider joining my Facebook reader group, **Onley's Oubliette**, and signing up for my newsletter on my website so you can stay up to date on freebies, release dates, teasers, and more. You can also always hit me up on my social media and find all my links here: **fans.link/OnleyJames**. You can find me literally everywhere, so say hi. I love talking to readers.

Finally, if you did love this book, (or even if you didn't. Eek!) it would be amazing if you could take a minute to review it. Reviews are like gold for authors.

Thank you again for reading.

ABOUT THE AUTHOR

ONLEY JAMES is the pen name of YA author, Martina McAtee, who lives in Central Florida with her children, her pitbull, her weiner dog, and an ever-growing collection of shady looking cats. She splits her time between writing YA LGBT paranormal romances and writing adult m/m romances.

When not at her desk, you can find her mainlining Starbucks refreshers, whining about how much she has to do, and avoiding the things she has to do by binge-watching unhealthy amounts of television in one sitting. She loves ghost stories, true crime documentaries, obsessively scrolling social media, and writing kinky, snarky books about men who fall in love with other men.

Find her online at:
WWW.ONLEYJAMES.COM

Milton Keynes UK
Ingram Content Group UK Ltd.
UKHW020043191223
434628UK00019B/570/J